HERE COMES THE SON

DAHLIA DONOVAN

-----------HOT TREE PUBLISHING-----------

LIST OF BOOKS

THE GRASMERE TRILOGY:
Dead In The Garden
Dead In The Pond
Dead In The Shop

THE SIN BIN SERIES:
The Wanderer
The Caretaker
The Botanist
The Royal Marine
The Unexpected Santa
The Lion Tamer
Haka Ever After

STANDALONES:
After The Scrum
Forged In Flood (M/M/M)
Found You
One Last Heist
The Misguided Confession (M/F)
All Lathered Up (Free—E-Book Only) (M/F)
Not Even A Mouse (Free—E-Book Only) (M/F)
At War With A Broken Heart (M/M/M)
Here Comes The Son

For information, contact the publisher, Hot Tree Publishing.
WWW.HOTTREEPUBLISHING.COM

EDITING: HOT TREE EDITING

COVER DESIGNER: FURIOUSFOTOG

FORMATTING: RMGRAPHX

E-BOOK ISBN: 978-1-925853-56-8

PAPERBACK ISBN: 978-1-925853-57-5

CHAPTER ONE

IGGY

THE MODERN DEMON USES EVERY TOOL AT THEIR DISPOSAL TO DRAW A FLOCK OF IMPRESSIONABLE MILLENNIALS INTO THEIR THRALL. INSTAGRAM, YOUTUBE, AND SOCIAL MEDIA SITES OFFER EASY PICKINGS.

~ JESUIT JOURNAL, 2017

Stowing both the journal and pen into his backpack, Iggy focused on the YouTube video playing on the library computer. *The Siren.* She was a beautiful, sultry vlogger who'd rapidly gained a cult-like following on her channel. No name, no history, no previous website. She'd sprung up from nowhere and catapulted to viral infamy.

Iggy hadn't needed a cryptic dream warning him of another demonic invasion in his beloved city or the strange shiver up his spine to immediately put her onto his list.

The whir of the printer behind him drew Iggy away from the video as the hairs on the back of his neck stood up. His dark-brown eyes scanned the library slowly. He'd apparently run out of time for research; somewhere in the city, a demon had come out to play.

Time to hunt.

Strapping on his bag, Iggy dragged a hand roughly through his short black hair. He winked at the librarian who grumbled at him when he leaped over a book cart in his path on the way toward the front entrance. She blushed, a response he was used to with his inherited looks and charm.

As one of his best friends from high school used to say, he had wickedly devilish good looks. He told her to stop reading Regency romances. From his jet-black hair to his deep-brown eyes, he knew his face balanced the angelic with the roguish.

I'd do me.

Blinded by the bright sunshine, Iggy took a moment to adjust after stepping outside. Denver's Central Library had always been a favorite of his for research, with its massive collection. Plus, he always thought the building seemed almost like a grouping of castle turrets.

He paused on the corner of Broadway and Thirteenth Avenue. Spring was supposed to have sprung in the Mile High City. Not that the weather had noticed; they'd only just thawed out from winter.

And judging by the crisp air and gathering clouds on the mountains, they'd be inundated with another blizzard before the end of the day.

Jogging down Thirteenth, Iggy skidded to a halt on Lincoln. He tilted his head, trusting his finely honed instincts. Half a block down, he spotted an alley between a parking lot and the Art Institute that was shadowed more than it should've been in the bright early afternoon sun.

One step into the gap between the buildings, and he'd plunged into nighttime. The smell of sulfur swirled around him. He slipped his bag around his body, reaching inside for a spray can.

"Ah, Son of the Morning Star. Half-breed. I hoped you'd sense my presence." Rastran stood at the end of the unnaturally dark alley. He leaned casually against the industrial air conditioner with one foot resting on a body, completely disregarding the dirt now staining his designer suit. Demons always enjoyed life's luxuries. "Ignatius Faber, we've saved you for last. Your father's brightest light. A beautiful irony. All of his hopes pinned on the one offspring who matched him most in appearance and strength. Pity he can't see the monster he created."

With a hard kick, Rastran sent the body rolling along the filthy ground to land barely a foot away from Iggy. *Titus.* One of his many half-siblings. Iggy hadn't seen his brother in weeks. They'd all assumed Titus was on a hunt.

They generally kept in close contact, particularly since hundreds of other half-siblings had been culled over the past eight years. Titus and Iggy were the only ones left. Rage erupted deep inside him.

"I'm the monster?" Iggy calmly stepped over Titus, shoving grief and anger viciously down to remain focused.

He had a demon to deal with. His fingers wrapped tightly around the canister of compressed holy water in his pocket. It resembled pepper spray but worked to stun creatures of Hell long enough for him to send them home. "You should've stayed away from my city."

Kicking a piece of brick at the demon, Iggy charged toward him, leaping over a dumpster. He caught Rastran in the chest with a kick, then doused him with the holy water. With the demon stunned, he swiftly dug the lighter from his bag and set fire to the expensive suit.

"Fuck off back to Hell." Iggy stared intently at the brilliantly red flames rapidly burning the demon into nothing.

Flashy, fiery piece of shit.

Demons, as a species, seemed drawn to anything expensive or shiny. Titus had joked about their being the Kardashian brand of hellspawn. Iggy swallowed down his desire to both laugh and sob uncontrollably.

When the last bits of ash disappeared on a sudden brisk breeze, Iggy twisted toward Titus. With Rastran banished, light had returned to the alley. He didn't have time to process his brother's death.

His shoulders dropped with the weight of sorrow. A dead man in the middle of the city would draw attention Iggy didn't need. He had no real explanation for how Titus had died.

Demons tended to kill without leaving a trace of evidence of their presence or method. Of their army of siblings, Titus had been the most dedicated to demon hunting. More than Iggy. Ironic, given fighting came a little too easily to Iggy.

With no way to transport Titus, Iggy gently removed the rosary from his brother's neck and fled the alley. He left no clues to his presence, making sure to avoid any cameras in the area. Catching a bus on Lincoln allowed him to quickly return to where he'd parked his vehicle earlier.

Poor Titus.

The good son.

And who am I?

Ignatius Faber—failed Jesuit. Demon hunter. Gay son of Lucifer, the devil.

Halfway to his studio apartment on Welton, Iggy changed his mind. Solace and solitude never suited him. He wanted wine, food, and a kiss for comfort, which meant one thing—Lalo.

Food and wine would be easy with Lalo.

The kiss might require a bit of flirting.

A lot of flirting.

Why does he have to play so hard to get?

I mean, I'd want me.

Is that weird?

It's weird.

Damn it.

Getting stuck in early rush hour gave him more time to process Titus's death. He grabbed his journal when traffic went to a crawl, flipping toward the back to find the section on his siblings. His heart hurt at having to write down the details of his brother's death.

Sharp honking and swearing from the car behind him refocused his attention on driving. *Impatient asshole.* Iggy pulled off the highway and took the long way to Lalo's house. He'd rather be driving than sitting in traffic for ages while Denver police figured out how to move damaged cars to the side of the road.

It wasn't technically Lalo's house.

Lalo Pavia had been one of Iggy's best friends since they met in school. Lalo had been around eight years old and the kid everyone picked on mercilessly; Iggy, three years his senior, had never been anything other than one of the most popular boys. They'd met in the cafeteria, bonding over a mutual obsession with putting potato chips in their sandwiches.

Almost thirty years later, they were as close as ever. Though not close enough for Iggy.

Iggy considered Lalo to be the strongest person he'd ever known. Lalo had lost his parents at a very young age after a car accident; one foster family after another had followed.

Even now as an adult, Lalo never talked about being in foster care. Iggy knew from Father Salvatore, who ran the garden at the Jesuit compound, that several families had given up on Lalo because he refused to conform to their standards. *Assholes. As if being autistic makes him an alien or something.*

He's not.

With dark-brown hair, golden-toned skin, and bright-green eyes, Lalo looked the spitting image of his Spanish father, at least according to the one picture he had. Iggy knew Lalo had a touch of insecurity around his heritage. Orphaned so young with no living family, he might never know what had brought his father from Spain to Colorado.

All Lalo had was photos and a name. Iggy, even with his questionable paternal link, had more of a solid family foundation. He didn't even know if being autistic came from his mother or father's side.

Lalo claimed his brain just worked on a different operating system than "the norms." He had a wicked sense of humor—and a great ass. Iggy had been hopelessly in lust with him for the last ten years.

And love, if I'm honest with myself.

But I'm not. Ever.

Maybe even in love longer than lust. And Lalo was hopeless when it came to anything even hinting at a romance. Or sex. Or even kissing.

WHEN THE DEMONS REBELLED AGAINST LUCIFER'S CONTROL, HIS CREATION OF AN ARMY OF CHILDREN HAD BEEN AT THE TOP OF THE LIST OF THEIR COMPLAINTS. THEY SEALED HIM AWAY AND BEGAN SLAUGHTERING HIS HUMAN OFFSPRING ONE BY ONE.

~ JESUIT JOURNAL, 2008

CHAPTER TWO

LALO

DEMONS PINPOINT WEAKNESSES. EVEN THE MOST INSIGNIFICANT DETAIL OF THEIR VICTIM'S LIFE CAN BE FODDER FOR THEIR VORACIOUS NEED TO SUBJUGATE HUMANITY.

~ *JESUIT JOURNAL, 1829*

Denver in spring didn't always lend itself to gardening, but Lalo loved the challenge of building a garden at high altitude with occasional—mostly—roller-coaster weather. If he were in Hogwarts, Herbology would've been his magical gift. *Still waiting on the damn owl.*

Vegetables, herbs, and fruits didn't stare when Lalo talked to himself. They flourished under his care, even in the harshest conditions. He thought they liked the sound of his voice.

Lalo sat back on his heels, wiping his hands on his jeans

and tugging the earbuds out of his ears. He glared up at the gathering clouds on the mountain range in the distance. "Don't you snow on me. I'm not finished clearing out these herbs."

"Are you almost finished, *pollito*?"

"I am not a little chicken," Lalo grumbled for the hundredth time.

"Ah, but you fluff up at me like one." Lydia Ruiz smiled at him. She waved him toward the house. "Come inside out of the cold. You'll catch a cold, and what will Ignatius say?"

"He hates being called Ignatius."

"Good." Lydia enjoyed ruffling Iggy's feathers as well.

In her sixties, Lydia happened to be the aunt of his favorite foster parents. She'd bullied him into moving into her home after his failed college experiment. He'd discovered rather painfully that higher education didn't have any pity for an autistic struggling with executive dysfunction.

"You're tempting the weather with all this gardening." She waved him impatiently toward the house for the second time. "Have coffee with me. I'll even add hot chocolate for you."

Lalo gathered up some of the old plants he'd pulled up. "If you want herbs, you'll thank me for doing this work, even before a spring blizzard."

Dumping the mess in his arms into the compost bin in the corner of the yard, Lalo started toward the back door, only to change direction at the sound of a vehicle pulling into the driveway. He scrubbed his fingers against his jeans and watched Iggy slide out of his Trailblazer. A single snowflake drifting in front of his face made Lalo glower at the sky overhead.

"Can't you fix the weather?" Lalo asked Iggy, who chuckled at him. He batted at another snowflake. "Fudgesicles."

"One day, you'll learn how to say fuck. Also, I don't control the weather." Iggy threw his backpack over one arm and draped his other across Lalo's shoulders, turning them both toward the house. "Did you miss me?"

"Saw you yesterday." Lalo tended to at the very least text with Iggy on a daily basis. He shoved the arm off his shoulder. "You smell of evil. Did you go hunting again?"

Technically speaking, Lalo wasn't supposed to know about Iggy's dark, demonic secret or his adventures. He'd happened upon Iggy practicing martial arts and witnessed an impossible demonstration of skill beyond what even the movies could create. The sulfuric cat had escaped the bag.

Iggy hadn't liked keeping secrets anyway. *And that's how I learned my best friend is the son of Lucifer.* Lalo had taken it well, mostly; he occasionally threw holy water at Iggy to see if he sizzled.

He didn't.

"Titus." Iggy twisted toward the street and covered his face with his hands. "My last sibling. The only one I knew. Damn demons."

"Shh." Lalo flapped his hands at Iggy when he practically shouted the last word. "Lydia has a vivid imagination."

"They are actually demons."

Lalo shushed him again with a smack against his arm.

"You know that. And I do too. She doesn't."

"Titus died."

"Yes, I realized." Lalo shifted uneasily in front of Iggy. "Giving myself time to figure out how to offer sympathy."

"And?" Iggy's hands fell away from his face. "What have you come up with?"

"Sorry."

Iggy dropped his backpack on the porch and hopped up to sit on the railing. "I got the demon."

He groaned dramatically, throwing his hands up in frustration. "Call them chilies."

Iggy seemed to brighten from his dark mood, grinning at him. "I got the ghost chili. Sucker went right up in flames. Spicy dickhead."

It seemed wrong to snicker, given Titus's death, even though Lalo knew Iggy had become somewhat immune to death after losing so many of his half-siblings. He worried about his best friend but had no idea how to help. None of the phrases he'd written down fit their particular situation.

"Was 'sorry' in the folder?" Iggy teased.

"Top of the 'grieving' page," Lalo admitted sheepishly.

The folder was a large binder that Lalo had kept since high school. He jotted down phrases, words, and conversation starters broken down into specific categories. Iggy, Lydia, and his favorite foster parents, Ramon and Maria-Estella Ruiz, had helped him to fill the pages over the years.

He'd memorized most of the phrases by his thirties. "Titus enjoyed a good feast. Why don't we salute him with food?"

"That on your list too?" Iggy slid off the railing to his feet.

"It's on Lydia's. Food solves many a pain in her mind." Lalo had firsthand experience with her grand solution for broken hearts. She'd even coaxed him out of moping when college had gone wrong. "I'll cook. You tell me about Titus."

"We'll cook. And you can tell me about this nighttime exploration of Denver." Iggy followed Lalo into the house.

"Denver at night in photos." He'd been planning a photography exhibition with a local gallery for ages, though the length of time had mostly been because of his fear of checking his email inbox. He'd ignored the first message for six months. "Still want to wander the city with me?"

"It's a *date*."

"Why are you saying date all weird?" Lalo picked up on emphasis Iggy put on the last word.

Iggy flopped dramatically onto the floor, groaning exaggeratedly. "You are hopeless."

"He's asking you out on a date, *pollito*." Lydia wandered by; she paused to wave down at Iggy, then returned her attention to Lalo. "You say yes. He picks you up. And my heart will be happy."

"I'm not a chicken."

"Is that a yes?" Iggy got to his feet and swung Lydia around in a graceful move. "Is he saying yes?"

"*He* is saying that *he* is not a chicken." Lalo made his way into the kitchen with a huff of annoyance. He didn't need the added stress of ruining his closest friendship with romance or sex or both, even if he'd stared longingly at Iggy for years. "What am I doing?"

"Saying yes to the half-chili?" Iggy followed him in and found his favorite spot, a chair in the corner of the room. "Let me spice up your life?"

"Okay, Baby Spice."

"Do we need to have the 'how two become one' conversation?" Iggy gave his first truly relaxed laugh since he'd arrived. "What do you really want?"

"This painfully 90s nightmare to end." Lalo knelt in front of the fridge to inspect the contents. "Iggy?"

"Hmm?"

"Yes."

CHAPTER THREE

IGGY

NECESSITY LED TO THE CREATION OF A HOME FOR CHILDREN ORPHANED BY THEIR MOTHERS DYING IN CHILDBIRTH AND AN ABSENTEE DEMONIC FATHER. JESUIT ELDERS HOPED TO PREVENT AN ARMY OF HALF-DEMON CHILDREN FALLING PREY TO TEMPTATION. THEY COULDN'T KNOW HOW LONG THEIR MISSION WOULD LAST AND HOW ULTIMATELY FRUITLESS IT WOULD BE.

~ *JESUIT JOURNAL, 2010*

After only the lightest blanket of spring snow overnight, Iggy ventured out to his favorite coffee spot. A double dose of espresso with a massive cinnamon crunch muffin woke him up sufficiently. He sat outside on a bench to watch the bustling downtown Denver traffic.

These were the days Iggy would miss Titus the most.

They'd often met over coffee early in the morning to exchange notes and share breakfast. His brother had been laser-focused on the task of stemming the flow of demonic power in the city.

Over the years, Iggy had struggled to build relationships with his siblings. He'd only known a handful of them personally. Titus had been the closest to him in age and personality.

According to the Jesuits written records, his siblings dated back hundreds of years. Lucifer had made a prolific attempt to build his army. After Iggy's birth, the devil had vanished from the earth; Titus claimed rebellious demons had sealed Lucifer away in Hell.

I'll miss him.

I'm truly without family now, unless you count Lucifer.

Fuck.

Me and my demonic, princely father, the fallen angel.

The door to his left opened, allowing the tempting scent of coffee blended with chocolate to drift his away. Iggy drained his cup and went back inside for a refill. Not even the brisk post-snow air had been sufficient to wake him up fully.

Was the first sign of addiction making automatic excuses for indulging?

With a fresh cup of coffee and a second muffin in hand, Iggy decided to return to the scene of his confrontation with Rastran. He'd been in such a hurry to avoid police involvement that he hadn't bothered to get a closer look at the alley. On the drive over, it occurred to him that Father

Ricci hadn't reached out to him about Titus yet.

Shit.

He parked a few blocks away from the alley. The walk allowed him to quickly text both Father Luca Ricci and Father John Lopez, who had been Titus's closest mentor. Their response made Iggy go from a casual stride to a straight-out run. A body hadn't been recovered from the alley.

What?

He skidded to a halt just beside the parking structure to check his beeping phone.

Father Lopez: Not only didn't we find a body, I checked with young Alexandra who works with the ME's office, and they weren't called yesterday. So, the police don't have Titus.

Father Ricci: See what you can find.

Restraining his automatic sarcastic response of "maybe I'll ignore the suspicious missing body of my brother just for fun," Iggy shoved his phone into his pocket. He yanked his hood over his head, ducking into the alley and carefully making his way to where Titus had last been. *Weird shit is getting weird again.* The only proof of his fight with the demon was the faint whiff of sulfur clinging to the frosty breeze.

In all his years of experience, Iggy had never known a demon to take an interest in a body. They enjoyed the theater of leaving their victims to be found, feeding off the tremendous grief it caused. If any others had been around after his defeat of Rastran, they wouldn't have been interested in Titus. They'd have been focused on finding Iggy for vengeance, not removing a corpse. If the police, Jesuits, and demons didn't do it, then where was Titus? Bodies generally didn't vanish on their own.

Using his phone as a light, Iggy crouched on the damp and grimy ground. He regretted leaving the Maglite in his Trailblazer. A glint of fabric drew his attention to the stack of crates nearby; he managed to snag the thick plastic after working his fingers underneath them.

"What are you?" Iggy sat back on his heels and twisted the black, rubbery piece of fabric in his hand. "A body bag."

Well, a demon isn't going to haul around a body in a cadaver bag.

And the police weren't called out, so the medical examiner hadn't gotten their equipment caught on the crates.

Iggy shoved the bag into his pocket. He glanced up toward the camera he'd spotted last time, only to find it broken. Whoever had stolen Titus's body hadn't done so randomly.

Shifting his attention away from the crates, Iggy didn't find any other signs of Titus, the fight, or the theft. He hopped onto the air conditioning unit and pulled his journal out of his backpack. He jotted down a few notes about the scene before sealing the black fabric into a container and dropping it and the journal into his bag.

He fished his phone out of his pocket to text an update to Father Ricci, who had been in charge of the orphans for over twenty years. The priest ran the Jesuit sect that had raised the children and trained many of them to hunt demons.

They also managed a retreat, a high school in Denver, and a community garden.

With nothing to go on, Iggy decided to locate the security office that monitored the cameras. He had to see if they'd captured any signs of his fight or the body snatchers. His luck held out when the only employee working turned out to be a young man.

Demonic powers, activate!

Despite being reprimanded by Father Ricci numerous times for using his "gifts of the devil," Iggy usually ignored the lectures. The priest's family had a long history of producing Jesuits who ran the orphanage for half-demons. A cousin, an uncle, even a great-grandfather, which had Iggy side-eyeing the man when he tried to scold him.

His charm magically softened even the most stubborn individual. He quickly talked his way into obtaining a copy of the footage from the previous day. *Demons use every advantage available, so I have to fight fire with fire.*

Literally and figuratively.

The phone number that had been snuck into the CD case got thrown in a trashcan on his way to his Trailblazer. *I may have overdone the charm—poor kid.* Iggy couldn't blame the security guard, a man in his early twenties; it didn't help that Iggy had stopped aging, appearing far younger than almost forty.

None of his half-siblings, going back centuries, had lived beyond their forties, dying young either from natural causes or murdered by demons. The priests had no idea whether Iggy might begin to age normally at some point. He felt like a bizarre cross between a vampire and Dorian Gray.

He'd just slid into the driver seat of his Trailblazer when his phone rang. "Lalo."

"Are you anywhere near the Voorhies?"

"Just south of it, why?"

"Swear I saw Titus walking by on the sidewalk," Lalo whispered into his phone. "I'm following him on Broadway, heading north away from the Civic Center Park. Did he really die?"

Iggy breathed through the sudden racing of his heart. "Lal, listen to me. Whoever it is isn't Titus. I can't find his body, though. Don't follow him."

"Just hurry and catch up with me." Lalo disconnected the call a second later.

"*Shit. Fuck. Shit.*" Iggy swerved by a stopped car and shot through a red light, barely missing a city bus before skidding around a corner into a rare open parking spot. He jogged down Broadway until he caught up with Lalo. "Damn it, Lal. So, where's the doppelganger?"

Lalo nodded toward the figure half a block ahead of them. "Did Titus have a twin? I know all of you orphans had similar features—same father, different mothers. But I don't remember anyone being as close in appearance."

"No twins, surprisingly, at all." Iggy almost swallowed his tongue when the doppelganger turned around and he saw what had drawn Lalo's attention. "Holy shit."

"Maybe he's a zombie."

"No more *Walking Dead* for you." Iggy nonchalantly led him by the Titus lookalike. He didn't believe in coincidences or reanimating the dead. "What the actual fuck is going on?"

"Zombies."

"He's *not* a zombie." He held his hand up to stop Lalo from disagreeing with him. "Can you try to get a video of him with your camera—without it appearing obvious?"

The short answer turned out to be no. Subtlety had never been a skill of Lalo's. He all but held up a sign that said "I'm staring at you."

"Right, we're not suspicious at all."

CHAPTER FOUR

LALO

~ JESUIT JOURNAL, 1972

Just sit in the tub. You don't even have to stand up.

Get off the bed. Walk to the bathroom. Turn on the water. And sit.

Why can't I do this?

Rolling onto his back, Lalo stared up at his ceiling. Managing his executive dysfunction, bouts of depression, and being autistic could often be a struggle. He hated days when even standing up seemed beyond his capability.

He kept running through all his plans for the day. His to-do list seemed impossible, though it hadn't the night before when he'd written it after returning home from being out with Iggy. The bed and blanket offered a comforting contrast to forcing himself into preparing for the day.

Compromise.

That's what Ramon is always telling me to do.

Compromise with yourself.

All I have to do is move the blanket.

Then shower.

I can do this.

As always, Lalo bribed himself to get out of bed. *If I stand up, I can head out into the garden.* He twisted around and sat up, his sock-covered feet touching the hardwood floor. *I'm halfway there, might as well do the rest.*

Taking a deep breath, Lalo leaned forward until he had to stand or topple over. *I'm up. Why does this always seem like a massive accomplishment? I wonder if allistics would feel as inspired watching me on an average day as they are by all those videos of extraordinarily gifted autistics doing amazing things?*

Probably not.

With a wry chuckle to himself, Lalo made his way to the bathroom, one slow step at a time. Staring at the taps for almost two full minutes, he eventually reached out to turn on the water. *Just shower.*

By the time he'd showered and dressed, Lydia had a hearty breakfast of seasoned rice with eggs waiting. She plied him with oversweet coffee as well. He appreciated her allowing him to slowly make his way through the fog in his mind without trying to pepper him with questions.

"I packed a thermos of coffee and a bag of cookies for you. Keep your strength up, *pollito*." Lydia waved off his muttered "I'm not a chicken."

"Ramon and Maria want to meet up for lunch at one. Don't forget."

Even though her nephew had been his foster parent, Lydia had taken him fully under her wing. She'd never married nor had children. He never quite knew how to respond to her unconditional love; part of him (a dark part deep inside) whispered that he didn't deserve such kindness.

Lydia obviously disagreed, and Father Sal, who managed the Jesuit garden, often told him those painful thoughts came from the devil. Lalo didn't necessarily believe him.

It seemed almost lazy to blame demonic powers for every negative characteristic. Leaving deep thoughts for another day, Lalo decided to return his attention to his morning of volunteer work. He spent at least three days a week caring for the yards and gardens of multiple senior citizens in the area.

He'd banded together with a few other young gardeners he'd met during his brief stint at college. They'd begun an unofficial charity, getting names from various places of elderly people who could no longer manage their yards. It was the most satisfying work he'd ever done.

They didn't take payment, though they were often given food or seeds to plant. Lalo found the elderly more accepting of his often stringent needs. If he had his earbuds in, they didn't chat with him.

Finishing up breakfast, Lalo gathered up his gear. His gardening tools already waited in the trunk of his little Scion. He shoved his wallet into his pocket, made sure his camera was secure in his backpack, and grabbed his keys.

"*Pollito.*" Lydia waited by the door for him, thermos and paper bag in hand. Lalo often forgot to take breaks for food; she'd begun sending him out with a snack just in case. "Hydrate."

"Not a chicken." He begrudgingly accepted her hug, then the thermos and packed snack. "Not a chicken. Don't have feathers."

Do the chilies have feathers?

I'll ask Iggy.

Everything went into the back seat except for his camera bag. Lalo preferred keeping it close. He never knew when something might catch his eye.

One of the things Lalo loved about photography was bringing the world into his sphere without all the clutter of allistic chaos to deal with. He found safety behind the lens. Sometimes, when forced to attend a party, he used his camera as a barrier.

College had almost ruined his love of the art. His professor had smothered Lalo with technique. He'd argued, failed his photography course, and ignored the grim-faced advisor who'd refused to listen to his complaints and continued to lecture him on paying attention in class.

Not surprising, allistics in authority tended to disregard autistic voices. Lalo had run headfirst into the same sort of barrier throughout his life. He'd given up on college; in the end, fighting against their lack of understanding had been beyond his ability.

Or maybe, they gave up on me.

Shaking his head, Lalo practiced the techniques he'd read about to acknowledge the sad thoughts and let them go. He'd left college, yes, but life had worked out anyway. Helping people, taking photographs; somehow what felt like the worst failure in his life had become a triumph.

The brief snow hadn't stuck around, so Lalo's drive went smoothly. He knew the side streets well enough to avoid any traffic. Denver had an organized grid that ran in diagonally in four cardinal points. Lalo was obsessed with it; sometimes, when Iggy had a night off from hunting, they drove around.

It made Lalo happy.

A full morning of working in the dirt, trying to clear away three different gardens in preparation for spring planting, and Lalo had completely forgotten his coffee and cookies. His phone buzzed in his pocket at one, a belated reminder that he should've already left for lunch. *Holy crumbs, I'm so late.* Making anyone wait for him was usually enough to send him straight into a panic attack.

Breathe.

It's Ramon and Maria.

They're never angry with me.

Thankfully, the drive to Alameda Avenue didn't take long. Lalo spotted their familiar, brightly painted cupcake food truck parked near La Calle Taqueria Y Carnitas, home of the best tacos he'd ever eaten. He'd been known to pick up twenty or thirty of them, or even more if Iggy planned to join him.

"Lalito." Maria waved him over to their truck. They'd set up a few stools outside for them to eat without having to sit in the restaurant, likely to save Lalo from further stress. "Ramon's ordering for us. The line was massive."

Lalo glanced over at the bright orange building, then shifted closer to let her hug him. She brushed the dirt off his shirt. "*Maria.*"

"I know. You're all grown up. All I see is your sad little face hidden by an oversized hoodie when they brought you to our house." She hugged him again, smelling of *dulce de leche* and coffee, two of the cupcakes flavors they made. "What's this I hear about a date?"

Lalo pulled away from her with a groan. "Fudgesicles."

"Where are you two going?" Maria dragged a stool over to sit and patted the one beside her. "Is it your first?"

Lalo shook his head, staring longingly at the restaurant in the hopes Ramon would save him. "No."

"With Iggy?"

Maybe I should've listened about how prayer works.

Dear God that I'm not sure exists, please save me from the woman beside me. Love, Lalo.

"Ramon. There you are," Maria called to her husband, who carried over several large bags along with three cups, carefully balancing them.

Prayer does work.

Lalo ignored the strange looks when he couldn't stop

himself from snickering. "Tacos?"

Ramon narrowed his eyes on his wife suspiciously. "Did she get too enthusiastic about your date?"

Prayer doesn't work.

CHAPTER FIVE

IGGY

RELATIONSHIPS ARE TO BE STRICTLY DISCOURAGED.
THEY PROVIDE A WEAKNESS DEMONS ARE FAR TOO LIKELY TO
EXPLOIT. THE SOLE FOCUS SHOULD BE TRAINING,
FIGHTING, AND WORSHIP.

~ JESUIT JOURNAL, 1986

Anyone who spent time with Lalo in a garden immediately recognized his devotion and capacity for love, even if it was all directed toward his plants. Behind a camera though, Lalo showed the depths of his soul for all to see. Iggy sat on the cold grass, enjoying the view of Denver from Lookout Mountain, eating dessert and watching his date photograph the bright skyline in the distance. They'd arrived as the sun went down and enjoyed dinner while waiting for the lights of the city to come on.

"Lal. Have some Nutella pizza?" He waved a slice at Lalo's back. They'd picked up one pepperoni and one of the sweet pies from Pizzeria Locale. "Help me help myself or I'll be licking the box clean before I know it. Do you know how much running I'm going to have to do to work all this off?"

"No," Lalo grunted abruptly. His attention focused intently on the viewfinder of his camera. "And don't eat my slice. Why are you so distracting?"

"Have you seen me?" Iggy licked the chocolate spread from his fingers, sighing when the move was completely wasted on Lalo, who hadn't bothered to turn around. "You're hard on my ego."

"Good." Lalo finally glanced over his shoulder with a grin. "Yours has needed deflating since high school. You've got Nutella on your cheek."

"Want to lick it off?" Iggy infused the question with all his charm.

"Are you this unsanitary on all your dates?" Lalo wrinkled his nose and turned back to his camera. "They put napkins in with the pizza."

Iggy fell backwards with an aggrieved sigh, staring up at the stars in the night sky. "Why do I bother?"

"No idea," Lalo muttered. "Don't know why you bother either. You're less obnoxious when you aren't using your chili senses to spice up your life."

They snickered together.

The slightly defensive tone in his voice caught Iggy's attention. He sometimes forgot Lalo misread teasing for seriousness. Silently kicking himself for not being more careful, Iggy got to his feet and walked toward him as their laughter faded away.

Great job, Iggy; put your foot in it on the first date. You've only known Lal for years.

Iggy brought his hands up, giving Lalo plenty of time to retreat, and gripped him by the shoulders. "I *bother* because you've had my attention since high school. Not that you noticed or cared."

"You were joking."

Joking?

Oh, right, the misunderstanding a minute ago.

"I was." Iggy tilted his head to put their lips closer, bending a little to close the two-inch height difference. "I'm not joking about wanting to kiss you."

"Your face is still sticky." Lalo's green eyes glinted with mischief in the glow of the moon and stars overhead. He reached up to grip Iggy by his hair and tugged him into a kiss. "Mouth tastes of Nutella as well."

Iggy smirked hungrily and sought Lalo's lips again. He only pulled back when oxygen became an issue; they stared breathlessly at one another. "Ever had sex under the stars?"

"Not—"

"Damn it." Iggy cut Lalo off when the telltale sensation of a demon on the prowl hit him, the strange, otherworldly rush of energy up his spine causing his hair to stand on end. "*Fuck.*"

"Chili on the loose?"

"Chili on the loose." Iggy gave him a crooked grin. "Rain check on the date?"

"Rain check?" Lalo scoffed, stepping away to begin

packing up his camera. "I'm coming with you."

"Lal."

"Igster."

"Fine." Iggy didn't honestly mind if Lalo joined him. Unlike his priestly mentors, he'd never seen a reason to keep secrets, not from his best friend. "Let's spice up our first date with a demon."

"Might want to wipe the chocolate from your face first." Lalo pointed to the napkins in the empty pizza box. "Can you open the back of your Trailblazer? I want to stow my extra gear."

Lalo drove, allowing Iggy to focus on feeling out where the demon had crossed over into his city. Despite centuries of journals, they'd yet to discover how or why the devil came to Denver in the first place. Nor did the Jesuits know how Iggy could sense demons.

Despite the Jesuits' reluctance to involve anyone outside their group, Iggy fully believed Lalo to be an asset. He tended to absorb everything around him, distilling the most complex issues into understandable ones. Iggy couldn't help wondering if his best friend had better luck studying the journals than he had.

Putting the idea aside for now, Iggy returned to pinpointing their demonic problem. *Let's not lose any souls tonight; might ruin our first date completely.* He couldn't help grinning at Lalo in the dimly lit vehicle as they drove away from the foothills toward the city.

Lalo understood his life. Youthful crushes and dick-driven lust aside, Iggy trusted every aspect of his life to Lalo.

What better foundation for a relationship is there? Who else is going to happily hop behind the wheel to play driver as I hunt down a sulfuric monster?

Focus, Ignatius.

Sex and romance after, not before.

As they moved through the city, Iggy leaned his head slightly out the open window. The cold air shook the slight haze that had filled his head watching the intense focus on Lalo's face. He had to quit thinking about how sexy Lalo was.

They were headed down Fourteenth when sulfur began to burn his nostrils. Iggy sat up, trying to get a hint of a direction. Lalo slowed the vehicle down to an almost crawl, much to the annoyance of the driver behind them, who honked in irritation before swerving around them.

"Right on Broadway." Iggy frowned at the familiar location. *Why do they keep appearing in the same area?* "Past the library."

Denver at night wasn't much different from during the day. Iggy preferred the brightness of the sun. He knew Lalo loved the opposite; evenings offered more quiet introspection.

Or so he claimed.

"Hang on." Iggy twisted in the seat, trying to pinpoint the location. "It's gone."

"The demon?"

Iggy slumped against the leather and massaged his forehead. "Let's head back to my place. I want to show you something."

"I'm not playing hide the salami."

Iggy barked out a surprised laugh, snickering helplessly.

"It's too big to hide."

MISTAKES MADE IN THE COURSE OF LEARNING HOW TO COMBAT DARKNESS CAME AT A JUSTIFIABLY HEAVY COST. NOT ALL AGREED WITH THAT ASSESSMENT. THE BITTER WAR AGAINST DEMONS HAD REQUIRED SACRIFICES, HOWEVER.

~ JESUIT JOURNAL, 1968

CHAPTER SIX

LALO

DEMONS HUNGER. FORGET THEIR POWER AT YOUR OWN DETRIMENT.

~ *JESUIT JOURNAL, 1868*

Street lights glinted off window panes with each passing building. Lalo maneuvered the Trailblazer quickly across downtown toward Iggy's fancy apartment. They both enjoyed the comfortable silence; he tried not to allow the sparkling lights to play with his vision too badly.

Denver at night often played tricks on Lalo's eyes but not as much as the bright sun. He'd always suffered from sensitivity to light; it often led to migraines if he wasn't careful. Lydia had made special curtains to help him deal with the issue at home.

"Lal?" Iggy brought him out of his thoughts. He gestured

toward the entrance to Cheesman Park. "Let's make a circuit. My spidey senses are tingling."

"You mean your spicy senses?" Lalo grinned before making the turn onto the street that ran through the park. He parked illegally on the side of the road when Iggy asked him to. "You realize we're going to get a ticket if DPD spot us. Is a demon out there?"

"Maybe." Iggy reached to the back seat to grab his backpack. "Grab your camera. Maybe you can capture something on film that I never see."

They crossed the two-lane street, jogging toward a small wooded area near the main part of the park. Iggy came to a halt, glancing toward a dark area in the distance. He whispered for Lalo to stay put and continued forward.

At times Lalo envied his best friend and crush for his athletic ability and brash confidence. Iggy made friends easily. He'd had a trust fund from an anonymous donor to pay for his apartment and shiny vehicle.

Anonymous.

They all had a strong suspicion who the money had come from. Iggy didn't care. The priests had complaints, but he ignored them.

Lalo had none of those things.

Though his life hadn't been perfect, Iggy hadn't struggled. Not like Lalo, who'd clawed his way to every single, tiny victory. Then again, Lalo never saw the point of dwelling on things out of his control.

"Iggy." Lalo froze with his camera focused on a shadow moving in the darkness at the edge of the wooded area on the opposite side from where they stood. "*Iggy.*"

Iggy ran back over to Lalo and then went past, in the direction his camera was pointed. "Shit. Stay here."

Lalo watched for a minute before following him. *Stay? How am I any safer if I'm over here than keeping close to the action? I wonder if I could do an exhibition called Demons at Night.*

Did demons always dress so impeccably? Lalo snapped a photo of the figure of a man who'd appear at home in any Fortune 500 office. He'd emerged from the shadow directly in front of Iggy, and the two appeared to be arguing.

Inching closer to try to hear, Lalo tried not to draw any unnecessary attention while also keeping an eye on the Trailblazer. He really didn't want a ticket. Granted, what would the police say about a demon vanishing, since they tended to pop in and out?

He switched to video mode, continuing to film. Iggy might get more information from a moving picture. The demon suddenly vanished, leaving Iggy cursing loudly in the darkness.

"If you're part chili, how come you don't get any of their superpowers?" Lalo asked while they trudged back to the Trailblazer. He tossed the keys over and slipped into the passenger seat to let Iggy drive. "You got a youthful appearance and what Father Sal calls a 'charming personality.' You can't vanish."

"Everyone's a critic." Iggy rolled his eyes, shoving the key into the ignition. "The sulfuric band noticed Titus's doppelganger. They thought I'd found a way to raise the dead."

"Are you sure Titus died?" Lalo had watched his cellphone video of the lookalike over and over. He thought the man had seemed younger than Iggy's half-brother. "Did he have a son?"

"Titus? No, no way." Iggy didn't sound completely convinced. "He would've told someone. His mentor, at least."

"Would he?" He'd noticed none of the siblings had been truly attached to the Jesuits, not the way he appreciated Father Sal, the gardener. Iggy was close to one of the priests but had been turned off by religion. *So, would Titus have confided in them about a child? I doubt it.* "Do you talk to your mentors about any issues outside of the chilies?"

"No." Iggy glanced sharply over at Lalo, pulling the vehicle into the street. "They raised me to fight. I don't know if it bred a deep trust toward the Jesuits. I'm angry about how they don't mind you working in the garden or me chasing demons for them, but some of them still judge us about our sexual preference."

"Maybe Titus felt the same. Either way, the demons want the lookalike. We need to find him first," Lalo said firmly. He knew Iggy had often felt alone, even surrounded by Jesuits and classmates. Lalo could relate. "I filmed your demon. Not sure how the footage will look."

"You're a fucking genius."

"Fudgsicle," Lalo corrected.

"You're a Fudgsicle genius?" Iggy shook his head, laughing hard enough that he had to pull to the side of the road to regain control of himself.

"Just drive." Lalo punched him in the arm when they'd both stopped snickering. "Ig?"

"Hmm?" Iggy checked for traffic before pulling back onto the road.

"Where do the demons live? Is there a physical Hell?"

"Jury's still out on Hell." Iggy dropped his hand onto Lalo's knee, squeezing tightly and leaving it there when Lalo didn't shake him off. "Father Ricci claims hell is in some dimension we can't reach. I'm not convinced. We don't know the origin of demons. The first demon I destroyed had an apartment in downtown Denver. Maybe they're spawned here on earth."

"Are they born young?"

"No idea."

"Aren't you curious?" Lalo had what seemed like an endless curiosity about the demons.

"Not overly. Not enough to question one instead of destroying it."

Stopping for a late-night snack at McDonald's, they made it through two large fries and nuggets on the drive to Iggy's place. He parked next to Lalo's Scion, left out front when he'd driven over earlier. They sat in a silence that suddenly turned awkward.

Lalo eased out of the seat, grabbing his camera bag from the floorboard and stepping out of the Trailblazer. "Lydia will be waiting up."

And she would, wanting to hear all the gossip to share with her niece-in-law.

Maybe I can sneak into my room without her hearing me.

Iggy raced around the vehicle and leaned against Lalo's car door, blocking his exit. "Want to come up? I've got leftovers."

"Not tonight." Lalo didn't know the details of all Iggy's relationships, but they'd ended quickly. He refused to throw away a friendship over a quick fling. Sex tended to muddle things up, in his experience. "Lydia's leaving for Phoenix tomorrow. I'll put my footage together, you bring your journals, and we can spend tomorrow evening together. We'll have a date of research."

A date of research?

A date of research.

Holy crumbs.

I'm a walking date disaster.

"Lalo?"

He'd barely lifted his head up when Iggy kissed him hard and deeply enough to almost change his mind. He pushed him away. "Good night, Igster."

"*Fudgsicle,*" Iggy muttered with a teasing grin.

CHAPTER SEVEN

IGGY

THE COUNCIL WAS CREATED OUT OF NECESSITY TO AVOID CORRUPTION. DEMONS SOUGHT TO PENETRATE THE CIRCLE AT EVERY STEP. THEY WANTED THE CHILDREN. OUR ORDERS FROM THE HOLY SEE WERE TO ASCERTAIN THE GOODNESS OF THE OFFSPRING AND TRAIN THEM TO FIGHT AGAINST EVIL.

~ *JESUIT JOURNAL, 1909*

"Your relationships impede your training, studying, and devotion. They have always been a distraction." Father Josiah tapped a finger against the table. Two other priests sat on either side of him, offering Iggy sympathetic glances. Josiah Wilson had always disliked Iggy—and Lalo. He'd somehow learned about their date. "You are not your father, to throw away so much of your time on sins of the flesh."

Sins of the flesh?

Self-righteous dick.

Iggy had mostly ignored Father Josiah over the years as much as possible. If their priestly order had been a military organization, Josiah Wilson would've been second-in-command. He also tended to be more closed-minded and rigid about rules than any of the other Jesuits. As a result, Father Josiah was usually the first to lecture or punish for supposed infractions. "As I'm the last half-demon standing, I'd say I'm more focused, not less. They haven't managed to snuff out my life."

"Lalo left the church. He's…." Josiah didn't appear to know how to finish his sentence. Or maybe he sensed the hostility building in Iggy. "Your every moment should be dedicated to training. We need you here."

"Do you?" Iggy had been struggling with his mentors for several years as tension built underneath the surface. "I came to talk about Titus's missing body. Not Lalo. And I left the church as well, or have you forgotten?"

Aside from the kindly older Father Sal who ran the garden, none of the Jesuits had dedicated much time to Lalo, though they hadn't been cruel to him either. Josiah had been particularly dismissive of Iggy's friendship with him. He wondered how they'd handle the changing nature of their relationship.

Fuck 'em.

"You will end your relationship with Lalo." Father Josiah completely ignored the mention of Titus. "He's a distraction."

"A distraction?" Iggy spared a look at the other

priests, who seemed resigned to whatever came from the conversation. He had too much experience being taunted by demons to simply blow his temper at a small-minded fool. They appeared surprised when he didn't immediately rush into a confrontation. "Titus disappeared, or his body died, and suddenly a younger version is wandering around Denver. Even the demons have noticed."

"Ignatius." Father Josiah always managed to make his voice drip with disdain.

Iggy got slowly to his feet, carefully easing the chair away from the table. He glared down at the three men. "I've said all along that I can fight demons with or without your input. You leave Lalo alone. He's none of your damn business."

"Iggy." Father Sal tried to draw him back, ever the calming influence.

Iggy didn't feel calm.

Striding away from the meeting, Iggy managed to avoid slamming the door. He breathed in the cool spring breeze coming off the mountains. *Right. If this goes downhill further, I'll lose all access to the journals and other archives kept at the retreat.*

The retreat in Sedalia had been run by Jesuits for anyone interested in Ignatian traditions. The compound within the retreat had been in the Rocky Mountain foothills for far longer, the retreat having been built up around it as a front to avoid unwanted attention. Iggy had always wondered how they kept it secret from the steady flow of guests coming in and out every year.

Passing through the outer gardens, Iggy made his way through a series of small buildings to reach a secure library. He entered a code into the lockbox and headed inside. The priests would eventually follow him, so he had limited time.

Priorities.

What journals have the most information about the demons, dear old Dad, and my siblings?

Iggy considered carefully before gently placing as many journals as would fit into his backpack. He kept it fairly light, not wanting to run with a heavy load, so an impressive number fit. They hadn't gone digital yet, for fear of hacking, so no online records existed.

Given the icy atmosphere at his weekly briefing, Iggy had no idea if they'd allow him into the library again. *Certainly not once they see I've run away with their journals. Screw them; Lalo's been with me for years. I'm not throwing him aside for a jealous old dick who's never even jacked off.*

Iggy made it all the way to his Trailblazer before one of the Jesuits caught up with him. He set his bag safely into the vehicle and turned to face Father John, who'd been the closest thing to a parental figure in his life. "What's the verdict?"

"I'm impressed you didn't lose your temper." Father John glanced at the backpack on the front seat of the Trailblazer but said nothing. "How is Lalo? Salvatore mentioned he expected the young man to come tend the garden either this week or next, depending on the weather."

"He's fine." Iggy crossed his arms and leaned against the vehicle. Of all the Jesuits, he didn't want to argue with Father John, not about Lalo or anything else. They'd probably sent him for that exact reason. *Talk some sense into him.* "What's the verdict?"

"Forty lashes with a wet noodle." Father John motioned for Iggy to walk with him. They made a small circuit around the gravel parking lot. "I disagree with my brother Josiah."

Iggy kept his eye on the Trailblazer, not wanting to lose the journals. He'd locked the vehicle, but stranger things had happened. "And?"

His number one lesson from dealing with Jesuits and demons was to never lead a conversation with more information than necessary. They might use different methods, but both could be tricky. Iggy waited Father John out, his gaze mostly focused on his vehicle.

"An apology might smooth things over."

"Lying is a sin." Iggy hadn't gone to church or attended confession since his teens. He'd tired of the politics and hypocrisy behind the scenes. "I'm not sorry for ignoring him or walking away. You'd definitely want an apology if I'd stayed behind."

"I've tried speaking with Brother Luca about Josiah. He claims not to see the problem." Father John tucked his hands into a fold of cloth when the sun dipped behind a cloud and a breeze picked up once again. "The loss of Titus hit us hard. Each death has made us doubt and question our decisions, but we keep our faith on the path before us."

Iggy tried not to roll his eyes. He didn't want to disrespect Father John. "You keep the faith. I'll kill demons."

"Ignatius."

He walked slowly back over to his Trailblazer. He wanted to avoid losing his temper, and they'd already tested it to the limit. "If you want me to focus, keep Father Josiah Wilson out of my way. He's more of a distraction than Lalo could ever be."

Father John followed him over and rested his hands on the open driver side window after Iggy had gotten inside the vehicle. "Anger won't help you."

Iggy tilted his head toward the Jesuit. "I'm tired, not angry. Maybe a little ticked off. He sits in his righteousness without having ever lifted a finger to help any of my siblings. What training did he offer? None. Is his job to judge us? It's all I've ever seen him do."

In the cold light of day, with the deaths of his siblings continuing to stack up, Iggy had lost his ability to be patient or understanding. He appreciated those who had helped, trained, and cared for him, but Josiah Wilson had done none of those things.

Having finished his gentle lecture, Father John stepped away from the vehicle. Iggy watched him walk slowly toward the gardens. He shook his head, sighing tiredly and wondering if he'd truly become an army of one.

Not that they'd ever fought with him.

His siblings had done their duty, some more willingly than others. Titus had occasionally told stories about some of their older brothers and their three sisters who'd lived that Iggy hadn't met. The ones who'd tried to avoid the fight, only to die anyway, and the others who'd been highly skilled fighters.

And died anyway.

Where is the training going wrong if we're all still dying?

An uncomfortable question, but Iggy couldn't help wondering. The Jesuits provided one view of the growing battle between Lucifer's children and the demons. He'd dedicated himself to reading through the journals in the desperate hope of finding one bit of information to give him an edge.

With each sibling death, Iggy had lost his trust in parts of his training. The demons had to be dealt with, but the Jesuit method hadn't really been an example of success. Of however many hundreds of children over a century or more, only Iggy remained.

Maybe Lalo can find the needle in the haystack.

I'm not walking blindly into the grave for anyone.

Making the drive down from Sedalia into Denver, Iggy decided to pick up another pizza. Lalo had mentioned spending the morning cleaning out Lydia's garden. He planned to reorganize part of it as a gift to her.

And then he'll hide, because he's always mortified of being thanked.

On his way to the pizza place, an all too familiar sensation drew Iggy's attention away from Italian deliciousness toward a strip mall several blocks over. He parked at the edge of the lot, trying to hone his senses to locate the demon. *Why the fuck is a demon hanging around clothing and craft stores?*

"Aw, shit." Iggy shifted his vehicle into Drive, slamming his foot onto the gas pedal when he caught a glimpse of Siren standing with two men in the distance. He threw caution to the wind, swerving around a row of parked cars to reach the opposite side of the strip mall. A flash of lights and a siren disrupted his attempt to catch the demon and her thralls. "Fuck."

A bit of charm got the police officer off his back. Siren and the two men had disappeared in the brief time it had taken. She'd obviously gone far enough away for Iggy's senses to fail at picking up on her location.

Time for pizza.

"You're early." Lalo glared when Iggy strolled casually into the backyard, pizzas in one hand and backpack in the other. "Two hours. Go away."

"I brought pizza."

"Go. Away. Two hours." Lalo stubbornly returned to kneeling in the grass with his headphones firmly plugged into his ears.

Well, cold pizza it is.

He should've known better. Lalo hated sudden changes in plans. It had been a particular nightmare during school on days when the weather interfered.

Lalo had panic attacks when his schedule changed. Iggy knew he went through each aspect of his day carefully, paying attention to every detail the night before. Any shifts out of his control (or even in it) caused him to shut down.

Kicking himself for not thinking about Lalo's needs, Iggy made his way into the house. He set the pizzas on the kitchen counter. After grabbing a slice and a can of soda, he made a workspace on the living room floor with a few journals spread across the coffee table along with his laptop.

Journals or the not-clone clone?

Clone.

With the video from Lalo, Iggy managed to get a better look at the man. The Jesuits had connections throughout the city. He sent a copy over to Father John; maybe his contact with detectives in the police department might lead to identifying their mystery man.

After watching the footage another ten times and learning nothing, Iggy closed the video and moved on to another mystery. Where had Titus's body gone? He searched every local news site, along with websites that tracked police scanner activity.

Nothing.

Shifting down slightly, Iggy rested his head against the couch cushion with a groan. Research had never been a strong talent of his. Lalo had always been willing to help.

Do I take advantage of him?

Fuck.

Have to do better.

CHAPTER EIGHT

LALO

Five songs after Iggy's arrival, Lalo felt the boiling emotions from his meltdown settling down. He no longer wanted to bite into his hand or kick a wall. The energy faded away, leaving him tired and unable to concentrate.

Sitting in the dirt, Lalo closed his eyes and let the music wash over him. He muttered one of his favorite phrases from a video game over and over. The familiar rhythm of the words settled him the rest of the way.

Did he say pizza?

Lalo gathered up his tools, set them in the small shed in

the corner, and went inside to ensure Iggy hadn't destroyed anything. He smiled sheepishly as Iggy waved a pizza crust at him. "Sorry, Igster."

"Don't." He pointed the pizza at him. "Grab a few slices. I even brought you a twelve-pack of your beloved blackberry soda from Rocky Mountain Soda. Had it delivered to my apartment yesterday."

Lalo had discovered the variously flavored sodas and become completely obsessed. He'd always preferred drinks with bubbles in them. "Want one?"

"No." Iggy took a second slice of pizza from the box Lalo had brought in from the kitchen. "Why are you working so much in the garden now? Aren't all your seeds in pots at the moment?"

"Gardening requires constant attention. Between the Sedalia retreat, volunteering, and Lydia, there's always something to do." Lalo kept seeds in pots from the beginning of the year through spring, getting vegetables ready to go in the ground right before summer. Colorado's weather and elevation required extra work, but seeing the flourishing plots made it all worthwhile. He paused at the stacks of journals on the coffee table. "Did you raid Father Luca's library?"

"Partly. They won't miss them." Iggy winked at him, patting the rug beside him. "Pizza and research. It's like college all over again."

"College didn't work out so well for me." Lalo stared grimly down at his soda bottle. "I failed."

Iggy waited until Lalo had sat down to place a hand

on his knee. "They failed you. You did brilliantly. They weren't prepared to accommodate your needs. That's not your fucking fault, Lal."

Picking uncomfortably at his pizza crust, Lalo tried not to let his emotions run away with him. He swallowed down the lump in his throat. Accepting support from others didn't come naturally to him.

Does anything come naturally to me?

Aside from awkward responses to every moment of my life.

"Lal?"

Lalo didn't want to rehash his post-high school nightmare again. He'd had the same conversation so many times before. "What are we researching?"

Iggy watched him for a few seconds. Lalo wondered if he'd let the subject drop. "We've three problems."

"Just three?"

Iggy scowled at Lalo, who grinned around a bite of pizza. "Three big ones. Daddy dearest, the demons, and Titus's clone, doppelganger, or son. Maybe connected, maybe not. My gut is telling me somewhere in these journals we'll find answers or help of some sort."

"Does your gut tell you things a lot?" Lalo's stomach hadn't ever told him anything aside from that he should stop eating junk. And he never listened. "One fart for yes, two for no?"

"You're not funny." Iggy scowled at him.

"Does your stomach seriously talk to you?" Lalo wanted to know if it was a frequent phenomenon.

"Figure of speech, Lal. Figure of speech."

"Oh, right, I knew that." He closed his eyes and tried not to flush at the familiar rush of embarrassment at having misunderstood an obvious fact. "I did."

"Could you imagine if we did communicate through farts?"

"We're not having a serious discussion about flatulence. Isn't your Daddy Dearest sealed up in Hell somewhere?" Lalo had trouble genuinely buying into the concept. If it wasn't for seeing demons with his own eyes, he'd think Iggy had hallucinated the entire story. "Why are you worried about Lucifer now? Aside from your speaking stomach. Did the Jesuits warn you about something?"

Iggy set his pizza down, wiped his fingers on his jeans, and grabbed one of the journals from the coffee table. He flipped through to a page near the end. "This is from a relative of Father Ricci. He was the one to first believe Lucifer had been sealed up because of the lack of children beyond my birth."

"You're child enough for anyone," Lalo joked.

A bad joke it turned out, when Iggy went into a ten-minute monologue about what he'd read about some of his siblings who'd died over a hundred years ago. Lalo always struggled to follow lengthy, detailed explanations, but getting irritated wouldn't help. He wanted Iggy to get to the point.

"Stop talking for five seconds. *Holy Crumbs.*" Lalo felt like words had been stuffed into his head through his ears.

"What?"

"Is there proof either way?"

Iggy stretched his legs out underneath the coffee table. He grabbed a different journal and flipped through the lined pages. "One of my siblings, when I was five or six, running around playing, had an encounter with a demon. A conversation. Father Ricci transcribed what Michael told him."

After washing his greasy hands off in the kitchen, Lalo returned to gently pick up the journal. He treated them with kid gloves, while Iggy tossed them around carelessly. Scanning through Father Ricci's notations, he thought the unwritten words more interesting than the multitude of paragraphs dedicated to the certainty of Lucifer's banishment.

"They assumed."

"What?" Iggy leaned forward to read from the journal resting in Lalo's lap. "How so?"

"Sounds more like the prince of sulfur allowed himself to be sealed up." Lalo read through Michael's account; he had been the eldest of the living siblings when Iggy had been born. "Overly confident and not very specific. And why tell the siblings? What did the demons hope to gain?"

Demons did nothing without a purpose. Offering up information for free would never have happened. They'd wanted the Jesuits to know Lucifer had been at least temporarily removed from the picture.

But why?

"What do demons want?" Lalo asked, mostly thinking out loud. He continued when Iggy frowned at him. "Aside from seduction and souls. Granted, we don't know what they gain from it. How many deaths have we witnessed outside of your siblings? They seem more interested in being worshiped and power. Not murder for the sake of murder."

"The journals…"

"Are written by Jesuits." Lalo completed the sentence when Iggy trailed off. "One side of the story. Whatever the demons are, however evil and powerful, the journals only show what the priests believe to be their motivation."

"Fuck."

Lalo set the journal aside and reached for another, checking the dates to find an older one, from when Lucifer had been free. "Why don't we read through all of these? Find the references to your father's imprisonment, anything related to his goals and demonic killings outside of your siblings."

Iggy didn't answer but sorted the journals into two piles on the coffee table. He set his laptop between them. "Remind me why the Jesuits refused to hire you for research? Oh, right, common sense isn't always their priestly duty."

Ignoring the question and the joke, Lalo got up to put the pizza boxes away. He grabbed a notebook and pen for himself along with a second bottle of soda. In truth, the only reason the priests allowed him to work in the garden was Father Salvatore's insistence.

For the longest time, Lalo had believed they thought an autistic wasn't capable enough. He'd learned later that it had more to do with his being gay. Both hurt—being judged harshly for something out of his control.

Judge not lest ye be judged, Father.

He'd thrown the words at Father Ricci during his interview before storming out of the office. It had been months before Father Sal had convinced him to return to the garden. Only his close friendship with the man had kept him from refusing outright.

Good enough for the garden.

"Lal?" Iggy grabbed the back of Lalo's calf, guiding him closer and patting the floor beside him. "You all right?"

"Fine." He shook Iggy's hand off and sat next to him. "Have you ever analyzed what's in your tranq darts?"

"The holy water?"

"Yeah, but have you ever actually tested it?" Lalo had wondered for ages about the clear liquid in the darts that could take down the otherworldly creatures. "What if you really know nothing?"

"We're fucked."

CHAPTER NINE

IGGY

DEMONS FEED OFF DOUBTS. THEY MAKE THE MOST DEDICATED OF THE DEVIL'S OFFSPRING QUESTION OUR TRAINING AND METHODS. GUARD AGAINST ALLOWING THEM TO DRIFT TOO FAR AWAY.

~ *JESUIT JOURNAL, 1958*

And the winner of the most boring date on the planet is—me.

They read through the journals until three in the morning. Iggy woke up with Lalo asleep on his shoulder. They'd drifted off, leaning against each other on the floor.

Iggy hadn't expected to be rushed out the door with a slice of cold pizza and mug of coffee. Lalo had rushed off, barely remembering to lock the house up. He stared after the departing little vehicle in bemusement. "My morning breath isn't that bad, is it?"

Most days, Iggy would've made his way to Sedalia for a morning briefing with his mentors. Not today. Their reading from the previous night had left him with more questions than answers. He had major doubts about the true nature of the Jesuit mission.

What are we really doing?

Finishing up his pizza and coffee, Iggy decided to make his way across the city to an old school friend, Wendy, who now ran a research laboratory at the University of Denver. She'd been a whiz at chemistry and had more than once gone out of her way to protect Lalo from bullies. He wanted her to run tests on the supposed holy water darts.

No more being led around by my nose; facts or nothing at all. I refuse to die for a cause that might not even exist.

What do I know for certain?

Demons exist; they're not human even in their physical form.

If I'm half-demon, what would my DNA show?

Finding parking around the university on a morning when school was in session always took forever. Iggy ended up walking for a good twenty minutes after finding a space. He found the door with Dr. Wendy Lewis on it and knocked before entering to find her sitting at her desk and frowning at her computer.

She banged her mouse on her desk. "Click, you little bastard."

"Morning, Dr. Lewis."

Her dark-brown eyes narrowed on him, and she pointed her mouse at him. "Don't even start with me, Ignatius Faber."

"Who, me?" Iggy waggled his eyebrows at her. She'd been the most beautiful girl at their high school, without question. "How goes the research, Stony?"

"*Ignatius.*" Wendy had earned the nickname Stony for her physical resemblance to Jada Pinkett in *Set It Off.* She'd had the braids and style to match at the time. "What do you need?"

"I…." He trailed off, not quite knowing how to ask for her help. It occurred to him that Wendy would need details on secrets he'd kept from everyone but Lalo. What if she didn't believe him? "Do you trust me? I need to talk to you about something… about Titus and myself."

Wendy stopped glaring at him. She glanced over at the closed door before sliding her chair around her desk and coming to a stop in front of the seat he'd taken. "Funny story. About six months ago, I saw Titus on campus. Hadn't seen him in years; he didn't give me a second glance. I followed him, being the curious scientist that I am. He went into an abandoned building just outside the university. I watched for almost forty minutes before leaving. He never came out."

"Did you try the door?" Iggy briefly forgot why he wanted to speak with her. "Where is the building?"

"I didn't try the door. There were cameras on every corner of the building, plus a biometrically secured entrance. Why would an abandoned building have so much security?" Wendy had always been one of the smartest people in school, tending to find the crux of a problem far more easily than anyone else. She'd butted heads with their teachers as a result. "I just wrote it off as yet another one of the oddities connected to the Faber siblings."

"Titus died." Iggy decided to start with the not-clone clone. "Saw his body. Then it disappeared; nothing at the coroner's office. A few days later, Lal and I spotted someone who looked like his twin—or a younger version of him."

"Do you have another sibling? One who especially looks like Titus?"

"They're all dead. And I'm the youngest," he answered confidently, despite the disbelief he could see on her face.

Wendy reached back to grab a notebook from her desk. She opened to a blank page and tapped her pen against the page. "If you're completely sure, have you considered Titus might've been in a relationship and had a son? Or, if not, maybe a one-night stand? Donation to a sperm bank? I know you all shared the same father. Could Titus's mother have had a second child?"

"I don't know." Iggy scrubbed a hand over his face. He pulled the vial of holy water out of his pocket. "Titus's doppelganger is only one piece of my puzzle."

"I'm not doing shots with you." She plucked the vial out of his hand. "What's this?"

"You're going to think I'm nuts." Iggy didn't know how to start explaining. Lalo had known because he'd seen a demon. Wendy would probably want to commit him for assessment if he blurted out the truth. "I'm not sure what the vial contains, either."

Wendy set it carefully on a stand beside her computer that held several test tubes. "Talk to me. Despite your charming ways, I've never known you to outright lie to me. Start from the beginning and finish with how I can help."

Shaking off the lingering doubt, Iggy plunged straight to the heart of the matter. He told Wendy about his birth and siblings, all of them. His brothers and the rare three sisters who'd survived their births. She barely blinked through his bizarre tale of demonic entities, Jesuit conspiracies, and his not aging and superpowers.

After graduating with her master's, Wendy had applied for a grant to research the connections between genealogy and genetics. She'd wanted to expand on discoveries already made to trace ancestries beyond what modern science had managed. He'd hoped her expertise might help with the questions he'd had for so long.

Wendy grabbed him by the wrist, dragging him across the room toward her part of her lab. "I'll test your clear liquid later. First, we're testing your DNA. I'm curious what I'll find. We'll also add it to the online DNA databases; it's entirely possible you have more relatives. I assume you'll want to know about your paternal side."

"You believe me?" Iggy opened his mouth to allow her to swab the inside of his cheek. He grimaced at the sensation. "Don't think I'm losing my mind or hallucinating?"

"Jury's still out." She shushed him with a sharp wave of her hand.

Taking his laptop out of his backpack, Iggy decided to see what information was available on the building she'd mentioned. Public records only showed a purchase twenty-three years ago, with no names or contact information. He typed the address into a simple internet search to see if he'd get lucky.

Nothing.

Well, not nothing.

He found a single mention on a Denver conspiracy website that claimed evil spirits haunted the building. Blurry photos offered up as proof did catch his attention. They reminded him of the images Lalo had taken of the demon at the park.

What were demons doing around the university? And why had Titus or his lookalike gone inside? He wondered if any of his questions would ever get answers.

"Has your blood ever been tested?" Wendy interrupted him after twenty minutes. She'd pulled on latex gloves and held a capped needle in one hand. "I want to run a battery of tests. You never know what might come out of it."

Iggy eyed the needle with distaste. "Seriously?"

"DNA testing is underway with your saliva. It'll take a few weeks to get all the answers. For now, I want to check your blood type for starters." She motioned for him to roll up his sleeve. "Once I get this going, you're going to tell me the rest of the story."

"The rest?"

"You're supposedly the son of Lucifer. Now, I'm not a Christian, but the Biblical mythology isn't foreign to me. What happened to the mothers? How did they die? And why do you only have three sisters across however many centuries? I know you're not sure that's important, but I do enjoy being thorough." Wendy gently withdrew the needle, having successfully distracted him from the blood draw. "How were the Jesuits able to find all of you?"

"Lalo used to ask about that. He never fully trusted the priests or their records." Iggy pressed a tissue to the crook of his arm to stem the bleeding. "I don't know. My mother died in childbirth. Every sibling I knew personally was the same. My aging has definitely slowed down. There are elements to this story that can't be explained by any test you do."

Wendy tossed her gloves into a small bin in the corner of the room. She glanced at her watch. "I'm also testing your age through gene expression. There's roughly a three-year margin of error, but if you've genuinely stopped growing older, this might show proof."

"You can't show anyone." Iggy knew at best they'd both be laughed out of the university. He hesitated to think what the government might do if word of superhumans existed; he'd seen too many movies not to know how badly that would end. "Anyone. I don't care how fascinating the results."

She grabbed her chair to sit beside him. "I can keep secrets. We both know the dangers of sharing our truth with the world."

Attending a conservative Catholic high school had been complicated for both of them. The world hadn't changed sufficiently for them to be completely out of the closet in the nineties. Wendy, Iggy, and Lalo had found comfort in one another, sharing some, though obviously not all, of their secrets.

"Does Lalo know?"

"He saw me fight one of the demons." Iggy twisted the laptop to show her the video, not that it showed much. "Not the strongest evidence in the world."

"About as strong as the footage of the Loch Ness monster." Wendy tapped a key to replay the video. "He vanishes. The blurry figure. Can you disappear?"

"No. Being part human seems to weaken abilities." Iggy leaned away from Wendy when she peered at him like one of her research projects. "I am not a slide under your microscope."

She snickered at his discomfort. "What about the liquid you wanted me to test?"

"Holy water."

Wendy glanced over at the vial and back to him several times. "Holy water? And what, they fizzle and melt like the wicked witch?"

"Stuns them long enough for me to set them on fire." Iggy waited for her to stop laughing at him.

"Holy water is just blessed water. Priest waves his hands over it and says some shit." She slid her chair back over to the desk to grab the vial, shaking it a few times. "Definitely throwing this into the mass spectrometer to figure out what it is. I bet you lunch there's nothing sanctified about your secret weapon."

Five minutes later, Wendy was staring between the results and several reference books. She muttered to herself repeatedly. Iggy waited patiently, not wanting to interrupt, taking a moment to text Lalo with the progress.

"Saline."

"What?" Iggy glanced up from the message Lalo had sent about wanting to meet up with both of them for lunch. "Saline? Salt?"

"Massive amounts of salt in this, along with a plant essence." She pointed to one of the lines on the printout. "Aconitum columbianum."

"In non-science English?"

"Monkshood."

"Not a fucking clue. Do I look like Lalo? I know nothing about plants." Iggy found the name humorous, but it didn't ring a bell.

"Wolfsbane, though technically that's a made-up plant based on the real deal—monkshood."

"Like from Harry Potter?" He grinned when she threw her hands up in exasperation. He texted Lalo to ask if the Jesuit retreat garden contained monkshood. "What's so special about your plant?"

"It's poisonous, for one." Wendy continued flipping through one of her massive books. "Also, some people believe both salt and monkshood can cause harm to demons and other evil beings."

"Anything else?"

"Anise. Other plant essences. It's not holy water." Wendy closed the book and reached for another one. "Though, technically, I can't say for certain without testing some. Think you can get some from a source other than your Jesuits? Maybe a local Catholic church not attached to them? We'd have a control to test against yours to make sure."

"Are you sure you want to get involved in this mess?" Iggy had lost all of his siblings, even though they hadn't been close. He cared deeply about Wendy and wondered if he might regret dragging her and Lalo into his disaster of a life. "Even if they aren't evil creatures from Hell, they're capable of murder."

"My little brother died trying to protect my mother from an intruder. Humans are capable of murder. I'm not running away from this mystery you've dumped in my lap." She grabbed her purse from underneath her desk. "The tests don't need me to babysit them. You owe me lunch."

CHAPTER TEN

LALO

THE FIRST CAPTURED DEMON FAILED TO PROVIDE SUFFICIENT ANSWERS TO THE IMPORTANCE OF THE CHILDREN. PRAYERS, RESEARCH, AND DEDICATION LED TO THE ANSWERS. WE DETERMINED RAISING THE CHILDREN TO BE BETTER THAN THEIR PATERNAL ROOTS WAS THE MISSION GOD HAD PROVIDED. GOODNESS FLOWED EVEN FROM EVIL ORIGINS TO TIP THE SCALES.

~ JESUIT JOURNAL, 1786

Iggy: Why don't we compromise? I'll call the order into Erbie Gerbie, and you pick it up. Just run in, pay, and run out. You barely have to talk to them.

Lalo: Fine.

Iggy: Are you sure?

Lalo: Why can't we just have them deliver to the park?

Iggy: Lal.

Lalo: Fine.

It wasn't fine. Lalo dug his knuckles into his upper thigh, trying to burn off enough energy to avoid a meltdown in public. Pain helped, sometimes.

He'd intended to spend the morning in gardens, and then work on photos for an upcoming exhibition. Instead, they were going to meet for lunch. With Wendy. He loved Stony, but they'd changed his carefully laid out plans for the day.

Even if it was my decision.

And adding a visit to a restaurant at one of the busiest times of the day certainly wouldn't help at all. Erbie Gerbie was Iggy's affectionate name for Erbert and Gerbet's Sandwich Shop. He consoled himself with the news that he'd soon have a chicken and cranberry wasabi sub in his hands.

A small consolation, when noon traffic forced him to park a distance from the restaurant and Lalo had to deal with loads of people inside. He grinned when the bag contained more peanut butter crispy cookies than was probably healthy along with the sandwiches and bags of chips. Somehow, he managed to carry the bag of food along with three drinks to his little Scion without dropping any of the sodas.

A miracle considering Lalo had been known to drop cups and bottles when he only had one to deal with. *Food, drinks, cookies. I wonder if they'd mind if I just ate all of it? Probably.* He made the drive to Washington Park to find Wendy and Iggy.

They'd found a bench near the lake. Lalo followed the

trail until he ran into Iggy, who quickly grabbed the drinks from him. He waved at Wendy when she pulled her hand out of her hoodie pocket to wave at him.

The weather had gifted them a cool but bright, sunny spring day. Lalo opted to sit on the grass in front of the bench, wanting to avoid being crowded. He'd stretched himself socially already; even a small amount of space felt like a massive relief to him.

"Are you going to hoard all the cookies?" Iggy tried to snatch one from the bag when Lalo hugged it to his chest. "Not even one?"

"Mine. All mine. My precious." Lalo patted the bag and hid it behind his back. "So? What's with lunch in the park?"

Wendy set her sandwich to one side, then reached into the satchel at her side. She pulled out a sheet of paper and handed to him. "Aconitum columbianum."

"Monkshood." Lalo glanced at the purple flower pictured on the printout. "I told Ig that there's a patch of these at the Sedalia retreat garden. In the sealed off part that Father Salvatore manages. There are several plants, but I've never touched the area. I only know about the monkshood because I had to help him obtain seeds a year or two ago."

Iggy held up one of the vials of clear liquid used in his dart gun. "Turns out, not holy water."

"We still need to verify for certain by comparing your liquid to actual holy water," Wendy cautioned.

"Lydia has holy water. Her sister brought some back from a trip to Rome." Lalo grinned, remembering how she had grumbled at receiving such a useless present. "She wouldn't mind offering it for research purposes. Is that your big reveal?"

"Not the only one." Iggy tried to steal one of the cookies, and Lalo knocked his hand away. "Sharing is caring, Lal."

"Says the man without the cookies." He continued reading the paper Wendy had given him. "Monkshood, salt, water, basil… to what end?"

"Knocks the demons on their ass." Iggy shrugged. "Why hide the truth under the guise of holy water?"

While they finished their sandwiches, Iggy filled Lalo in on the other discoveries and mysteries. The supposedly abandoned building seemed of particular interest. He hadn't been able to shake the idea of the Titus lookalike being more important than they realized.

Lalo glanced from Wendy to Iggy. "If Stony's the brain and Iggy's the brawn, does that make me the quirky sidekick who gets captured because they ran into a wall?"

"You'll always be more than my sidekick." Iggy grunted when Lalo whacked him on the shin. "I demand cookie payment for my pain and suffering."

Drawing them back to the matter at hand, Wendy ran through the small amount of information on the building. They hadn't learned much. Iggy thought a nighttime visit might provide the best opportunity to get inside.

Wendy disagreed. She thought they should take a measured approach, learning more about the owner and mapping out the security cameras to prevent them getting busted trying to investigate. "How would you even explain to the police what you're doing snooping around in the first place?"

"They'd have to see me." Iggy popped the last of his sandwich into his mouth, wiping his hands off on his jeans. "At night, dressed in black, moving as fast as possible, they'll see a blur but not much else. They'd get no identifying features."

"So, all you have to do is get through the massive security door with the biometric scanner?" Wendy burst the bubble in Iggy's master plan. "Can you walk through walls?"

While Wendy and Iggy bickered like they were back in high school, Lalo returned to studying the plant data. He wondered if Father Sal would stop him from a cursory inspection of the plants in the secret garden. What else might he find other than monkshood?

"Deliver a pizza." Lalo folded the paper and placed it inside his pocket.

"What?" Iggy stopped arguing with Wendy midsentence. "Deliver a pizza to where?"

"The warehouse. See if anyone answers." Lalo averted his eyes when both Iggy and Wendy stared at him. "What? It works in movies. If you're worried about them getting you on camera, why not anonymously pay for pizzas to be delivered, and we can watch from a hiding spot?"

"We're going on a stakeout." Wendy grabbed the cookie Lalo held out to her, laughing when Iggy grumbled. "When are you two going on a second date?"

"*Iggy.*"

"What? Were we keeping it a secret? She tortured me for information." Iggy snagged the cookie from Wendy and shoved the entire thing into his mouth.

"Is the sex good?" Wendy asked.

Lalo stared at the plastic bag from the restaurant, briefly considering pulling it over his head. "Nonexistent. And none of your business."

Getting to his feet, Lalo gathered up all the trash. He tossed Iggy one of the last cookies. His legs had gone numb from sitting on the grass for so long, and he stumbled slightly, trying to shake off the annoying sensation.

"I've a research lab to lead in twenty minutes. You two fuck, and then figure out when we're staking out the warehouse. I vote for tomorrow night." Wendy dropped kisses on both their cheeks before taking off at a jog. "Call me later."

"We could—"

"Eat your cookie," Lalo cut him off, already knowing Iggy's thoughts tended to live permanently in the gutter. "And, no, not a euphemism."

"Spoilsport." Iggy followed him down the path toward the parking lot. "Want to head up to Sedalia with me tomorrow afternoon before the stakeout? See Father Sal? I'm hoping to *borrow* a few more journals before they realize I've taken them."

"Fine." Lalo double-checked his car was locked, grabbed his camera bag, tossed the trash into a garbage can, and climbed into the Trailblazer. "Am I making you move too slowly?"

Iggy frowned at Lalo for almost a full minute. "Sex isn't everything."

"But, am I?"

Iggy twisted in his seat. He reached out to cup Lalo's face gently, dragging his thumb across his bottom lip while his fingers ran across his five o'clock shadow. "I'm in no rush to get you naked, Lal. You'll better appreciate my sexual mastery if I take my time."

Lalo bit Iggy's thumb and shoved his hand away. "Just drive."

CHAPTER ELEVEN

IGGY

DEMONS IN MODERN TIMES HAVE CHANGED MUCH FROM PREVIOUS DEALINGS THROUGH THE CENTURIES. NO LONGER CONTENT WITH STARTING WARS AND CAUSING MASS DEATH, THEY APPEAR TO CRAVE DOMINATION THROUGH ADORATION. A DANGEROUS ENEMY TO COMBAT IN AN AGE OF IDOLATRY,

~ JESUIT JOURNAL, 1996

The drive from the park up to Sedalia the next day was a quiet one. Lalo had shoved headphones into his ears, tuning everything out. Iggy wondered if the crowded restaurant, impromptu picnic, and teasing yesterday had been too much for him; Lalo sometimes needed days to recover.

Kicking himself for not doing better, Iggy focused on the drive. He kept the radio turned off, not wanting to exacerbate the situation. Lalo at least had time to decompress a little before they arrived.

Do better.

Through the many years they'd known each other, Iggy had watched Lalo adjust to situations thrown at him. The world rarely, if ever, accommodated his needs. Iggy promised himself that he'd pay more attention.

I could've picked up the sandwiches. We could've ordered from closer to the park. Lal didn't have to go into a packed restaurant at lunch.

I could've come up to Sedalia on my own.

Damn it.

He always remembered Lalo trying to explain to a teacher why he didn't want to attend a school event. *Just because I'm capable doesn't mean I'm not negatively affected by forcing myself to go.* Iggy hadn't understood at the time.

"Whatever you're thinking about so loudly, stop." Lalo broke into his self-recrimination. "We might work with Catholics, but we're not practicing. So stop with the guilt. And don't say sorry."

With that out of the way, Lalo put his earbuds back in and closed his eyes. No response required. Silence filled the Trailblazer once again, leaving Iggy with nothing but his thoughts.

Traffic didn't hinder them much, making the thirty-minute drive down the interstate to the foothills relatively painless. Iggy pulled into the private parking at the rear of the Jesuit retreat center. He nudged Lalo with his elbow to wake him up.

"Ready?"

Lalo stretched and tugged the headphones out of his ears with a grimace. "Going to see if I can sneak into the sectioned-off portion of the garden. I'll get samples for Stony to test."

"Not sure Dr. Lewis appreciates her high school nicknames anymore." Iggy knew Lalo was probably the only other person Wendy would allow to get away with the moniker. "I suppose it's better than calling her Rainbow Bright."

"Wonder if she still has those rainbow-colored laces that went in her Converse?" Lalo lifted his leg to show his battered sneakers with the hole in the top. He refused to replace them, and Lydia had even tried sewing a patch to fix the problem.

"Not everyone is opposed to buying new shoes."

"These are comfortable." Lalo petted the top of his blue shoes. "Do you know how hard breaking in new sneakers can be? They make weird sounds and squeeze my toes. These work."

"What happens when they fall apart and you can't superglue the bits together anymore?" Iggy had watched Lalo reattach the soles at least three times.

"Doom. Wailing and gnashing of teeth."

"You're not allowed to attend Mass anymore." He turned off the vehicle, pocketed his keys, and got out of the Trailblazer. "Ready to infiltrate?"

"Is it infiltration when we have an open invitation?" Lalo wandered past him, already putting his headphones into his ears once again.

Iggy's gaze followed Lalo, who disappeared through the wooden gate leading into the garden. He sensed a presence and glanced over. "Father Sal."

"Ignatius." He smiled as always. He was the most open and welcoming of all the Jesuits. "You both seem tense."

"Do we?" Iggy didn't think he appeared overly stressed. Lalo tended to live with a permanent level of anxiety when not at home or in a place he considered to be safe.

"You might, if so inclined, read journals by Father Xavier Ricci, a cousin of Luca's and a close friend of Josiah's. Xavier found a kindred spirit in the latter more than his own relative." He mentioned a priest Iggy had never heard of. "He was excommunicated in the 70s. You'll find his writings on one of the top shelves in the library, hidden behind false paneling. The others are currently on the retreat side of the compound. I'd imagine you have thirty minutes or more to retrieve them."

Iggy stared stupidly at the priest, who walked away without another word, heading toward the garden. "What the actual fuck?"

"Mind your language, Ignatius," Father Salvatore called over his shoulder. His dark-brown eyes twinkled with amusement.

"What the *actual* fuck?" Iggy whispered to himself.

Of all the Jesuits, Father Sal had grown quite protective of his gardening protégé. He'd never approved of his fellow priests' less tolerant attitude toward Lalo. Iggy didn't know his motivation in sharing secrets, but he instinctually trusted him—on this at least.

As time was of the essence, Iggy jogged across the parking lot and down the gravel path to the library. How had he never noticed a hidden panel when so much of his youth had been spent reading the journals? Childish curiosity had led him to snoop through everything else.

Once inside, Iggy tossed his backpack on one of the study tables and turned his focus to the tall shelves lining the walls. He scanned the dark antique wood in an attempt to find any visual clues from a distance. *Nothing. Let's get up close and personal, shall we?*

A sturdy chair provided an ideal stepstool. Even at his height, he couldn't quite check the panels on the top shelves without it. He climbed up to the first one, carefully running his fingers along the sides and back behind the rows of books and journals without noticing anything out of the ordinary; a light knock on the wood sounded solid enough.

Nothing.

Three shelves in, his inspection hadn't revealed anything aside from dust bunnies. He shifted the chair down to the next one and again got up to tap his knuckles against the wood. The slightly muffled thud, duller than the previous attempts, immediately caught his attention.

Not wanting to destroy the shelf, Iggy gently traced the edges of the panel to find a release trigger. His finger caught a small notch along the right corner, and he pressed it. The trap door slid open and revealed a small linen sack holding a stack of four, slender, leather-bound journals.

"Well, well, well." Iggy gingerly removed the linen bag and resealed the panel. He used his sleeve to wipe the entire shelf to avoid the obvious marks his fingers had left behind in the dust. "What are you hiding in your pages?"

"Shameful secrets."

Iggy moved away from the shelf and placed the sack securely into his backpack, then turned to face Father Luke Martin, the oldest of his mentors, though not the oldest of the priests. His white hair and beard made him more a cross between a benevolent Santa and Kurt Russell than a skilled fighter. "How do you always manage to sneak up on me?"

"Silence is my superpower." Father Luke had a gentle way about him, belying his years of police training before joining the Jesuit order in his late twenties. He waved Iggy toward two comfortable armchairs on the opposite side of the room from the shelves. "I was forbidden to speak with you about the contents of those journals, despite my belief in their importance. I was overruled."

Iggy lowered himself into one of the chairs, focusing so intently on the priest that he almost missed the seat. "Why?"

"Telling you about their contents requires admitting to a lie by omission." He seemed genuinely pained and his fingers worried at the rosary dangling from his wrist. "Of all our young students, you asked the most probing questions. Your curiosity was never sated. Brother Luca refused to allow us to answer. Or, me, in any case. The others agreed with him, aside from Salvatore, who lives to be contrary."

"Josiah lives to be contrary," Iggy countered. "Father Sal only argues with his plants."

Father Luke chuckled and shuffled more comfortably into his seat. "Salvatore is very fond of you."

"Because I'm nice to Lalo—and the plants."

He laughed for a second time, then gestured to the backpack where Iggy had hidden the journals. "Those belong to an excommunicated priest, as I'm sure Salvatore told you. Luca's cousin. Xavier had wild ideas on how to solve the demonic issue. He thought we didn't go far enough in fighting fire with fire. He believed your siblings provided the perfect soldier for a holy war, never caring at all about the damage done to young souls. I may have trained many of you to fight, but only ever out of a desire to ensure you could protect yourselves."

Iggy wondered how wild ideas from a priest could actually be. "And he was kicked out on his ass?"

Father Luke shook his head at the language. "He was. And he disappeared."

"Dun, dun, dun," Iggy murmured dramatically. "Disappeared? Did you kill him?"

"*Ignatius.*"

"Fair question. Excommunicated could mean anything." He'd been trained to destroy demons. It didn't seem much of a stretch for those who taught him to be capable of killing. "How do you know all of this anyway?"

Father Luke didn't answer, posing a question of his own instead. "How old do you think I am?"

Iggy blinked at the sudden change of subject. "Isn't vanity a sin?"

Father Luke stared at Iggy until he stopped snickering. "I've lived through both world wars."

Iggy's jaw dropped in shock. "So, I'm not the only one

of Lucifer's children left."

"No. Technically, yes. I'm a grandchild. Not quite as strong or capable as you and the other siblings." He reached into his cassock pocket to retrieve a small embossed book. "My journal from the early days. You'll find details of the way the order here in Sedalia grew into an official program for the orphans and myself. It also details how we determined Lucifer's purpose."

"What the fuck is happening?" Iggy almost dropped the book when he reached out for it. "Why didn't you tell me?"

"Father Ricci and his predecessor both believed I might prove to be a distraction." Father Luke shrugged. "You are *not* alone, Ignatius. We might not all agree on the path forward, but at the very least, Salvatore and I will put every ounce of our beings into you succeeding—and surviving."

What. The. Actual. Fuck.

Iggy traced the embossed initials at the bottom right of the journal. "You're worried."

"Aren't you?" Father Luke gestured toward the book in Iggy's hand. "Read them, all of them if you can. One of our greatest weaknesses was disregarding certain brothers who didn't fall into the mold of the perfect Jesuit. You may discover answers on the fringes of our order—rather than those like Josiah who rose up the ranks to find a way to fully take control."

"Dissension in the ranks?" Iggy teased.

"Yes." He nodded seriously. "And not for the first time."

CHAPTER TWELVE

LALO

Becoming attached to the children leads to a dangerously slippery slope. Objectivity is absolutely necessary to maintain control. We train. We teach. We cannot become emotionally involved. Our mission remains far more important.

~ *JESUIT JOURNAL, 1988*

"These might help you."

Lalo dropped the small garden shears in his hand, narrowly missing his foot. "Father Sal."

"You'll find these might keep your samples secure." He held out several small plastic containers. "I raided the kitchen cabinets for you."

Lalo bent to retrieve the scissors, double-checking they hadn't cut his beloved sneakers. "I'm experimenting with grafting herbs."

"No, you aren't." Father Salvatore set the small tubs on a wooden shelf in the greenhouse. They kept pots of various plants inside during the colder months to get them prepared. "Or rather, I highly doubt the reason you came to take samples was for gardening experiments."

"Might be," Lalo insisted stubbornly. He fidgeted with the shears and almost lost a finger trying to get a small clipping. *Okay, let's not sacrifice a body part in the process.* "Stranger things have happened."

"They have. I'm sure." Father Salvatore reached out to gently take the shears from Lalo's fingers. "Why don't I clip them for you?"

This is the opposite of snooping. I'm robbing a bank with the security guard helping fill the bags with money. Is this normal?

This can't be normal.

"You should breathe, young man. Ignatius won't believe you passed out all on your own." Father Sal knelt in front of Lalo when he sank down on a wooden crate. "Put your music on and readjust your mental plan for how your day was supposed to go."

The solitude of the garden always drew in Lalo. Father Salvatore, true to his word, quietly moved around the small section of the greenhouse, clipping various plants and placing them carefully in the little pots. He stayed sitting with his music playing until Iggy wandered in with Father Luke close behind.

"The plot thickened," Iggy whispered when he walked

by Lalo. He went over to take the little tubs from Father Salvatore and placed them in his backpack. "Ready to go, Lal?"

"Yes" seemed a simple word. Lalo couldn't quite get his brain to connect to his mouth. He nodded instead.

Lost in his head, Lalo managed to wave. Getting in the Trailblazer and leaving Sedalia was more of a blur than anything else. Iggy had immediately turned on the "Lalo hates peopling" playlist, allowing the music to soothe him.

Resting his forehead against the glass, Lalo watched the foothills slowly shift into the city proper. They slowed to a crawl in the midafternoon traffic. As they turned onto a side street near the university, he noticed a familiar figure stopped at the light.

"Ig." Lalo reached out to turn the music down. He pointed to the driver of the flashy Dodge Charger who seemed more focused on a conversation on his phone than the cars around him. "Am I seeing things?"

"Yes, but no." Iggy kept just to the back of the Charger. "Get the license plate for me. We might get a name if we're lucky."

Since neither of them believed in luck, Lalo ignored the comment and focused his camera on the vehicle. He tried to keep from making it obvious while ensuring they had a clear view of the license plate along with the Charger itself. When their doppelganger made a right turn, Iggy continued forward to follow.

He drove further down the street, easing into a packed overflow parking lot the university students used. He angled the Trailblazer so they could continue to watch their target who'd parked on the side of the street. "Too early for a stakeout. Someone from campus security will eventually want to know why we're sitting here. We should've gotten Wendy to get a pass for us. What time is her lab over?"

"What?" Lalo didn't bother looking away from his camera viewfinder where he watched the not-Titus walk down the sidewalk and disappear through a heavy door. His brain caught up with the question before Iggy had a chance to repeat himself. "Her last lab of the day should've ended ten minutes ago. I'm sure students will have questions for her. And she said there was a faculty meeting afterward. Hungry."

"Stakeouts don't have snack breaks."

"He went inside the building already. We're not going to see anything now. Also, I'm hungry." Lalo was preparing himself to argue vehemently for an early dinner or late lunch when Iggy froze beside him. "Sulfuric senses tingling?"

Iggy nodded.

He eyed him in concern, carefully setting his camera down on the dashboard. "Ig?"

"Demons. Maybe more than one? I've never sensed such a strong presence. It has to be more than one of them. Fuck." He unbuckled his seat belt. "Whatever they're doing can't be good. I haven't…."

"Ig?" Lalo grew anxious as Iggy paled further. "What the fudge is going on?"

"I have to get inside the building."

Lalo grabbed his arm to stop him from immediately

leaping out of the vehicle. "Think. You can't sneak into a secure building without a plan. I doubt they went to the trouble of installing a state-of-the-art security system to not make it difficult to enter. Let me use my drone."

"Stay here." Iggy ignored his rambling.

Because of course he ignores me when I'm making sense. Son of a fudgsicle.

With a groan, Lalo decided not to waste further energy attempting to stop Iggy. He grabbed his drone to follow from a distance. His mouth dropped open in shock when Iggy sped up, moving faster than humanly possible.

Holy crumbs.

Forget Usain Bolt.

Ig's quicker than the Flash.

Theoretically, Lalo had known Iggy had gifts from the special portion of his DNA. He'd never seen him take off at full tilt. Whatever Iggy sensed had to be more dangerous than the average demon.

He guided the drone beyond Iggy, getting a clear view of every side of the building, including the roof. They might be able to use the footage to their advantage later. He enjoyed watching Iggy as well.

"Magnificent, isn't he?"

Lalo dropped his tablet. *What the fennel? I didn't hear anyone.* He watched in stunned amazement as a hand shot out to grab it midair as it slowed impossibly to almost freeze by his waist. "He is."

"My most magnificent creation." The stranger stood almost a foot taller than Lalo and appeared to be an older, gray-haired, more beatific version of Iggy. He'd never seen a man so beautifully angelic, yet danger and darkness practically oozed out of his pores. *He's terrifying.* "Most like myself in almost every way. The closest to perfection from my original attempts. Pity, really. Those fools twisted him around. His mother's humanity poisoned my hopes for him."

Lalo's mind went blank even as he grabbed the tablet to carefully guide the drone back. He found words an impossibility, frozen because his brain was sometimes a jerk in a crisis.

"And you?" The stranger smiled wickedly—a twisted version of Iggy's grin. "You're his weakness."

CHAPTER THIRTEEN

IGGY

Half a block from the building, Iggy skidded to a halt on the sidewalk. *Wait. Where the hell did it go?* He twisted around in an attempt to pick up the demon's location. His heart froze in his chest when he spotted Lalo not far from the parking lot with a stranger by his side.

Though Lalo likely didn't see, Iggy noticed the slight shimmer of demonic energy around the man. He ran the short distance as quickly as possible, only to arrive too late. Lalo stood alone, looking completely shell-shocked.

"Lal?" Iggy grabbed him gently by the shoulders. He shook him slightly. "Lal? Are you all right? Did he hurt you?

Fuck. Talk to me, damn it."

Realizing a silent Lalo likely meant he'd gone into a shutdown from stress or fear, Iggy shifted his hold to wrap his arm around Lalo's shoulder, guiding him down the sidewalk toward the Trailblazer. He wanted to get him safely out of sight.

The tall stranger had felt and appeared demonic. Iggy had never sensed such strength before. He'd never seen him before either.

Lalo slid into the passenger side. He pulled his feet up on the seat and wrapped his arms around his legs, staring at Iggy, who was leaning against the open door. "Lucy's come out to play."

"What?" Iggy wondered if the demon had messed with Lalo's mind. "Lucy?"

I don't know any…. Oh fuck.

No wonder he seemed so familiar.

"Lucifer?"

Lalo nodded. "He said you should be careful not to interfere in his plans."

Iggy reached up to rest a hand firmly on Lalo's shoulder. "Well, we'll just have to be smarter than him."

"Than the devil?"

"Questioning my abilities?" Iggy teased, pleased to see Lalo crack a smile. He decided not to lean in for the kiss he wanted, not after their stressful experience, and walked around the vehicle to hop into the driver seat.

"No, your sanity."

Tapping his fingers against the steering wheel, Iggy

decided maybe a stakeout did require a snack break. He made the short drive to the Ramen House, one of Lalo's favorite restaurants. They both needed something warm to chase away the icy chill of fear.

Two bowls of roast duck noodle soup and a triple serving of furikake french fries would definitely get them through the evening. Iggy picked up ramen for Wendy as well. She'd texted while he'd been inside the restaurant to say her meeting had ended early.

"Think Wendy will want fries?" Lalo had the first container open and proceeded to shove a few into his mouth.

With a shrug, Iggy leaned forward and opened his mouth with an impatient grunt. Lalo flicked a fry at his face. He snickered when it caught Iggy in the eye.

"*Lal.*" He grimaced before wiping the grease and seasoning off his face. He was relieved to see Lalo smiling. "We'll head back to the parking lot and wait for her there. I doubt she'll miss the fries."

A complete lie, since Wendy had specifically asked for an order of them when he'd texted her. *You snooze, you lose.* Iggy had always found it impossible to deny Lalo anything. He wanted him to have the world, or at least all the seasoned fries available.

I'm such a romantic.

Grabbing one of the containers of fries for himself, Iggy waited in silence. Lalo would eventually tell him about Lucifer's conversation. He highly doubted his father had kept to a one-sentence warning.

All these years, Iggy had tried to separate his dangerous

world of hunting from Lalo. He'd kept them apart, at least in his mind. He had the sinking feeling all pretense of safety had disappeared.

"I agree with him on one thing." Lalo picked absently at his fries, not eating them. "You are magnificent."

"He said I was magnificent?"

"His greatest creation. Said something about you basically being plan A."

Iggy didn't quite appreciate the wording. Creation made him seem like a specimen created in a laboratory. His gaze shifted toward the large building in the distance. "Maybe our Titus doppelganger isn't a random lookalike."

"Clone?"

"Maybe." He wondered if Titus had been old enough to have a son in his early twenties. "What do we know for sure?"

"Lucifer isn't locked up. Titus is dead. Someone who looks like him is wandering around. There's a not-abandoned abandoned building with a lot of fancy security. And I've eaten all my fries in record time." Lalo reached slyly into the bag for the extra container of fries that Wendy would definitely miss. "Also, the Jesuits are part of some massive conspiracy. Holy water might not be holy. And you run really fast."

"Did you save up all your words for that?" Iggy grinned when Lalo inhaled deeply to catch his breath. "Not succinct, but accurate."

"Are you two eating my fries?" Wendy banged her fist against the passenger window, making them both jump.

"Fuck."

"Fudgsicle."

"Open up." She moved to the back door, trying the handle a few times before Iggy managed to unlock it. Lalo waited for her to get seated before offering her bowl of ramen. "And the fries?"

Lalo handed over the container holding the remnants of what were supposed to be her fries. "I was hungry."

While Lalo and Wendy argued over potato morsels, Iggy dug out his ramen. He'd gotten halfway through before the two declared a truce. Lalo had always been more comfortable around Wendy than anyone else in school.

What had Lucifer wanted? When had he gotten free? And most importantly, why had he decided to speak with Lalo?

Do the demons know he's free?

"This is a dream, right? You're going to wake me up, and I'll realize I shouldn't go to sleep watching Buffy anymore." Wendy had taken several minutes to process everything when Iggy filled her in on their afternoon, starting with the surprise admissions from the Jesuits and ending with the surprise appearance of his father. "Your blood work is strange."

"Define strange."

"Strange enough that if I showed the results to anyone, the government would have you locked up in a secret facility for testing before I even finished reading through the first page." Wendy fished around in her purse and came up with a small plastic bottle. "One of my students is religious. I asked them yesterday and they brought holy water in for me today. It, as expected, didn't match your vials. Though, now my news seems even less shocking."

As the parking lot slowly thinned out, Iggy decided to focus on one issue at a time. The warehouse first. He wanted in the abandoned building. They'd find answers inside, some of them, at least.

He'd find. Wendy and Lalo would not be going. Their idea of fighting was trying to beat each other in contests naming the uses of various plants, with the loser having to do a shot of soy sauce.

They didn't stay in the parking lot. He knew they wouldn't. Wendy got behind the wheel to move closer to the building for a quick getaway; Lalo had unpacked his drone, letting it fly high above to offer an aerial perspective with the thermal mode active on his camera.

"Stay inside the vehicle." Iggy already regretted agreeing to the stakeout. He should've come by himself. "This isn't a video game where you get to restart if you die."

"We're not helpless," Lalo snapped indignantly. His gaze was focused completely on the tablet he used to control the drone.

"No, you aren't." He slipped out of the passenger seat and moved to the back of the vehicle to retrieve his dart gun. "You're also no match for a demon."

Neither Wendy nor Lalo had a response for him. If nothing else, they'd stay inside the vehicle. Iggy had seen enough not to want them coming face-to-face with any of the shadowy creatures that stalked Denver. He made a mental note to give them some basic training with the dart guns.

If a sulfuric war started between Lucifer and his former legions, he wanted them to have at least a fighting chance.

"Ig."

"I'll be fine, Lal. I've hunted demons for a long time. How hard can sneaking into one building be?" He grinned at Lalo, who didn't appear to find any humor in the situation. "Just stay here. And keep an eye in the sky for me."

Throwing on his hoodie, Iggy shoved his hands into his pockets. He took the long way around, avoiding the security cameras. An alley between two smaller buildings offered a blind spot for him to hide in.

Once blended into the shadows, Iggy crouched down and patiently scanned every angle of the building, thanks to Lalo's drone footage from earlier. They'd already determined the roof and front didn't provide a viable entrance for him.

Shame.

I always do well in the front door.

Movies always made sneaking into a secured facility so easy. From his vantage, Iggy thought the small window near a boarded-up door at the back had the best chance. Whatever the risk, they had to get answers.

You can't win a war by fighting on three fronts.

Said no one ever.

Iggy sensed the atmosphere around him change, the shadows almost flexing in the alley. He immediately got to his feet. "You're not welcome in my city, demon."

"How adorable are you? All grown up. A warrior for

the righteous. Claiming a city as your own. Brings a tear to my eye." The silky voice came from a few feet behind him. "I rarely remember the mothers. Too many to count, and they served as a means to an end. Yours, however, stood out. Fiery, strong. Made me work for it. Humans are so frail. Weak bodies. Still, I almost regretted her inevitable death in childbirth."

Iggy shifted to put the wall to his back, allowing himself a view of both ends of the alley. "Did you?"

"No. Why bother?" Lucifer closed the distance between them, giving Iggy the first view of his sperm donor. *Do demons actually ejaculate?* "Have I amused you?"

"Since you're you, do your seedy little swimmers have super sperm in them?" Iggy snickered at the stunned expression on the devil's face. "How many over the centuries?"

"Hundreds. Maybe thousands. Pity they're all dead. Most of the girls died in the womb. None of the mothers survived. Before modern science, I'd considered women the weaker sex, so obviously, they couldn't survive. Now, with technological advances, I've begun to wonder if genetics played a part." He sounded annoyed at the loss, though without an ounce of grief. "Your brothers had such potential. A beautiful army of beings in my own image, only to fall so quickly."

"So, not super sperm?" Iggy listened to Lucifer's egotistical monologue, keenly aware of the drone hovering above their heads. *Not now, Lal. For fuck's sake.* "How did you escape?"

"Escape?" Lucifer narrowed his red-rimmed brown eyes toward him. "They couldn't hold me."

"And what? You voluntarily took a vacation in a sealed underworld somewhere, stopped fucking anyone you could charm, and allowed your demons to run free?" Iggy didn't believe for a moment Lucifer had simply opted to disappear for an extended period, allowing his army to be destroyed one child at a time. "We're not your children. Not your sons and daughters. Just pawns. A demonic version of the Cybermen."

"The who?" Lucifer frowned in confusion, and Iggy felt the completely inappropriate urge to laugh in his face.

"Why reveal yourself to me? To Lalo?" Iggy wanted answers. *Am I ready for them, though? And can I trust the prince of lies to give me honest ones? Eight ball says I'm fucked.* "So, what will it be, Dad?"

CHAPTER FOURTEEN

LALO

Lalo had scooted to the edge of the back seat with his tablet angled so Wendy could watch and listen with him. They'd panicked at first when Lucifer appeared, then focused on trying to get a better look at him. "Genetics. Did your tests reveal anything other than just Iggy not being completely human?"

"How long until your drone takes a nose dive?" Wendy ignored his question, which Lalo had discovered usually meant yes to an allistic. "Lal?"

"Another six or seven minutes." His drone had been a gift from Iggy last Christmas; he'd given him the best one on the market with the longest battery life. "Wendy?"

"*Lalo.*" She lifted her gaze away from the video. "What?"

"Genetics."

"What about them? Can this wait?"

"Would a hair and blood sample from Lucifer himself help with figuring out the mystery of what he is?" Lalo, despite having seen Iggy's abilities and been in the presence of the big bad himself, still didn't entirely buy into the idea of a supernatural creature. "Aside from saliva, that's what you'd want, right?"

"Yes, let's waltz up to Satan and ask him to say 'ahh' for an oral swab." Wendy turned her attention back to the video. "Even if we ask nicely, it's not happening."

"Maybe." Lalo grabbed the tablet and eased into the seat. "Right. Don't mess this up. What if he hears it?"

"Your drone sounds like a swarm of buzzing bees. If we're lucky, traffic will drown out the majority of the sound before he even notices it," Wendy encouraged.

With a careful bit of flying, Lalo rammed the drone directly into the back of Lucifer's head. He was tempted to go in for a second pass but didn't want to risk it. The drone wobbled slightly when Lucifer shot out a hand to grab for it, but Lalo finally managed to steer it safely back toward the vehicle.

"What— Holy shit." Wendy bent forward until she almost obscured his view. "Did you seriously crash your drone into the skull of Lucifer?"

"Yes." Lalo hopped out of the Trailblazer to catch the drone. He hadn't mastered landings as well as takeoffs.

"Gross."

"Success?"

Lalo held the drone up carefully to show the glistening red smear with hair along the edge. "I've got your sample."

Grabbing her leather satchel, Wendy lifted a container out, opened it, and picked up several swabs. She collected the sample. When she finished, Lalo carefully wiped the drone clean before putting it away.

"You terrify me." Lalo watched her make notes with a Sharpie on the plastic covers of the swabs. "More than Lucifer. You're going to dissect me in my sleep, aren't you?"

"*Lalo.*"

"Iggy." Lalo spotted movement on the sidewalk in the distance. "Start the vehicle. He's running for a reason."

A breathless Iggy yanked the front passenger door open and leaped inside. He urged Wendy to drive. Lalo slid across the seat wildly when she took off and immediately made a sharp U-turn to head away from the university, almost rolling the Trailblazer in the process.

"Try not to kill us, Stony." Lalo righted himself with a pained groan. He buckled himself in and gripped the bar above the window tightly. "Maybe Ig should drive."

"Who thought dive bombing the devil was a good idea?" Iggy asked when they'd put a few miles between them and the university.

"Lalo." Wendy immediately ratted him out. She snickered when he grumbled at her. "Worked, though. We got a decent sample for testing."

"You crash landed a drone on Beelzebub's head."

"Yes."

"You whacked the devil with a drone."

"And?" Lalo shrugged. He held a hand up when Iggy opened his mouth. "Repeating yourself won't change the facts. Where are we going anyway?"

"I can't believe you assaulted the devil." Iggy laughed with Wendy.

Lalo shrank back into the seat, wrapping his arms around his upper body. "Can you drop me off at Lydia's?"

"Lal." He twisted around as far as his seat belt allowed. "I'm not complaining. And I swear I'm not laughing at you."

"Sounded like you were," he grumbled.

"Lal." Iggy stretched a hand out to touch Lalo's knee, but he shifted out of reach. "Your idea *was* fucking amazing. You should've seen the shock on his face. Epic. Priceless."

"Yes, yes. He's genius personified. Can we focus? What the hell did the devil want? Pun unintentional but hilarious." Wendy waved a hand to cut them off. She drove through the lessening traffic. "Wait. Actually, this is definitely a food conversation. Where are we going?"

They argued for several minutes.

"Chicken."

"What?" Iggy and Wendy both twisted their heads around to stare at him.

"Chicken. Nuggets." Lalo had an obsession with them.

Pulling yet another ill-advised turn off University Boulevard, Wendy made for the nearest fast-food restaurant. They ordered more nuggets and fries than could possibly be healthy for three people. By mutual agreement, Wendy drove across the city to Lydia's, even though it technically was the furthest.

Lalo wanted to be comfortable.

Comfortable meant an environment he had control over. Food, no shoes, and his space. When they arrived, he sank on his preferred recliner across from the sofa. Wendy tossed him one of the paper sacks and handed over a large soda, warning him the sugar would make his teeth fall out.

She stuck her tongue out when he suggested her ten packets of dipping sauce probably had more sugar than his soda. "Eat your nuggets."

Lalo glanced over at Iggy, who'd sat on the sofa with a box of nuggets balanced on one knee, fries between his legs, and a drink on the other knee. "Well? Tell us about daddy dearest."

Iggy's long-winded reply almost put Lalo to sleep. He tried to listen. Mostly, he ate two boxes of nuggets and his fries, completely dazed by trying to keep up with the conversation.

"Lal?"

He dropped the empty fry container in his hand when fingers snapped in front of his face. "What?"

"You've been holding an empty container for thirty minutes. Wendy grabbed an Uber to head home." Iggy crouched in front of his chair with his hands resting on Lalo's jeans-covered knees. "She'll be up all night trying to decipher the ins and outs of my paternal genetics. Not sure she grasps that no one other than us can see it. Who'd believe her?"

Lalo stretched his hand out to cover Iggy's mouth. "Please, for the love of the chicken. Say fewer things for five seconds."

Maybe more than five seconds.

"Why don't I go? Yeah? We can catch up tomorrow." Iggy went to stand, but Lalo caught him by the wrist to stop him. "Or?" he asked carefully.

"Or you could stay." Lalo ran a finger along the underside of Iggy's arm, feeling the muscle flex underneath his touch. "Sin a little with me?"

Iggy's eyes darkened. He licked his bottom lip before sliding his hand down Lalo's arm to grip his elbow and lift him to his feet. "Father, forgive me, for I have sinned."

Lalo covered his ears with both hands. "Bad thoughts, bad thoughts, bad thoughts."

"Catholic guilt not a kink, then?"

"We're not Catholic." Lalo grabbed Iggy by his hoodie to drag him through the house toward his bedroom. He refused to engage in anything under the watchful gaze of the multitude of photos lining the walls with their creepy eyes that always felt like they followed him. "Do you still snore?"

"Who says you'll be sleeping?" Iggy followed more gracefully than Lalo would've managed, into the bedroom, and watched him pace the room nervously. "Or we could just sleep? Maybe kiss, mostly sleep."

"Ig."

Iggy caught his wrist again, fingers artfully gliding against his skin. "I don't know about you, but I've certainly imagined a number of creative ways this might go the first time. I'd rather you be a confident, consenting participant and not a nervous wreck."

"Kissing. I can manage kissing." Lalo almost jumped out of his skin when Iggy dragged him over, closing the distance between them. He'd certainly fantasized about his best friend, but acting those out hadn't ever occurred to him. *Oh, my crumbs.* "I think."

CHAPTER FIFTEEN

IGGY

~ JESUIT JOURNAL, 1990

Waking up in bed beside Lalo had been nice; the panicked call from Wendy had been the exact opposite. The building with her lab had been burnt to the ground. Iggy woke Lalo up, and they watched the news footage together.

Flames billowed out of the windows in the science building. *The devil walks among us. And apparently he sets shit on fire.* Iggy had no doubts the stunt with the drone hadn't been missed by Lucifer, nor had his connection with

Wendy—and her research.

"Is she okay?" Lalo whispered. He had a mug of coffee clutched in his hands. They hadn't managed breakfast yet. "Did she get burned at all?"

"She sounded more distraught about the loss of her equipment and research." Iggy drained his own cup before setting it on the table. "She wanted to meet for breakfast. Are you up for a restaurant, or should we grab something to go and find a quiet park?"

"You want to talk to an excited Wendy about her research in a crowded restaurant?"

"Good point." Iggy grabbed his phone from the coffee table to send a quick text to Wendy. She wanted to be picked up. "Her vehicle is missing as well."

"He's thorough."

"He's sending a message. Two, probably." Iggy knew the devil was in the details, after all. "Warning her off, and letting me know my friends are in as much danger as I am."

"And?" Lalo nudged him with his knee. "What are we going to do?"

What Iggy wanted to do was return to bed. A little time jump to before they knew about the fire, and he'd be able to enjoy Lalo without interruption. Facing reality required so much more effort than he wanted to expend.

"Have you ever seen a demon's true form?" Iggy asked, not surprised when Lalo simply shook his head. "Shadow. An oppressive blanket of darkness you can almost taste, suffocating the life and goodness out of you. I've always wondered if the mythology of succubae and incubi came from a close encounter with our sulfuric monsters."

"Too many words, Ig." Lalo grabbed both their mugs and disappeared into the kitchen. He returned a moment later, tossing one of the two granola bars in his hand over to Iggy. "Why do I need to know what they look like?"

"You'll be as much of a target as Wendy. More so, probably." Iggy knew either Lucifer or the demons would place Lalo high on their list. They'd made their connection too obvious. "What's the first thing you'll do if you see or feel a demon's presence?"

"If last night is an example, suck them off."

"*Lalo*." Iggy choked on a granola chunk. They snickered together for a second. "Half-demons don't count. What would you do?"

"Poop my pants." Lalo shoved the wrapper of his granola bar into his pocket and went around the living room picking up their mess from the night before. "I'd say fight or run, but in times of great stress, when have I ever done anything aside from freeze?"

That was both true and terrifying. Any intense stress required time and space for Lalo to process. And on bad days, he might not need extreme pressure for him to shut down.

"Ig. Are we going?"

He stopped mentally plotting out how to train Lalo and found him waiting patiently by the front door. "He bashes the devil in the head with one little drone and suddenly he's ready to rush out into the world."

"Food."

Right.

Food.

Iggy had learned the hard way not to get between Lalo and a full breakfast. He took hangry to a whole other level. "You're not starving."

"*Food.*"

"Patience is a virtue."

"I'm being patient. I haven't crash landed a drone into your head, have I?" Lalo patted his backpack that contained the freshly charged gadget. "Have you tried vanishing like Lucifer does?"

"Yes."

"And?"

"According to Father Luke, I looked like I was constipated. Nothing happened. If there's some sort of trigger, I've yet to find it. Maybe the human half dilutes the demonic genes enough to prevent me inheriting any of the powers outside of ones related to my physical body." Iggy had hoped Wendy's findings might shed light on the differences in his makeup and Lucifer's, but he feared all of her work from the night had been lost in the fire. "Let's go. We might be in time for you to fly your drone over the scene of the crime."

The gods of traffic hadn't been kind to them. *Or maybe the demon of traffic has snarled us into a trap.* Iggy had expected to run into some of the morning rush. He hadn't anticipated accidents to completely jam up Logan Street while Broadway was blocked off for roadwork. Trying I-25 didn't offer much luck either, with additional construction on the highway.

Tired of crawling down the road, Iggy decided to make the less than legal decision to drive down the emergency lane to get to the closest exit. He charmed the officer who pulled them over into letting them go with a warning. Lalo admonished him for taking advantage of his powers and risking lives.

"You can have food, or we can sit in traffic for another thirty minutes." Iggy laughed when Lalo immediately moved the conversation on to breakfast. "Hey, Lal?"

"Hmm?" He stopped fidgeting with his puzzle key chain. He glanced over, though his gaze lingered more on Iggy's forehead. "What?"

"Are we dating?"

"We are engaging in pleasurable activities outside of the auspices of normal best friend behavior." Lalo perfectly mimicked the tone and inflection of Father Edward, one of their old teachers. He'd always been impressively gifted with accents and mimicry. "Does it feel like we're dating?"

"I want more—"

"Satan." Lalo cut him off. "The science building went up in flames. Figure us out later."

"After Armageddon then?"

"At least after breakfast, I can't decipher allistic-ese on an empty stomach." Lalo sat up and stopped fidgeting when they ran into a roadblock of fire engines and police vehicles. "Oh, my basil."

"We really need to work on your swearing. I can't believe it's still fucking burning." Iggy followed the instructions of the officer directing traffic away from the university. He made a loop around, eventually trying to find a parking spot off York. Students and faculty had obviously detoured from their usual spaces. "Longer walk than I wanted, but Wendy wanted us to meet here near her lab."

And they would.

The police had cordoned off numerous streets around the university. The radio claimed the fire was not believed to be an accident, and authorities had increasing concerns about the flames spreading to nearby buildings.

Iggy eventually spotted an open space to squeeze his vehicle into. "Are you coming or waiting here?"

"I…." Lalo hesitated, shrugging a shoulder.

Iggy tried never to pressure Lalo into going places, not always successfully. He'd seen firsthand the toll a meltdown took on him. *Never again, if I can help it.* "Stay if you want. We won't take long."

"I'll be fine. Let's go."

Fine.

Sure.

My definition or his?

And is mine any better?

Over the years, the priests had all harped on Iggy for his bad habits, selfishness being the worst of them. He thought of himself first in most situations. The Jesuit cure had involved prayer, scripture, and community service.

His teenage self hadn't bought into any of it. Father Luke had always said the devil in him was showing. Lalo had been the one to change him.

In their teens, Iggy hadn't really understood or appreciated that being autistic meant Lalo processed life differently. He had always blended in so easily. And they'd all pushed him too hard with their expectations as a result.

Until one day, they'd skipped class with Wendy. Lalo had required significant convincing. They'd been busted by Father Josiah, who'd ranted and raved at them. Lalo had gone into an immediate meltdown, muttering to himself and biting his hand.

Father Josiah hadn't been satisfied with punishing him for skipping class. Lalo had been given detention for "not fitting in." Iggy had felt awful for not only being the cause of a meltdown but for leading to additional trouble.

When Father Sal had taken Lalo under his wing, Iggy had breathed a sigh of relief. It kept him far away from Josiah, who'd prescribed to a method of therapy that even in his teens Iggy had found cruel. Father Sal had encouraged Lalo to be himself.

Years later, Iggy held on to the lesson from that day. He never allowed his selfishness to cause pain to others. And with Lalo, he'd tried to go out of his way not to mess up again.

"I'm going." Lalo hopped out of the vehicle and slammed the door before Iggy had a chance to respond.

Well, okay then.

They walked down York until they could cut across Wesley and finally up toward the building. Wendy waited for them on the edge of the crowd of gawkers. They blended in easily enough with the students.

The fire had burned hot, too hot to be of natural origins, in his opinion. Iggy used his height to see over the heads of the gathered onlookers. He'd seen demonic arson in the past and wanted to know for certain.

"Lal? Can you get your drone out?" Iggy didn't have a clear enough view.

They crowded around the tablet, watching as Lalo maneuvered it carefully into the sky. He steered clear of the firefighters and well underneath the circling news helicopters. A roaring fire at Denver University was definitely big news.

Wendy stepped back over, having finished her conversation with several other members of the faculty. "My whole damn life is in my office. Memories, samples, photos, all gone in a flash. Thank the fucking goddess I back everything up when I leave the lab."

Iggy wrapped an arm around her. "I'm so sorry."

"Wendy?" Lalo drew his attention to the tablet. "Isn't your lab on the far left side of the building?"

They easily noted that the extreme intensity of the fire and smoke appeared strongest near her office. The flames had obviously spread, but Iggy would bet his entire bank account they'd begun there. Wendy had been targeted, or her research at least.

"What time did you leave last night?" Iggy asked.

"Three in the morning? Maybe close to four. I left with several students who'd been working on their midterm project. We went for a late-night snack and coffee." Wendy rubbed at her eyes, coughing slightly from the smoke when the wind shifted direction. She pointed toward a group of teachers off to one side. "Angela discovered the fire when she arrived at six to open up the administration office. She spotted smoke coming out of my window."

Confirmation of what Iggy had already believed.

"Why isn't the fire spreading?" Lalo flew his drone back for a wider perspective. "The water hasn't done much to put the flames out, so where are the embers?"

Iggy looked away from the screen up into the air. "Fuck."

"What? Iggy?" Wendy caught his arm when he began to walk away.

"No embers. Water isn't putting the fire out." Iggy grabbed the tablet from Lalo, trying to shift the drone, only to send it crashing into the building. "Fuck."

"*Ignatius Faber.*" Lalo snatched the tablet away from him in a desperate attempt to save the drone. "For the love of mulch. What are you doing?"

"He's here. Has to be." Iggy raced away with his friends chasing.

He didn't have time to stop them. The fire wouldn't burn out. The firefighters were wasting water at this point.

The few times Iggy had seen hellfire in action, it had burned hot until the demon controlling the flames released them. Lucifer had to be nearby. Not close enough for him to sense, but within range to see the building.

I can't believe I missed the lack of fucking embers.

Damn it.

Picking up speed, Iggy left Wendy and Lalo behind. They had no chance of keeping up with him. He skidded to a halt, glancing up for any nearby buildings tall enough to provide a view of the university.

Ahh.

There you are.

How the fuck did you get up there?

Iggy stood at the side of the building, trying to figure out how to get to the roof without access to inside. He was assessing his options when Lalo and Wendy joined him. "You two really need to work out more."

"You are an asshole." Wendy punched him in the arm. "You are also not Spider-Man, so I don't see how you plan to get on the roof."

"Watch me."

Grabbing a nearby dumpster, Iggy dragged it across the alley to rest against the wall. He sent an apologetic glance to Lalo, who covered his ears against the high-pitched screeching sound. Leaping on it, he managed to scramble up to grab the lowest rung of a maintenance ladder and then pulled himself along the wall.

"Don't fall!" Lalo shouted.

While Wendy shushed Lalo, Iggy swung himself onto the roof. He'd half expected to be knocked off the building immediately. Instead, Lucifer stood facing away from him, focused on the raging fire.

"Beautiful, isn't?"

Iggy brushed his hands off on his jeans and stepped closer to Lucifer. He risked a glance toward the university. "I've always found the city to be beautiful from any angle with the mountains in the distance."

"Not anything so mundane as this planet." Lucifer waved his hand with an impatient growl. "Look at the flames. Beautifully controlled. Almost a living creature, with the power to utterly decimate anything in its path."

"Except for water."

"Watch." Lucifer brought his hand up, and suddenly the fire exploded.

Fuck.

Making a rash decision, Iggy launched himself at his father. He tackled him to the ground and immediately rolled away from him to crouch in a defensive position. Lucifer rose to his feet, straightened his suit, and vanished in a shadow flash.

Well, damn.

Iggy stood up. He glanced over toward the university. The fire had definitely increased, but now the firefighters appeared to be making progress. "I hate playing cat and mouse with demons. Bastard."

Getting down went far more easily; Iggy simply dropped to the ground to find Lalo and Wendy sharing a bag of Skittles. Lalo tossed one at him, which he caught in his mouth. They made their way back to the university.

"Oh my…." Wendy trailed off, horror evident in her voice when they came around the corner and saw the utter devastation the final surge of power from Lucifer had caused. Her building had been gutted, and embers were definitely spreading. "Why?"

Iggy didn't answer. He led her away with Lalo following close behind. "Let's grab coffee and something to eat. Staring at the fire won't make a difference."

CHAPTER SIXTEEN

LALO

It has become clear over the past century that demons are more blatant in their ambitions. Unchecked, we risk losing all of our trained fighters. Some argue children must be allowed to be children. Can we risk their dying, unable to protect themselves from evil?

~ *JESUIT JOURNAL, 1948*

"Oh, son of a carrot." Lalo was in the middle of breakfast when he remembered his photography exhibition. He chugged down his iced coffee. "I need to get home."

"Maybe finish your sandwich first?" Iggy tried to keep him in his seat. "What's wrong?"

"My photos, the ones I was supposed to take the other night, are due to the gallery tonight. I promised to be at the exhibition." Lalo usually managed to talk his way around attending events in person. He never knew how to speak with people. They swanned around with drinks, wanting to know the deeper meaning to his art. "What am I going to do?"

"Eat. Get another coffee. I'll drive you home. Wendy and I can go over what she found last night while you put your photo package together." Iggy pushed the plate back in front of Lalo and got to his feet. "Actually, I'll order three more coffees and donuts to go."

"Extra donuts. The cinnamon sugar ones with extra sugar." Lalo held up his hand to stop Iggy. "Wait. Let's get cupcakes from Ramon and Maria. They'll be better than donuts."

"I could eat my weight in cupcakes," Wendy readily agreed.

"Can you? Wait, never mind, figure of speech." Lalo kicked himself mentally for making the mistake. "I'll text Ramon to see what they've got in the oven today."

His foster parent texted back with the list for the day. Lalo ordered one of everything for the three of them, plus two extra *dulce de leche* cupcakes. Wendy had stolen his in the past, so planning ahead seemed wise.

"Lalito." Maria greeted them enthusiastically before they'd gotten out of the Trailblazer. She hugged him tightly, then went to greet Wendy and Iggy. "Are you behaving yourselves?"

"Always." Iggy grinned charmingly at her. "Is Ramon treating you right?"

"That is not behaving yourself." She waved them over to the food truck. "Did you hear about the fire at the university?"

Lalo decided to deflect the conversation, since Iggy wouldn't want to talk about the fire. "We drove by picking up Wendy."

That's not deflecting.

Ugh.

Moving away from the others, Lalo ducked into the food truck. He found Ramon sautéing diced apples. They smelled amazing.

"Want some?" Ramon spooned up a portion of the apples into two small cups. He leaned against one of the counters and offered one to Lalo. "You need some quiet time, Lalito."

"I'm fine." He carefully avoided the knowing look Ramon sent his way.

When the court system had finally gifted the Ruiz family to Lalo, he'd already spent a significant amount of time in the foster care system. They'd been different. Ramon and Maria had gone out of their way to make him welcome.

Early mornings and late evenings had often been spent in the kitchen. They'd snack while baking; Ramon invested a lot of time teaching Lalo how to not only cook for himself but also just cope with inevitably becoming a self-sufficient adult. He'd understood, for the first time, what being a family felt like.

Cooking and baking had become a tradition, one Lalo had missed after moving out on his own. The kitchen held some of his truly joyful childhood memories.

In his mind, Lalo had been lucky. Many older foster kids found themselves turning eighteen and shoved out into the world with little to no support. He'd found a family in the Ruizes; they'd been there for him even into his thirties.

He'd tried calling them Mom and Dad. It hadn't worked for him. The words always came out stilted and unnatural. They didn't seem to mind.

They loved him.

"Lalito?" Ramon rested a hand gently on his shoulder. "Don't forget you never owe anyone an explanation for needing time to yourself. Your health matters as much as whatever mess Ignatius drags you into. You can say no. To him. To the gallery. To me speaking my mind."

Lalo shrugged. "I'm fine."

"Ah, yes. Lalito speak for anything from actually fine to dead." Ramon shook his head. "Come on. Help me fill these cupcakes with apple. Maria hasn't finished her interrogation of Ignatius over his intentions toward you."

"Oh, mother of rosemary." Lalo squeezed by a chuckling Ramon and dashed out of the food truck. "Maria."

Tripping over his own feet, Lalo stumbled right into Iggy, who appeared to be sweating. He glared at Maria's nose. She didn't appear at all bothered by his aggravation.

"I've faced demons. Hell, I tackled the prince of them. This tiny five-foot woman terrifies the fuck out of me," Iggy whispered in his ear. "If I'm facing the family firing line, I'm claiming you as my own."

"Not an object to own."

"Romance isn't literal, Lal."

"Romance is apparently disturbingly possessive." Lalo drew away from Iggy. He refused to have a relationship conversation with both Wendy and Maria trying to eavesdrop. "Time to go. Exhibition. Photos."

"Always in such a rush," Maria teased.

With limited additional parental embarrassment, Lalo managed to escape with cupcakes, hugs, and his two tagalongs. Ramon had watched him with a hint of concern on his face. Lalo kept telling himself he could manage their intrusion.

Their drive through Denver to his home in Five Points took forever. Every light seemed to be red; random roadwork and accidents blocked off usual routes. They had to dodge one-way streets.

Most days, Lalo loved the grid of Denver's streets. They made sense to his mind and he never worried about getting lost in the city. Iggy had grown tired of the forced excursion and cut up through a neighborhood to get to Lydia's home. Between Wendy's singing and regular road noise, Lalo was slowly reaching the end of his ability to deal with external sounds.

By the time Iggy pulled in behind Lalo's vehicle, half of the cupcakes had been sacrificed to their sweet teeth. Lalo was reminded of high school, when they'd eaten enough sugar to rot their teeth while studying for exams. They'd emptied the Ruizes' fridge on several occasions.

"How can we help?" Wendy asked. They'd gotten cushions off the couch to get comfortable around the coffee table with their laptops in front of them. Iggy also had a stack of journals next to him. "Want me to look through your photos to help select some?"

Go away.

Lalo had learned the hard way not to voice every blunt thought that crossed his mind. He was mostly successful. "Help Iggy with the journals. I can manage my photos."

Was that nice enough?

He tried. None of his images seemed right. He hated all of them.

Why am I so useless?

Why are they even giving me a spot in the exhibition?

It's sympathy, right?

Why do I suck so badly?

"Lalo?"

He shoved his laptop across the table, knocking a plate of cupcakes to the carpet and sending a can of soda into Wendy's lap. "Son of a cabbage."

Ignoring the concerned exclamations from Wendy and Iggy, Lalo raced down the hall into his bedroom. He slammed the door behind him and yanked on his hair in raw frustration. All of his efforts to avoid a meltdown in front of them had gone to waste.

The feeling of humiliation only intensified the overload of emotion and energy running through his mind. He hated the lack of control. His body was trembling as if he'd drunk a gallon of espresso.

He punched his pillow over and over until finally the need to bite his hand faded away. He tried so hard to avoid self-harming while dealing with a meltdown. "Crumbs."

Collapsing backwards onto his bed, Lalo stared up at the ceiling. Exhausted. Every part of his body ached as though he'd run a marathon. *Why am I like this?*

Lalo lay there until his mind settled enough to think clearly. *Time to face the music.* He opened the door to find Iggy sitting across from it on the floor. "Hi."

"Feeling better?"

"No." Lalo couldn't manage more than one word. "No."

"Wendy took an Uber home. She has to check in at the university." Iggy leaned comfortably against the wall. "We didn't want to both leave and have you worried about our reaction. Want to binge the *Avenger* movies? Eat our weight in cupcakes while watching Thor swing his hammer?"

Rolling his eyes, Lalo wandered down the hall into the kitchen. He grabbed a fresh bottle of black cherry soda. The familiar fizz of bubbles in his mouth made him feel slightly better.

Lalo glanced over at the clock above the sink. He groaned at having lost an hour. "I don't have time for Thor. The exhibition needs my images—"

"Stony called the curator to cancel for you."

"*What?*" Lalo slammed his can down on the sink, ignoring the soda that spilled out.

"She wanted to help. We didn't know how long you'd need to recover, and just not showing up wouldn't look good." Iggy seemed confused by his obvious anger.

Lalo wanted to scream in frustration. He hated being helped without someone asking if the assistance was even wanted. "I'm not a child."

Iggy grabbed a towel to wipe up the soda flowing down the counter. "No, you aren't. You're capable, intelligent, and sexy as fuck. You also hate phone calls and disappointing people. Wendy spared you both. No shame in needing help or accommodations to have even footing in the world. It doesn't make you weak or a child."

"Stop being logical," Lalo grumbled.

"Can we watch Thor's hammer now?"

"Fine. But I'm not touching *your* hammer. Not sure I like you right now."

CHAPTER SEVENTEEN

IGGY

An hour into the second *Avengers* film, Lalo had fallen asleep under a heavy blanket on the rug in front of the television. Lydia had gotten the soft rug specifically for him to curl up on. Lalo had frequently struggled with sitting in chairs and sofas.

Turning the sound down on the movie, Iggy reached over for one of the smaller journals. He ran a tired hand across his face when he realized how bad the handwriting was. It might as well have been some obscure, forgotten language.

How am I supposed to read this chicken scratch?

A snuffling grumble drew his attention to Lalo, who'd

rolled over to face him. Iggy couldn't help smiling. Lalo felt relaxed enough in his presence to be able to fall deeply asleep.

The trust meant more than any declaration of love. Iggy knew Lalo rarely slept well in the presence of others. He had a phobia of being attacked while unaware, something likely a direct result of the accident that took his parents' lives.

Trust.

Iggy decided Lalo's trust was worth more than anything else.

Returning his attention to the journals, he tried for a second time to decipher the handwriting. He gave up after ten minutes; maybe Lalo or Wendy might have better luck. *Why am I bothering with all of these? Not one has offered a useful ounce of information.*

The journals were mostly self-indulgent lectures.

Jesuit self-gratification.

This is more useless than those geography lessons in fifth grade. When am I ever going to need to know about maps from ancient history? Never, that's when. Almost as pointless as algebra.

Fuck math.

"Ig?"

He glanced up to find a bemused Lalo watching him. "What?"

"Did you know you're doodling penises on a journal from the 1600s?"

"Shit." Iggy dropped the pen. He'd always had a bad

habit of doodling nonsense when bored. "Think anyone will notice?"

"Yes." Lalo grabbed the journal, flipping the pages. "Can you believe this? 'Sexuality, as they grow into teenagers, appears increased.' Why did they even need to write it down? Who is shocked that puberty leads to attraction and exploration?"

"Who knows?" Iggy had made a rule for himself to ignore any and all advice from the church on sexuality. "Wendy texted while you were getting your beauty nap. Her lab, as expected, went up in smoke. All of her data in the cloud is safe. She has a temporary office for now in another building and wants us over as soon as possible. She wouldn't tell me why."

"And you're dying of curiosity, of course."

"Aren't you?"

"No, I was sleeping." Lalo shrugged.

Iggy covered his face with his hand and groaned. "You know what I meant."

"Not really."

Iggy knew better than to get into a debate about the meanings of words or phrases. Those always ended badly with Lalo. He remembered getting thrown out of a class for laughing when a teacher had attempted to correct Lalo with little success. "I ate the cupcakes."

"We had six left."

"And now we have none."

Lalo leaned forward to poke him in the stomach. "How the hell do you maintain a six-pack while eating six cupcakes?"

"Good metabolism." Iggy tended to burn through calories, especially on days when he used his inherited strength and speed. His grocery bill was more than an average family's. "I run hot."

"Can you run hot without destroying my cupcakes?" Lalo complained bitterly. "You're buying dinner."

"I always buy."

"Well, some of us don't have trust funds." Lalo got to his feet, facing away from Iggy. He stretched slowly, revealing a glimpse of the large apple tree tattooed on his back. Iggy had been with him when he'd gotten the ink, to represent both of his families—foster and birth. "You can afford it."

And he could.

The priests had provided for all of the siblings through the centuries. Iggy had graduated from high school and discovered a trust fund waiting for him, given by an anonymous donor. Father Ricci hadn't wanted him to accept, but why refuse a generous gift?

The trust fund hadn't offered a life of luxury. He had been able to afford a nice apartment, vehicle, and there was enough left to never worry about a day job. Father Ricci had been disappointed.

Father Ricci always seemed to find a reason to be disappointed in him, particularly after he'd begun dating men and separated from the church. He believed in hunting demons. Religion just didn't attract him.

I can be the son of the devil, destroy demons, and fuck men.

Maybe not at the same time.

The church hadn't felt the same way. The reaction to his sexuality had been the final nail in the religion coffin, so to speak. He'd never looked back.

"I'm out of soda." Lalo had wandered over to the kitchen while Iggy got lost in thought. He stood in front of the open fridge, staring mournfully at the contents. "How can I be out? I buy in bulk."

"How do you even have teeth left?" Iggy had bad eating habits, but his paled in comparison to Lalo's. "Do you buy toothpaste in bulk as well?"

They bickered like an old couple all the way to the university, pausing only when Iggy had pulled into a drive-thru for burgers and fries. Wendy wanted comfort food. Losing her lab had hit her hard; she'd spent more time there than in her home.

It wasn't until they pulled into one of the overflow parking lots near the main campus that Iggy remembered the clone. He banged his head against the steering wheel. *I am a complete fool.*

Lucifer had completely taken his focus from the mystery. Iggy wanted to try to get inside the building, hopefully without the reappearance of his demonly father. He did wonder if the distraction had been purposeful or merely a coincidence.

Then again, Iggy didn't necessarily believe in coincidences when it came to the behavior of demons.

"Ig?" Lalo slid his hand between the steering wheel and Iggy's forehead. "Don't damage anything important."

Iggy laughed despite knowing Lalo had been serious in his concern. "Just kicking myself for falling into a trap."

"What trap?" Lalo eased his hand away when Iggy sat back in the seat. "Did I—"

"Nothing you did." Iggy cut him off, knowing immediately what direction Lalo's mind would go. He always seemed to blame himself for things. "We all completely forgot about the clone with the fire and Lucifer."

"The clone." Lalo blinked at him several times. "The clone. And the weird building. And the cameras."

"Yes." Iggy mentally kicked himself. They'd thrown away a perfect opportunity with the fire to get a closer view. "Was your drone damaged by the up close and personal with the devil?"

"No."

"Think you could dive bomb the clone if we saw him again?" Iggy thought the idea was a long shot, but it worked the first time. Might prove successful a second. "Let's see what Stony has for us."

"She hates being called Stony when she's in her lab." Lalo followed him out of the Trailblazer and down the street. They dodged the students on foot, bike, and in vehicles. They'd shown up at the end of classes for the day; not the best timing on their part. "Why are there so many people? Make them go away."

"I'm not a magician." Iggy wiggled his fingers at Lalo. "Not the Scarlet Witch either. Things don't happen when I twitch my nose."

"She doesn't twitch her nose."

Iggy stared up at the cloudy sky for several seconds. He tried hard not to laugh when Lalo took a joke as a serious statement, because it tended to embarrass him. "Ready to wade through the collegiate throng?"

"No." Lalo stared across the street at the campus still filled with students. "Why couldn't she meet us at that parking lot?"

"Come on." Iggy looped an arm around Lalo's shoulder and guided him through the milling students. The strong, acrid scent of smoke still lingered in the air. They'd driven by the burned shell of the science building. "I'll buy you a steak, bacon, and potato pizza."

"My love of pizza doesn't extend this far." Lalo shrank away from a group throwing a football around. He'd never been fond of athletic pursuits outside of hiking in the mountains.

"I'll take you to Paulino's off Broadway and buy whatever planty things you want." Iggy smirked when Lalo stopped grumbling under his breath. The way to Lalo's heart tended to either be food- or garden-related. "We'll make a date of it."

Not his idea of the most romantic date in the world, but a relationship with Lalo was always going to involve compromise on his part. Iggy knew that despite, or even because of, his half-demon side, his life had a lot of advantages. He could afford to bend and sway with whatever Lalo needed from him.

"Fore."

Iggy's hand shot up to catch the football before it

smacked into Lalo's face. He flung the ball back toward the players, harder than required. "Assholes. It's not fucking golf."

"Language. You might corrupt the youth of the world," Lalo teased.

They made the rest of their journey unscathed to Wendy's temporary new office in the administration building. She was scowling at her laptop with a row of coffee cups around her, a few knocked over. Her fingers flew across the keyboard while she cursed creatively under her breath.

"How many double espresso lattes have you drunk in the last hour?" Lalo gathered up all the empty cups, dropping them in a recycling bin in the corner.

"My bladder hasn't floated me out of the room yet." Wendy grinned at both of them. "Feeling better?"

Lalo shrugged. He wandered across the room to stare out the window through the blinds. Iggy exchanged a glance with Wendy; they both decided to leave him in peace.

"Well?" Iggy sat on the edge of the desk and tried to peer around the edge of her computer. "What was so damn important you needed to drag us across Denver at the start of rush hour?"

"You're not human."

Iggy stared at her, almost falling off the desk. "To borrow from Lal, I'm going to need a few more words."

Wendy shoved her laptop out of the way and spread out several pages of charts. "When I tested your blood and saliva, I expected to find a normal DNA strand. Maybe a little blip of abnormality, but I can't compare. My entire career could be spent trying to decipher your bizarre genetics."

Iggy didn't understand the charts at all. "Smaller words."

"Those were small words." Wendy went off on a five-minute rant of technical terms that made Iggy's head spin as Lalo snickered at him from across the room. "Clear?"

"As a mudslide." Iggy rolled his eyes at the two who snickered at him. "Oh great Stony with your genius mind, please explain what the fuck you're talking about to my lowly self."

"This is my DNA chart. See? This is a student's who was part of my project that went up in smoke. And another student's." Wendy laid out page after page before finally showing the final one. It looked nothing like the others. "Yours makes no sense. My equipment kept telling me I'd made a mistake. Are you sure you weren't crossed with an owl?"

"Fairly certain. What about my mom?"

"Ah." Wendy slid her laptop back over. "I expected a standard combination of your mother and whatever Lucifer is."

"And?"

"It's like your mother never existed. You might as well have been spawned outside of the womb." Wendy scrolled through lines of what felt like a bizarre coded language. "I compared the swabs of matter from the drone. None of it registered as blood."

"It was blood." Lalo shifted from his spot by the window to join the conversation. "Red and sticky, from his head."

"I know, I collected the sample." Wendy patted his hand reassuringly. "But standard testing showed no recognition either of human or animal. The blood wasn't blood."

"So?"

"You're basically an alien." Wendy gave him a look that made Iggy feel like a specimen in a test tube. "Can I run more—"

"I am not a frog to dissect." Iggy cut her off before she could ask the inevitable question. He grinned despite himself when Lalo reached out to hold his hand. "What does any of this really mean?"

"What if demon reproduction is completely different?" Wendy spread out the various charts again. "Cloning might be far simpler. If they managed to put a scientific mind and research into it, they'd easily be able to create an army like you or Titus without waiting nine months and the issue of dying mothers. Less children dying as well. I'd bet, though I've no proof, the lack of Y-chromosome is what caused the majority of your sisters to die. If you're not human, not taking any of your genetic makeup from your mom, their bodies might not cope."

Iggy struggled for breath as though she'd slammed her fist into his stomach. *Fuck.* "We need to get into the building we saw the clone enter. Modern science might've provided them with the perfect method...."

Trailing off, Iggy found the implications completely horrifying. He wondered again at Lucifer's sudden reappearance and his distracting them away from the heavily secured building. The demons hadn't been thrilled with the clone popping up.

His glib comment of a war on three fronts came back to

haunt him. When had Lucifer escaped imprisonment? The goal had always been to populate the earth with his children. Had he come up with an easier way of achieving his plan?

Or had that never been the plan at all?

"We're so fucked." Iggy ran his fingers roughly through his hair. He had an army of demons to fight and potentially a second one as well. Alone. Lalo squeezed his hand again. Not alone; he had a gardener, a scientist, and several old priests. *Yep, I'm fucked.* "Reading journals isn't going to do a damn thing to help."

"You never know." Wendy gathered up her papers into a stack. "If I could…."

Iggy's sigh of frustration made her sentence fall away. "Research my blood after we've stopped Armageddon."

"I don't want to be an astronaut," Lalo interjected.

Iggy and Wendy both glanced over at Lalo. Iggy glared at him, then had to smile. "I'm having a panic attack. And you two have all the jokes."

"Yeah, but you're the son of the prince of hell; we expect you to be a little overdramatic." Wendy winked at him with a wicked glint of humor. "You might say you're flaming."

"I'm never speaking to you again." He couldn't help snickering when Lalo literally fell to the floor in a fit of breathless laughter. "I need a barrel of coffee to deal with this."

Wendy gestured to the recycle bin containing her used cups. "I feel your pain."

"No, you don't understand." Iggy shook his head. "You're not thinking in larger circles."

"What?"

"It's not theoretical." Iggy instinctually knew Lucifer had found a way. "He's already started."

"Son of a soda." Lalo seemed to pick up on what he meant. "How many do you think are already wandering around?"

"Maybe the lookalike is his first test run?" He wondered if the demons had been led to Titus by Lucifer. "We need more information."

"He's not doing press releases." Wendy closed her laptop, carefully stowing it with the papers into a bag. "Keeping this with me in case of another fire. Also, let's not get ahead of ourselves. We only have theories at this point."

They were severely outnumbered. Iggy knew no matter what he said to them, neither Wendy nor Lalo would stay away from the fight. They had to find some angle to get an advantage.

How many more fires will there be?

How many more deaths?

The journals, as useless as they were, in some ways had provided a view into Lucifer's preferred methods. Fire. Flames had definitely been at the top of the list. Early wildfires in Colorado had been attributed to him by the Jesuits.

Without proof.

All we have is theoretical bullshit on all sides.

Yeah, we're so screwed.

CHAPTER EIGHTEEN

LALO

FOR THE GOOD OF THE WHOLE, OUR BROTHERS WHO DISAGREED FOUND THEMSELVES SENT AWAY. SOME EXCOMMUNICATED FOR RADICAL IDEAS.

~ JESUIT JOURNAL, 1977

"I was promised pizza and plants." Lalo had waited through Iggy's panic, and his stomach overruled his desire to be patient. "And, no, Stony, I'm not talking about going around the corner to the closest pot-brownie bakery."

"Picky, picky."

"I struggle enough to figure out my brain. I don't need anything messing around with my efforts." Lalo didn't even enjoy a casual beer with Iggy. "And, yes, before you start on me, I know sugar has a detrimental effect on the mind. I'm used to it."

"Addicted," she retorted.

Lalo pointed to the overflowing recycle bin. "And your coffee problem?"

"Are you two done arguing about your addictions?" Iggy sat up from where he'd lain down on Wendy's office floor to contemplate his existential crisis. "I vote for pizza before the end of the world."

"Is it definitely ending?" He'd only half paid attention to the muttering between them. "Today? Can we put it off until pizza? I'd rather die on a full stomach."

Iggy tilted his head toward Lalo. Pizza was one of Lalo's comfort foods, guaranteed to reduce the stress from what he sometimes referred to as "allistic nonsense." They shared a grin. "Food first. Apocalypse later."

"Father Sal said we'd have horses."

"Pretty sure that was four horsemen." Iggy got to his feet, brushing his jeans off.

"Don't horsemen have horses? And why are they only men? Aren't women responsible for death and destruction?" Lalo liked picking apart doomsday theories, whether religious or otherwise. He found allistics tended to go to extensive lengths to prove their points to his simple questions. "Is pineapple on pizza the first sign?"

"Definitely."

They argued over where to get the pizza and what to have on it. Lalo won. His argument hadn't been the best, but it had definitely been the most confusing.

Is confusion my superpower?

Pizza, in his humble opinion, made everything better.

End of the world? Basic cheese with a thin, floppy crust. Demons walking the earth? Pineapple and ham. Farting while Iggy tried to sneak a kiss in the university hallway? A chocolate overload pizza drenched in fudge ganache.

He needed all three washed down by cherry soda.

If I'm going to die anyway, I'm going out on a happy food high, holding Iggy's hand.

Maybe not while eating the pizza, though.

Holding hands and kissing had become his new favorite hobbies. "My apartment is going to smell like chocolate and grease for days." Wendy slouched in a beanbag across from Lalo, who'd slipped into a food coma on her sofa. "I'm dying."

Over their massive meal of pizza goodness, they'd come up with a slightly insane plan. Lalo had gone online to order several different drones—small and large, their first and safest option to trying to gain access to whatever was happening inside the building. *The building. It needs a better name. An official name. The building that has no name.*

I'll work on it.

His thoughts flew around in a circular spiral, trying to come up with a name. Lalo managed to reel himself back in with years of practice. He glanced over to find Wendy had drifted off to sleep.

"She's a lightweight." Iggy waved a slice of garlic bread at Lalo from the table. "Want another piece of pizza?"

"Only if you want to see the inside of my stomach."

While Iggy polished off another slice, Lalo scanned

through the to-do list Wendy had made. She'd organized their plan into sections. Thanks to overnight delivery, the drones should arrive by the following day; he hoped that of the various sizes they'd ordered, one would suit their purposes.

The loud silence started to weigh on Lalo. He struggled to think through the little sounds around him. Wendy's breathing, Iggy's chewing, the ticking of the clock, a barking dog in the distance, and the humming from the overhead light. All of them combined to strain his already exhausted nerves.

Grabbing the remote, Lalo turned the television on. He wanted something to drown out the quiet sounds no one else seemed to hear. Before he could switch to a channel other than news, the breaking story caught his attention.

"Ig." He threw one of the pillows on the couch at Iggy, who'd dozed off at the table. "Ignatius Faber."

Iggy shot up, glancing around wildly. "What's wrong?"

"The retreat." Lalo gestured toward the footage playing on the television of familiar structures engulfed in overly bright flames. "Father Sal. My garden."

Iggy staggered over to drop on the couch beside him. "Why? Don't answer. Stupid, rhetorical question. Stony. Wake the fuck up."

Wendy slowly opened her eyes. She sat up instantly when the news actually filtered through her sleep- and food-induced haze. "We should head to Sedalia."

Lalo couldn't move from the couch. Iggy appeared to be just as frozen as they watched memories of their childhood burning. "Holy crumbs."

"Okay." Wendy snatched the remote away from him, turning the news off and tossing the controller aside. She grabbed their hands to pull them off the couch. "Sitting here won't solve anything. If Lucifer is involved, the fire won't stop without intervention. You *have* to get to Sedalia. Now."

They stumbled to the door, struggling to get out while Wendy still had hold of their hands. She came to a stop when her neighbor came out of the apartment across from hers. Lalo glanced in confusion from the suddenly stammering Wendy to Iggy, who snickered under his breath.

"Ignatius, Lalo, meet Alexandra. She teaches religious studies with a focus on ancient mythology and deities." Wendy sounded strangely breathless to Lalo as she introduced the curvy thirtysomething woman with dark-brown eyes and wavy brown hair, who said hello with the barest hint of an accent. "She transferred from a university in Athens."

"Georgia?"

"Greece." Alexandra smiled, and Wendy leaned forward a little.

"Oh." Lalo glanced between the two of them a few times. "Is she the crush you mentioned?"

"I hate you."

"She doesn't, really," Iggy whispered to him. He grabbed Lalo by the hand to drag him off. "We should run away."

And they did, leaving Wendy to chat with her not-crush.

CHAPTER NINETEEN

IGGY

Science may lead to answers. Not all of our brothers agree on involving those outside of the Jesuit order, or the church itself. We never imagined the consequences of allowing them to go free—free of constraints to research.

~ *JESUIT JOURNAL, 1985*

Their pleasant evening of planning and pizza disintegrated into ash. Iggy kept calm on the drive, ditching the completely gridlocked I-25 and construction zone of 85 for smaller side streets through Highlands Ranch until they reached the Jesuit compound. He went off the road to get around the blockade of fire trucks amassed around the buildings.

Focus, Iggs.

We've more than a destroyed retreat and lost lives at stake.

"Use your drone." Iggy grabbed Lalo's backpack from the rear of the Trailblazer and handed it to him. "Any footage of the fire and the area surrounding. He has to be here, somewhere he can watch the flames. Line of sight seemed important."

"Okay." Lalo nodded jerkily. He was probably in shock but managed to keep hold of his bag. "Okay. Okay. *Okay.*"

Leaving Lalo muttering to himself for comfort, Iggy started walking. He knew the priests and the compound like the back of his hand. He rushed through the wooded area around the compound and leaped over a small fence into the garden.

Iggy paused to figure out what to do next. *Right, find Father Luke first. Then, I'm going to hunt for the sulfuric bastard responsible. The easiest way to fight the flames will be to stop him.*

If the fire department spotted him, Iggy knew they'd do their best to keep him away from the fire. The heat from the flames made focusing on Lucifer almost impossible. *I should've stayed by the vehicle to hunt for the dickhead.*

Retracing his steps, Iggy went back over the fence. He raced at top speed around the boundary to a small incline at the north end of the retreat. *There you are, you flaming piece of sulfur.* Lucifer had the audacity to smirk at him when Iggy slid to a stop a few feet away.

"Shouldn't you be playing the hero? Rescuing the frocked sheep?" Lucifer taunted.

"How's the head?"

"Amusing." Lucifer glanced back toward the retreat.

"Save your priests, Ignatius. The world will burn around you eventually."

"Not if you do first." Iggy dug his fingernails into the palms of his hands to keep from launching himself at his father.

A scream drew Iggy's attention. He wanted to fight. To take Lucifer on and destroy him. Every fiber of his being raged at not even attempting it. Only a lesson from Father Luke stopped him.

Only a fool attacks when an enemy is prepared for battle and has the higher ground.

Iggy smothered his fury while a chuckling Lucifer vanished into the shadows once again. "I will fucking end you—you sulfuric piece of shit."

To his surprise, the fire didn't immediately explode as it had at the university. Iggy jogged down the hill, launching himself over the fence. He turned toward the raging flames engulfing the building where the priests lived.

The Jesuits lived simply. Not spartanly; they had a few luxuries. He darted by the busy firefighters to head inside.

Clambering underneath a fallen beam, Iggy squeezed by a collapsed wall until he reached the long hallway leading to the bedrooms. Open and closed doors lined his path on either side. He didn't want to consider how many of the priests, particularly the more elderly, might be trapped within.

His worry lessened with each empty room. Iggy hoped the priests had received sufficient warning to escape or perhaps had been in the chapel for prayers. *Fuck. What if he set the church on fire?*

How much would that appeal to the damned devil?

Pushing past the discomfort from the oppressive heat and smoke burning his eyes, Iggy cleared each room until he reached the last door. Father Luke's. He pulled his sleeve over his hand to avoid burning himself on the handle, which turned, but the door didn't budge.

"Fuck." Iggy put his full strength into ramming his shoulder against the door. He managed to shift it open enough to squeeze through. "*Fuck.*"

With flames closing in, Iggy didn't have the time to process seeing Father Luke on the floor. He lifted him up, glanced around the room, and decided to kick out the side door leading out into the garden. Firefighters rushed over to him when they spotted him coming around the side of the building.

They took the limp body from him. Iggy closed his eyes, trying not to breathe in too deeply to avoid the acrid smoke. His lungs burned from the short amount of time spent inside the burning building.

"Ig?" Lalo raced up to him. His hoodie and T-shirt were ripped and singed, while both his hands and face were caked with soot. "Oh, my absinthe. They're all...."

A tiny part of Iggy wanted to laugh. Lalo only pulled out absinthe as a curse in the direst of circumstances. He lunged forward to catch Lalo when he collapsed into himself.

"Easy, Lal. I've got you."

"They were praying." Lalo pushed away from Iggy, turning toward the small but beautiful chapel attached to the retreat. "All but three of them."

He found his tongue practically glued to the roof of his mouth. Words seemed almost impossible. "Father Luke."

The wail of a siren and screeching tires kept him from having to come up with a full sentence. Additional firefighters and paramedics rushed by them, all desperate to find survivors and stop the flames from moving to other buildings—or worse, into the hillside behind the retreat.

"Ignatius." Father Sal limped weakly toward them, ignoring the paramedics following him. "Lalo. We saved as many of the journals as we could. Brother Josiah placed them in our van."

Iggy didn't care about the journals. "How can we help?"

Lalo reached out hesitantly to grasp Father Sal's hand. "Were you hurt?"

Father Sal patted Lalo's hand, but his eyes were on Iggy. "Find what he wanted so desperately to destroy. The journals obviously contain some insight of great interest, enough to burn all of us to the ground."

The paramedics bustled the injured priest toward a waiting ambulance. He'd sounded so convinced that Lucifer hadn't any other motivation to set the retreat on fire. Iggy didn't have the same confidence.

Lucifer didn't need any motivation to murder priests aside from creating pain and chaos. Iggy had no doubt any demon would relish turning all of them into ash. Pain, chaos, and death came naturally to the sulfuric.

And what does that say about me if my DNA is more demon than human?

CHAPTER TWENTY

LALO

~ JESUIT JOURNAL, 1962

Lalo had quickly realized his interference was more of a hindrance than a help. He left the firefighters to do their work. The night had taught him an important lesson— his fight or flight response tended to be more freeze than anything else.

Something he would need to work on, given the state of the world. Between Lucifer and the demons, Iggy had more than enough to focus on without worrying about Lalo every second. Maybe a martial arts course might help him with his response time? Were there autistic-friendly self-defense classes?

How do I help? What do I say? Are there any words to make any of this better?

What would Lydia say?

In his limited experience, Lydia handled emotional moments better than anyone else. Lalo didn't know how to deal with his own feelings, let alone those of people around him. He could barely breathe with the heavy weight on him.

Tired of standing and doing nothing, Lalo found an undamaged wooden bench to sit on outside the garden. Iggy had disappeared in an attempt to find Father Josiah and the journals—more the latter than the former. He hadn't returned, which was worrying.

The chaotic explosion of sound, scents, and lights had frozen Lalo in place. He dug his fingernails into his palms, trying to center himself. *You can't zone out in the middle of a fire, Lal. They'll notice.*

For so many years, Lalo had visited the retreat. Even after graduating from high school, he'd gardened for the priests. Aside from Josiah's obvious dislike, the other Jesuits had mostly either ignored or at least treated him cordially even when he'd rejected religion.

They hadn't bothered with him much.

The compound in Sedalia had been home to some of the gentlest people Lalo had ever met. Not perfect, but kind and caring. In one night, Lucifer had ruined the tranquility.

The ugliness of hatred had burned through the beauty of the foothills, leaving a trail of death and ash. *Why do*

I want to sob? Father Sal's alive; I only really knew him. Lalo scrubbed at his eyes, blinking rapidly when dirt got into one.

Not my best idea.

Crumbs.

Iggy wandered up to rescue him. He had two bottles of water for them and helped rinse Lalo's eye out. "You okay?"

Lalo shrugged. He didn't quite know what the emotions in him were at the moment. "Fine."

"Father Josiah and the van disappeared." Iggy dropped on the bench beside him, holding out a pair of earbuds. "Had these in my pocket. Thought you might appreciate a reduction in all the fucking noise around us."

"You keep these in your pocket?" Lalo grabbed them gratefully, carefully pushing the soft-tipped buds into his ears. He instantly appreciated the dampening of aural input. "Did Lucifer take him? Or the demons?"

"Maybe." Iggy didn't sound convinced. He dragged dirt- and ash-covered fingers through his dirty hair. "The fire is contained."

Way to state the obvious, Ig.

Lalo had to strain to hear Iggy through the earbud silence. He tuned Iggy out. His gaze narrowed on the coroner's vehicle pulling up between two fire engines. "They're dead. Most of them."

Iggy took his hand and shifted down the bench until their legs pressed together. Their fingers were both caked with grime. "He won't get away with this."

Lalo snorted in disbelief at Iggy's confidence. He rested

his head against Iggy's shoulder. "How many hundreds of thousands of years of experience does your dear old dad have over us? He's not even human. What chance do we really stand?"

"About 5 percent."

"Yeah." Lalo snorted again, this time in amusement. "Don't give a speech. It's just you and me, and I won't be impressed that you've memorized Aragorn's from the last film. You're not in *Lord of the Rings*, and the world is already burning around us."

"Right. Not putting you in charge of morale. Ever." Iggy stood up, dragging Lalo up with him. "We need fresh air. Acrid smoke isn't good for us."

They checked with one of the police officers who told them where the surviving priests had been taken. They gave their names and numbers for any further questions. Iggy seemed adamant on getting away from the retreat quickly.

"Are we running from something?" Lalo barely had time to buckle up before Iggy had slammed his foot onto the accelerator. "Or someone?"

"The police are going to start to wonder why we showed up when we did. I suppose we can just say we saw the fire on the TV and jumped into action. Can you text Stony for me? Let her know we're stopping by since she has the journals at her apartment."

Barely a mile from the retreat, Iggy made a hard right and pulled to a screeching halt on the gravelly shoulder. His hands gripped the steering wheel so hard it cracked under pressure. Lalo slowly eased Iggy's fingers away before more damage was done.

"Ig."

"I'm the great fucking hero who hasn't saved a single goddamn soul. Pun intended." Iggy dropped his forehead against the steering wheel with a thud. "All my training, for what? None of my family has survived. Who have I saved? Father Luke."

"You're only human, Ig."

"Except I'm not, am I?" Iggy shifted back to lean into the seat with a tired-sounding groan. "Not completely."

Lalo struggled to find the right words to comfort Iggy. He'd never heard him sound so lost before. Confidence, or cockiness, had always been one of Iggy's closest friends. "To err is human, to revenge is sulfuric?"

Iggy tilted his head to the right to stare at him before snorting loudly and laughing so hard his shoulders shook. "Not the catchiest of phrases. I wouldn't put it on a T-shirt."

"Coffee mug?" Lalo mulled the words over in his mind. "Probably not the most grammatically correct either."

"Lal?"

Lalo's heart skipped a beat when Iggy reached out to touch his face, sliding to cup the back of his head. Their lips met in the darkness of the vehicle. Iggy growled in frustration when Lalo eased back for air. "We're covered in ash, grass, and mud from crawling around at the retreat."

"And?" Iggy's fingers gripped Lalo's hair, tugging him across the center console for another kiss. "I *am* human."

"Does kissing make you human?" Lalo asked seriously. "Does that make dogs and cats human when they lick people?"

"Lal." He chuckled and rested his forehead against Lalo's. "Way to kill the mood."

"What? You said it." Lalo genuinely wanted to know how kissing led to a sense of humanity. "What does—"

Iggy shut him up with his lips. And tongue. "Makes *me* feel human."

But how?

Lalo decided not to question further. But he decided the foray into helping Iggy remember his humanity had to stop when his body got wedged across the console. "We're not attempting to engage in anything on the side of road, even if its pitch-black outside. Not happening."

It became apparent Iggy believed his mind could be changed. No amount of kissing made either of them flexible enough to create a pretzel shape out of their bodies. Lalo batted away Iggy's hands and reseated himself, pulling down the seat belt that had somehow gotten unbuckled.

"Why don't we swing by my place to shower?"

Lalo didn't even look up from where he was typing in a text to Wendy. "With or without a side of playing with your penis?"

"Definitely with."

He sent a half-hearted glare at Iggy, who stretched his hand out to drop on Lalo's lap. "*Ig.*"

"Yes?" Iggy squeezed Lalo through his jeans, smirking when Lalo moved in his seat. "Are you sure we can't stay here?"

Lalo grabbed Iggy by the wrist and lifted his hand away.

"I am *not* getting arrested on the side of the road outside of the retreat. Not tonight, not ever, I hope."

"You're never any fun."

Lalo batted away the reaching fingers. "Will you focus? Is this how you handle traumatic events? Sex."

"Ever heard of sexual healing?"

"For the love of oregano. Stop it." He tried hard not to reward Iggy with a laugh. They shared a grin despite his intentions.

With a somewhat resigned sigh, Iggy settled back into his seat. He grumbled to himself while Lalo tried to reach Wendy by text again. She had yet to respond to his first one.

As the lights of the city grew brighter, Lalo became increasingly worried. Even in the middle of research, Wendy had a phone within reach. She'd never not responded to him within minutes, particularly since he tended to avoid messaging unless necessary.

A two-word response finally arrived when they'd gotten within a few blocks of the university. **Skate park.** *Skate park?* He exchanged a glance with Iggy. Why did she want to meet there?

He knew exactly what park. They'd gone to the same one all through high school. *Rebellious teens that we were.*

Doesn't the park close at eleven anyway?

Lalo tapped his fingers against the door handle repeatedly. All the chaos messed with his carefully ordered world. He was struggling to cope with the constant upheaval. "Aren't we too old for skating?"

"Can we call what you did skating?"

"Don't be a jerk." Lalo had spent more time falling off a board than going forward, backward, or doing tricks. "Why the park, though?"

"Wendy's natural habitat."

"Maybe at sixteen. Now it's in her lab." Lalo glanced down at his phone when a second message arrived with a lot of extra exclamation points added. "She says hurry the f-word up."

"One day, Lal, you'll learn that saying fuck won't cause the sky to collapse on your head." Iggy grinned at him. "Auntie Lydia can't even hear you."

"She might." Lalo glanced down at his phone when a third text from Wendy arrived with more exclamation points and words he refused to repeat. "Stony *really* wants us to hurry up."

"We're a damn mile away."

Lalo knew instinctively that their nightmare of a day hadn't ended. How many more surprises were in store? And would any of them be happy ones?

Any idea of kissing, showering, or finding clean clothes flew out of their minds. Iggy hit the accelerator, skillfully navigating the familiar narrow side streets. Lalo hoped they didn't draw any unwanted attention from the police.

They'd certainly be pulled over for going twenty miles over the limit, never mind the state of their clothes. They defined suspicious. Lalo's mind whirled in circles until Iggy reached over to turn on some music.

Strains of his de-stress playlist filled the vehicle. Lalo rested his head against the glass, closing his eyes against the dizzying blur of vehicles and buildings flying by. He wanted the madness to stop.

He wasn't ready for whatever had sent Wendy to the park. Or *whoever*. Lucifer had been the first name that came to his mind. If not him, they had other demonic possibilities.

I just want to garden.

With Ig.

Maybe naked.

Can't we all get along?

Oh, my basil.

Brain, shut up.

CHAPTER TWENTY-ONE

IGGY

PREPARATION MUST BE MADE FOR THE INEVITABLE DESTRUCTION OF OUR ORDER. OUR ENEMY IS POWERFUL. IF THE ORDER FAILS, OUR MISSION FALLS TO THE CHILDREN AND THEIR TRAINING. DEDICATION AND STRUCTURE ARE REQUIRED.

~ *JESUIT JOURNAL, 1926*

"Did you roll around in the debris after the fire?" Wendy greeted them from her cement bench. Alexandra waved at them with a bright smile. "Had a visitor at my apartment while I happened to be next door visiting with Alex."

"Visiting? Is that what we're calling—" Iggy cut himself off, grinning mischievously when Wendy flipped him off. "Sorry. So, who was your mysterious visitor while you were definitely not doing the naughty with your new friend?"

"*Ignatius.*" Wendy glared at him with a look that

promised revenge at some point. "Father Josiah Wilson. He had friends with him."

"Stony, so help me…." Iggy's jaw dropped open as she smiled smugly at him. She drew out an unnecessarily long pause to mess with him. "Was it Daddy Lucy?"

They all snickered, even Alexandra, who seemed slightly confused.

"Titus 2.0," Wendy answered when they'd calmed themselves. "Another two—man and a woman. Never seen either before. She was drop-dead gorgeous, though. They knocked. When I wasn't there to answer, she vanished into this weird shadow that drifted through my door."

"A d-thing." Iggy had believed they didn't have any involvement with the doppelganger and mysterious warehouse. "Maybe two."

"Here. I grabbed a copy from the webcam attached to my doorbell from the mobile app." Alexandra held out her phone to show the image. "Best I could get of them. The Titus 2.0 refused to cooperate and turn fully toward the camera, but Wendy recognized him anyway. She explained about your demonic problem."

"Well, fuck me." Iggy snatched the phone, holding it closer for a better angle. He made a mental note to talk to Wendy about spilling the beans. "What a motley crew. Josiah Wilson, an ex-Jesuit, our lookalike, and the Siren. What is she doing with a Jesuit?"

He'd wondered when they'd have to deal with Siren. Her viral fame had only continued to grow. She was probably the most successfully famous and integrated demon of the bunch.

"Or what is a Jesuit doing with a demon?" Lalo peered over Iggy's shoulder to see the screen. He grinned when Iggy stole a kiss. "Who's the ex-Jesuit?"

"Xavier Ricci." Iggy had never met him personally, but he bore a striking resemblance to his cousin, and Father Luca had a photograph of them in his office. "So, we know where he disappeared to."

From his recent reading of the journals, Iggy knew the Siren to be one of the oldest demons in existence, rumored to be a lover and second in command of Lucifer.

And Father Josiah. He wondered if the sulfuric rebellion knew a snake had snuck into their midst.

"So, why the park?" Lalo returned his attention to Wendy, clearly losing interest in the photo.

"We climbed out the back window of Alex's place. The park seemed safe—and close." Wendy shrugged.

Iggy glanced over at Alexandra. "You're taking all of this really fucking calmly."

"I've studied mythology and religion since I was a child. This? Demons being real? It's a wet dream. The chance to study flesh and blood creatures." She accepted her phone when he held it out to her.

"You have wet dreams about demons?" Lalo shuddered. "Weird. Am I the only one who thinks that is strange?"

"Lal."

"Oh, *right,* not literally. Allistics are such a pain." Lalo crossed his arms and huffed at Iggy. "I smell like a furnace."

"When have you ever smelled a furnace?" Wendy asked.

"If they found my place, they'll know where you and Iggy live as well. We need somewhere safe."

"We brought research materials. And journals." Alexandra lifted a large duffle bag.

"You showed her the journals?" Iggy rolled his eyes when Wendy grinned shamelessly at him. "We can't hang out at the skate park into the early hours. Someone will notice and call the police on us for loitering."

"Lydia's?"

Iggy shook his head at Lalo's suggestion. They had to find somewhere to stay with no connection to any of them. "Wendy? Does Shell still work at the front desk of the Four Seasons?"

"Even with Shell, we can't afford a stay." Wendy had already pulled her phone out and appeared to be scrolling through her contacts. "Can we?"

Iggy never bragged about the size of his bank account. He couldn't afford a month of living at the Ritz, but a few days at the Four Seasons wouldn't even put a dent in his savings. "Get the two-room Presidential Suite."

"We're going to need clothes." Lalo patted his shirt, sending a cloud of dust flying. "Unless you think we can swing past your place and mine for clothes."

The fire, the deaths, and the sudden visit to Wendy's had all combined to make Iggy paranoid. He didn't want to risk going anywhere near his or Lalo's homes. They had a better chance of avoiding any issues elsewhere—aside from Lucifer, who according to the journals could track his children no matter how hidden.

A run to a twenty-four-hour Target solved the clothing dilemma for all of them. Iggy shopped through his grief. Lalo, for once, enjoyed a store, given the lack of other customers.

They hadn't processed the deaths. Not yet. Iggy knew Lalo might take weeks to truly register the loss. He'd always struggled with stronger emotions.

Like I'm any better?

I'm pretending nothing happened, which is a ridiculous coping mechanism.

Lalo and Wendy argued about what constituted a necessity. Alexandra had grabbed four notebooks, two six-packs of pens, and clothing for herself already. She seemed to find their brand of madness entertaining.

"Why are we arguing about socks?" Iggy dodged the Iron Man T-shirt thrown at him. "Just get the crazy socks. I don't care."

"Ignatius." Wendy groaned when he tossed the T-shirt into the cart. "We don't need completely new wardrobes."

"These are soft." Lalo clutched a ten-pack of socks to his chest. "I fingered them."

"He fingered them." Iggy tried not to laugh. He did. Lalo grinned, and they both collapsed into each other giggling. "Less disagreeing, more buying."

Thirty minutes later, they managed to lug far too many bags over to Alexandra's car. They'd left the Trailblazer in a lot near the skate park. Father Josiah knew his vehicle. And Lalo's.

And if they'd made a connection to Wendy, they'd likely

know hers as well.

So Alexandra had made the sacrifice. They squashed into her little four-door car. Iggy had moved all of his equipment out of the Trailblazer into her trunk, which made getting their purchases in a tight fit.

The two suitcases Iggy bought made it slightly easier. They'd be a more subtle way of taking their bounty into the hotel. They didn't need to draw any extra attention to themselves.

Shell, thankfully, hadn't asked any questions when they arrived at the Four Seasons. They did send a glance at Iggy that promised an interrogation later. Iggy had a feeling Shell would find a way to sneak up to the room once their shift was over.

"Always causing trouble." Shell handed over the information for the Presidential Suite. "Want a fruit basket?"

Iggy ignored the snickering behind him. "I'm guessing room service is closed."

"Definitely not. We're fancy." Shell shooed them toward the elevators. "Don't make a mess. And don't order fish."

"Who, us?"

"Shell looks good. Haven't seen them in ages. When did they shave their head? Very sexy. Makes their blue eyes pop and their jaw all well-defined like a model." Wendy slipped into the elevator in front of him, holding the doors open while Iggy, Lalo, and Alexandra carried their bags. "We could—"

"I won't risk another person being caught up in my mess." Iggy forced himself not to clench his hand into a fist.

He didn't think Shell would appreciate having to replace a broken room card. "Even if Shell would find the concept of demons to be fascinating and *wicked cool.*"

Sheldon or Shelly, depending on the day, usually went by Shell. Lalo had met Shell in foster care. Where Lalo went, Iggy and Wendy had followed. They'd stayed in touch over the years.

"So." Lalo rushed out of the elevator first. He'd never enjoyed enclosed spaces. They made their way through into the lush sitting room, standing awkwardly around. "Shower."

With a shrug to the two women, Iggy followed Lalo in the direction of one of the two bedrooms. He found Lalo sitting on a chair with his head in his hands. *Damn.* Setting the suitcase on the floor, he crouched in front of him.

"Lal?" He gripped the arms of the chair, not wanting to add stimulus to Lalo by touching him. "Want to talk about it?"

"They're dead." Lalo brought his hands down, staring at the dirt on them. "And all I did was stand there."

"Lal."

He waved impatiently to stop Iggy from responding. "Don't. We walked away from the dead without a word. Are we terrible?"

Iggy kicked himself for not considering how grief might confuse Lalo. "What would Father Luke say about mourning?"

Lalo scratched at his knuckle, not meeting Iggy's gaze. "He's on to the next adventure. And his wisdom lives on in us."

"Well, the last one sounds more like something the grand dickhead Josiah would say." Iggy smiled when Lalo gave a watery chuckle. "The priests all say they move on to a better place. We're not churchy, but they believe with their whole hearts. Lives dedicated to a perceived higher purpose. Are they right? I don't know. Nothing short of a near-death experience will ever provide the answers."

"Yeah." Lalo found a clean part of his shirt to scrub his face. "Shower with me?"

Iggy's mood, despite the circumstances, lifted instantly. His lips turned up in a wicked smile. "Time to clean up."

Any other time, Iggy would've taken full advantage of being naked in a massive hotel shower with Lalo, but tonight, touching each other seemed more comforting than seductive. If they hadn't been in a hurry, Iggy wondered if they'd have simply stood holding each other under the warm water forever.

Grief poured out of him unchecked. The steady flow of water allowed them both to pretend tears weren't tears. Iggy had never mourned, not really, and strong emotions made Lalo intensely uncomfortable.

They grieved.

Together.

Awkwardly.

Eventually, their tears dried up. Lalo dried himself off, complaining about the towel the entire time. Despite the softness, it still triggered his sensitivity to touch. Iggy sat on the edge of the tub watching him.

With the priests alive, Iggy had always left the planning to them. They tended to point him in the right direction. They'd been decimated in a single evening.

And their plans didn't always work, did they?

Maybe we'll do better.

Iggy caught the boxers Lalo flung into his face. "Is that a hint to get dressed?"

A T-shirt and jeans followed. Iggy caught them too. He ducked the belt and glared at a grinning Lalo.

The small living room between the two bedrooms became their work center. Having cleared everything off the glass table, they spread out the journals, along with Alexandra's and Wendy's laptops, Iggy's iPad, and Lalo's battered tablet. They each had a notepad to jot down any scrap of information.

Lalo had dug out a bag of Doritos and a six-pack of soda from one of the other suitcases. He disappeared behind the couch with two drinks, his snack, and a journal. Iggy exchanged an amused glance with Wendy; even as adults, some things never changed.

Lalo often enjoyed being in the same room for the company—but not necessarily right next to or even in the middle of the conversation.

Snagging a drink and chips for himself, Iggy continued reading Xavier Ricci's journals. He'd seemed to have had a scientific approach that the other priests hadn't appreciated. The man had been driven to understand the truth of Lucifer and his children.

Xavier Ricci hadn't been blinded by belief, superstition,

or faith.

My brothers' lack of understanding and inability to see the magnitude of our danger along with the potential of these partly human children frustrates me greatly. We can harness their power. Use them to defeat the demonic hordes. Create our own holy army. Defeat the devil at his own game with his own plan.

The handwritten journal made Iggy's skin crawl. Xavier had a callous disregard for the lives of the children, no matter their age. He had no issues with attempting to experiment on them.

In the 70s, modern science hadn't quite caught up to the dreams of Xavier. Iggy knew that modern genetic research and cloning could offer the former priest a solution. *Is that what's going on in the warehouse?*

Is Titus 2.0 actually a clone?

He had to get inside to see for himself.

One other aspect of the journal had caught his attention. Xavier frequently wrote of an unnamed woman who'd offered, amongst other things, financial support. They needed to know who the mysterious ally was.

I will end the sulfuric dickheads, once and for all.

"Ig?"

He pulled his tired gaze away from the journal to meet Wendy's gaze. "What?"

"You don't age." She gestured to one of the journals. "They made notes about you and your siblings."

"I'm aware." Iggy was too tired to fish the information out of her a piece at a time. "What's your point?"

"Lalo *is* getting older." Wendy tapped her finger against the page. "He'll continue to do so. And you won't."

"Fuck."

"Something to think about, Ig. And talk to Lalo about. Shit. I can't see straight." Wendy put a slip of paper into a journal to mark her place. "It's been the longest night ever. I'm going to bed."

Think about?

I'm not going to be able to think about anything else.

The two women disappeared into one of the rooms. Iggy leaned over the back of the couch to find Lalo had dozed off on the soft carpet. Lightweights. He gently lifted Lalo off the floor to carry into the second bedroom; they all needed rest.

Tired eyes never see the world clearly.

Stretching out on the bed next to Lalo, Iggy watched him sleeping. *Do I live a life without love because Lal will inevitably die before me? Just fuck around for fun? Can I live that way?*

Without Lal?

He deserves better.

"Iggy. Stop worrying about what Wendy said." Lalo opened his eyes suddenly. "And quit staring at me when you think I'm sleeping. It's creepy."

"She—"

"First, no one knows for sure if or when you're going to age. Second, you don't make decisions for the both of us on your own. It's my life. I get a say in whether or not I want to spend what time I have with you. Third, we haven't even had a real relationship discussion yet." Lalo shifted around with a tired grunt. "So go to sleep. For fennel's sake."

Well, he told me.

Will it really be as easy as that?

"Go to sleep."

CHAPTER TWENTY-TWO

LALO

WE ARE ON THE BRINK OF SUCCESS—OR ULTIMATE FAILURE.

~ JESUIT JOURNAL, 2008

Lalo awoke to Iggy's lips exploring the lower half of his body. He didn't recall ever waking up with someone pleasuring him. *Weird. Not bad, but a little disconcerting.* "Are we dating or screwing around or boyfriends?"

Iggy tilted his head up to stare at Lalo. "Seriously? Right now? You want to have the 'what are we' conversation while my mouth is on your dick?"

"Well, it's not on my dick now, unless you've developed skills as a ventriloquist." Lalo wanted things set in stone—especially considering their conversation before drifting off. "Well?"

Iggy shifted on his side. "If I were a ventriloquist, I'd

make your dick talk."

"*Ig.*"

"What? I was all set for a pleasurable start to the morning, but you want to have the talk." Iggy snagged a pillow to rest under his head. "I would *never* just fuck around with you, Lal. Ever."

"Does two dates make a relationship?" He didn't even know if you could count what they'd had as an actual date.

Iggy stayed quiet for so long, Lalo looked up to his eyes to see if he'd gone to sleep again. "I'm in love with you."

Lalo covered his face with a pillow. He couldn't handle the intensity in Iggy's eyes. "You aren't."

"One, I can't hear you. I don't speak pillow." Iggy tugged on the pillow, but Lalo held it firmly. "If you suffocate, I'm going to be laughing too hard to do CPR."

Lalo swatted Iggy in the face with the pillow. "Jerk."

"I'd like to do some jerking."

Lalo hit him again for good measure. "Awful pun is awful."

"But true." Iggy had always been far more at ease discussing anything of a sexual nature, even just with flirting. Lalo tried but usually failed. "No jerking, then?"

"So, love?" Lalo shifted uneasily. He might feel the same but saying it was an uncomfortable feeling. "Love. And you're going to outlive me."

"Yes." Iggy sounded sad, but Lalo wasn't completely sure of his tone. "Probably."

"Then, we better make the most of our time."

"Jerking?" Iggy asked hopefully with a grin.

"Breakfast first. Jerking later."

"Lalo…." Iggy trailed off, seeming uncharacteristically unsure of himself.

"We've barely gotten beyond jerking, Ig. What's the point of worrying about me dying of old age before you?" Lalo always preferred a pragmatic approach. Iggy was getting wound up in future possibilities. They had years of life to live before it even became an issue. "I'm hungry."

Rolling off the bed, Lalo wrapped the soft blanket around his pajama-covered body. He stumbled out of the room to find both women already in the middle of researching. They'd ordered room service, given the plates on the table.

Lalo lifted the silver domes to find one that appealed to him. He pieced together breakfast for himself with bacon, eggs, and a few pieces of toast. "Morning."

"Ordered coffee for you." Wendy slid over a large cup from his favorite coffee shop. "It's amazing what the concierge will do for someone in the Presidential Suite."

Lalo grabbed the coffee with both hands, taking a long sip. "I no longer feel the urge to smother all of you with a pillow."

"Comforting." Iggy stole a piece of bacon from his plate.

"You two okay?" Wendy's gaze flicked between Lalo and Iggy.

"He's in love with me." Lalo realized after blurting out the words maybe he shouldn't have been so honest. He always forgot allistics didn't appreciate total honesty all the time. "Crumbs. Sorry, Ig."

Wendy's face blossomed into a massive smile.

"Ignatius Faber—in love and blushing. I didn't even know he could."

"Blush or fall in love?" Iggy stole another slice of bacon while Lalo wasn't paying attention.

He struggled to tell if Wendy had been joking or not. He forced a smile, deciding to be on the lighthearted side. *It's always less embarrassing than not laughing when everyone else is.* "Both."

Iggy winked at him, reaching out to ruffle still sleep-mussed hair. "We need a plan."

"Living in a fancy hotel suite forever?" Wendy had her face practically buried into her coffee. Alexandra seemed far more awake seated beside her. "Alex suggested I share her office at the university. I can work on studying the genetic angle while awaiting additional results. She can see what ancient mythology has for us, given her access to original texts."

"Sharing office space already?" Iggy cupped his face with his hands and swooned slightly. "Aren't you both adorable?"

"I can kill you without leaving a trace. I'm a scientist." Wendy pointed a slice of toast at him menacingly. "We're not finding anything useful in the journals. So you two can hide in the hotel reading while we head to the university."

"Can't." Lalo inhaled the rest of his breakfast to avoid the thief better known as Iggy. "The weather is good. I have three gardens to clear out this morning. I need to check in with Father Sal to see how he's doing."

"Lal."

Lalo narrowed his eyes on Iggy, who'd opened his mouth, likely to argue against the idea. "Divide and conquer, Ig. Alex can drop you off at your vehicle. Shell gets off in an hour. They'll be able to give me a lift to Lydia's."

He refused to argue.

And refused to change his mind.

Ignoring the three allistics exchanging glances with one another, Lalo returned to the table with the food to hunt for more toast. He wanted time to himself to process, and Iggy hovering wouldn't provide any opportunity to simply breathe. *They mean well.*

Allistics always mean well.

After scarfing down the toast, Lalo found his notebook from the night before. He hadn't jotted anything important into it, so he used the first page for a to-do list.

Iggy didn't argue with him.

Iggy stared, which was almost as bad. Lalo tried not to fidget under his worried gaze. He stood his ground.

The demons, or Lucifer, or genetically mutated superhumans, whatever they were, would not change Lalo's schedule. His elderly clients depended on his help in their gardens. For some, his visit might be their only one for the week.

"I'm not being brave." Lalo interrupted a whispered conversation between Wendy and her new friend about his amazing strength in the face of adversity. *Can they hear themselves? For fennel's sake.* "Do you know how condescending it is when non-autistics go on and on about how courageous I am for getting through the day? I'm not your inspiration to be better or do more. I'm going to garden—not fight in a war."

"She didn't mean—"

Lalo set the plate down hard on the table, cutting Wendy off. "I'm not your inspiration, Stony. Or hers. Is my life hard at times? Of course. I love you, but don't patronize me with how heroic I'm being."

The sudden tension in the room was too much for Lalo's nerves to handle. He retraced his early steps back to the bedroom. Shell wouldn't mind him hanging around in the lobby for a while.

Unlike Iggy, who'd always been Mr. Popular, and Wendy, with her amazing intellect, Shell could relate to Lalo's experience. Maybe not exactly but more than their other friends. And what he needed at the moment was understanding.

Taking one of the shopping bags, Lalo threw on the clothes they'd bought for him. He squashed it into his backpack. Iggy slipped into the room while he hunted under the bed to find his phone.

"Lal?"

Lalo wrapped his fingers around his phone and slid out from under the bed. "I am not angry."

"You sure?" Iggy sat on the edge of the bed. "They're sorry."

"They think I'm courageous."

"You are." Iggy held a hand up to stop Lalo before he responded. "Hear me out, all right?"

"Fine." He continued gathering up his belongings,

anything to avoid eye contact. He found listening easier when not stressed by social norms. "*Fine.*"

"Everyone has struggles. We all have our fights. Our issues. You face your mountains with the quiet strength of someone who doesn't see an issue but a simple fact of life. It's courage, Lal. Maybe it's because you live your battle. The world was designed for non-autistics, and we don't always make things easy for you. And I'm sorry. I am. I'm not trying to patronize you." Iggy moved from the bed, getting closer and holding his arms out. Lalo grumbled but accepted the embrace. "I admire your strength."

"Fudge off."

"I admire you even though your idea of swearing makes no sense at all." Iggy snickered. "Texted Shell. They're waiting downstairs for you. Caught them just before they left for home."

"Good." Lalo grabbed his backpack and wandered off without another word. He ignored Iggy's amused chuckling.

As the elevator descended, Lalo wondered if he should've at least said goodbye. He sent a short text to Iggy, who probably hadn't stopped snickering. Shell stood in the lobby waiting when the doors slid open.

"Ready?" Shell asked wearily. "Night shift is the worst."

Lalo decided not to say a church full of dead priests might be more awful than a long night at work. He'd learned slowly not to allow every thought to come out of his mouth. "Yes."

Shell led him through the hotel toward the employee parking lot. "What did Iggy say now?"

"What?"

"You're playing doubting Thomas."

"What?" Lalo blinked at Shell, trying to figure out what they meant. "I don't understand."

"I adore Iggy. You know I do. But he has a terrible habit of making you doubt yourself. What has Mr. I'm-too-sexy-for-myself done now?" Shell looped their arm through Lalo's, dragging him over to the beat-up old Volkswagen bug in the farthest corner of the parking lot. "Wait. Don't tell me. This conversation will require donuts."

"Shell."

They grinned winningly at Lalo. "Are you telling me you don't want a voodoo doll donut?"

"No."

"Seriously?"

"I want three." Lalo had no problems eating his weight in chocolate-covered, raspberry-filled donuts. He could use the pretzel stake to stab it in the eye and pretend the doll represented Lucifer. "Fine. Coffee, sugar—"

"And gossip," Shell added helpfully.

CHAPTER TWENTY-THREE

IGGY

~ JESUIT JOURNAL, 1994

Iggy had told Wendy and Alexandra to head out without him. They'd offered him a ride, but they'd run late for work. He didn't want to drive around in his Trailblazer anyway.

With the hotel room to himself, Iggy fought the temptation to catch up on sleep. He wanted to lounge in luxury. An hour or two in the Jacuzzi tub might do wonders for his mood.

I can always say the devil made me do it.

His amusement faded rapidly in the face of the cost of the previous night. Lucifer had intended those deaths. Iggy had no doubt his father planned to murder all of the Jesuits.

The two survivors had likely gone to the top of Lucifer's list of humans to deal with. They were a sign of failure. *And he doesn't like to lose, does he?*

Forgoing the Jacuzzi, Iggy opted for a quick and cold shower instead. He wanted the jolt of adrenaline to wake himself. Three extra-strong cups of coffee hadn't been enough for him.

After gathering up the journals to carry with him, Iggy made his way out of the hotel room. None of their reading from the previous night or the morning had brought any clarity whatsoever to solving their sulfuric infestation. He was coming to the conclusion the answers would come from his own experiences.

Did Lucifer honestly care about the written words of old priests?

Doubtful.

The Jesuit traditions had guided him to this point. His difficulty came from all of his dead siblings having followed the same path. What fate waited for him if he traipsed along after them?

What the fuck are we even doing?

Lucifer had set fire to a university. He'd decimated the retreat. Murdered people. *He'll kill more if he's not stopped.*

Leaving the Four Seasons, Iggy glanced out at the rainy, cool spring morning. He called for an Uber, getting a lift across town to the library, his favorite place to sit and think.

They needed a plan.

A real plan.

One that didn't involve praying for a miracle.

They weren't going to get one.

Is it a miracle if you make it happen on your own?

Sitting at his usual spot in the library, Iggy pulled out his own journal. He added all the names of the dead to a section near the back. Up to this point, the pages had only contained his siblings, a tangible reminder written in red ink of the blood on the hands of the enemy.

Iggy flipped toward the middle and found a blank page. He considered making a "to be killed" list. A random stranger stumbling on his journal might not get the joke. "Number one? Daddy Lucy."

One of the librarians shushed him on her way past with a cart of books. Iggy had to bite the inside of his cheek to stop laughing. He jotted down the names of Josiah, Siren, Titus 2.0, and a few additional demons, separating the list into two sections.

Daddy Lucy had his potential allies on the left, with the demons who'd definitely rebelled against Lucifer on the right. Siren and Josiah had been working together. He didn't know for certain whose side they were on.

He'd bet on them cooperating with Lucifer.

The demons had been quite obvious in their intent to kill *every* half-demon. Why would they suddenly change their minds? Iggy hated not being able to see the entire picture clearly.

How do I fight the half-known?

He drew a bold line underneath Titus 2.0. If answers were required, he had to get into the warehouse. Subtlety had failed; maybe brute force might be more successful.

So that's the plan then?

Target Lucifer and his allies, if they are allies.

Target the demons who aren't his allies.

Figure out what the hell is going on with Titus—and target him if necessary.

Shoving his journal into his backpack, Iggy exited the library quietly. He zipped up his new hoodie and walked down the street to the bus stop. *No time like the present.*

After a short wait, Iggy hopped on the bus for the twenty-minute drive down Broadway. He briefly considered walking when the bus stopped what felt like every few feet for another passenger. His patience evaporated by Evans Street, and he hopped off to walk the rest of the way.

Or jog.

Traffic and lights meant Iggy quickly outpaced the bus. He ran through the campus to the burned-out wreckage of the science building. Caution tape still cordoned off the area.

Iggy drew to a halt. Security likely had eyes on the building, so ducking inside might draw unwanted attention. He regretted not grabbing Lalo's drone to get a peek at the rubble.

With the building being declared dangerously unsound, the university would likely tear it down and rebuild. The structural supports had been too badly damaged for anything else. If the large dumpsters were a sign, they intended to start the cleanup within the next day or two.

Move on, Ig. You're not going to find answers in ashes and rubble.

A familiar tingling slid up his spine. Iggy adjusted his backpack and began to jog again. He followed the intensifying sensation until Siren appeared before him on an empty street, leaning casually against a wall.

"Oh, you are delicious, aren't you? Pity we chose your brother. Boring in life and in death. Both father and son." Siren flicked her burgundy hair over her shoulder. Her black eyes focused on him intently. "Have I given the game away? Did you wonder? Your brother had a child. Three-quarters demon."

"Three?" Iggy didn't quite think the math worked out.

She smiled wickedly at him. "You are just a pretty boy, aren't you?"

Iggy bristled at her tone. He had to remind himself to stay calm. Mistakes happened when he allowed his emotions to carry him away. "It's the devil in me."

"Clever boy. I imagine you'll quickly figure out how the son of a half-demon might become closer to a complete one than his father." Her hand shot out to grab him by the chin, her nails digging into his skin. "I've watched you for so many years. The youngest. The runt. The last of the weakest versions of Lucifer's great plan. Your little friends. He told me to wait. I want to show you the ruin. Torture was always my greatest gift."

Iggy wrapped his fingers around her wrist to ease her hand away without getting scratched for his trouble. He wanted to end Siren right there on the street, but the street was too crowded to manage it without drawing unwanted attention. "Scurry off back to Lucy."

"I wonder if he'll be angry if I play with you first." Siren vanished before Iggy had a chance to respond.

Son of a bitch.

How the hell is the son of a half-demon more genetically sulfuric than his father?

Half plus none equaled a quarter, not three. Unless the mother happened to be a demon.

No.

Could she—

No.

Oh my fucking God.

"You knew my father."

Iggy barely managed to keep from starting in surprise. He glanced down the sidewalk toward the warehouse to find Titus 2.0 standing a few feet away from him. "I did. My brother."

"You could join us. My uncle."

Iggy wanted to reach out to the young man. Up close, he realized Titus's son appeared to be in his early twenties at most. When exactly had his brother betrayed them? "No, I couldn't join you."

"You'll die."

"Maybe." Iggy adjusted the strap of his backpack. He kicked himself for getting drawn into these discussions on a public street. There were too many witnesses for him to drag his nephew away for questions—or to have attacked Siren. "We'll all die eventually."

"You're throwing away the gift Grandfather gave us."

"Grandfather gave us?" Iggy wanted to laugh in the

kid's face. He did. His youth showed despite physically being a broad-shouldered, tall adult. "Is that what your mother told you? You're nothing more than a foot soldier to them. Cannon fodder. A test run to see if the new plan works better than whatever his first one was."

The kid ranted for almost five minutes. Iggy let him. His ramblings offered more insights into the plan than he probably knew.

"Do you have a name?" Iggy interrupted when he grew bored. He wondered if this was how the priests felt dealing with his angst as a teenager. "I can't keep calling you Titus 2.0."

"Titus."

"They named you Titus?" Iggy failed to stop his laughter. "Run along home, baby demon. Tell your mother that I'll be coming for her eventually."

And then your grandfather, when I figure out how the fuck to defeat him once and for all.

An idea occurred to Iggy as he began to walk away. He pulled a confused Titus into a hug, reaching up to yank some of his hair out. He explained his actions with the flimsy excuse of a bug.

What can Stony tell us based on this sample?

Has to be something, right? New plan.

Stop Siren's madness. Then the other demons. And then I'll figure what to do with Lucifer.

Also, find time to take Lalo on a date.

Many dates.

CHAPTER TWENTY-FOUR

LALO

EVERY GENERATION OF THE ORDER HAS BELIEVED THEIRS TO BE THE END TIMES. WE TEACH AND TRAIN TO PREPARE AS IF SURVIVAL RELIES ON OUR ABILITIES TO COMBAT EVIL.

~ JESUIT JOURNAL, 1918

Three gardens into his day, Lalo had mentally plodded through his emotional quagmire. He'd gone over and over the conversation with Wendy, Alexandra, and Iggy. Embarrassment flooded him as he acknowledged to himself that he'd overreacted a little.

Had the conversation been tinged with a hint of patronization? Definitely. Was it intentional? Definitely not.

Not the first time a misunderstanding led to a meltdown, and likely not the last either.

Something to work on. Relationships, particularly

romantic ones, according to Lydia, required a lot of communication. He loved Iggy enough to do better. *Be more flexible. For Iggy?*

I can do just about anything.

His energy had flagged by the time the last garden on his list came into view. He'd crisscrossed the city, making quick work of his to-do list. Mr. Jackson was the last stop.

Seventy-year-old Mr. Jackson had hired Lalo to care for the garden after his wife passed away several years earlier. He almost always had a box of cookies as payment. Lalo generally refused to take cash from his clients.

Mr. Jackson lived at the end of a cul-de-sac at the top of a steep hill. A thick grouping of aspen trees circled the yard, making a natural fence and shade for the garden. Lalo loved the quiet isolation, free of noise and people.

He usually loved it.

Today, however, the air weighed oppressively on him. Lalo wanted to go home, or maybe to the hotel for at least another night. Iggy hadn't let up on his paranoid desire to keep all of them safely away from their own places.

I don't like this.

I don't.

Gathering up the clippings from having trimmed a few bushes around the house, Lalo carried them over to dump into the compost bin. He kept one in every garden he managed as a way to save money on nutrients for the plants. His teeth chattered against the inexplicably cold air.

I'm just cold, not scared. Stop being a baby. There's nothing wrong. You're letting Iggy's paranoia get to you.

Lalo brushed his hands off on his jeans before digging into a pocket for his phone. He'd usually send a text, but the uneasiness had him spooked enough to call Iggy instead. His foot tapped a restless rhythm against the ground while waiting for an answer. "Ig?"

"Lalo? You all right? I can count on one hand the times you've voluntarily placed a call—and I'll have most of my fingers left." Iggy's velvety voice soothed some of his unexplained anxiety. "Lal? What's wrong?"

"I don't know." Lalo's panic came rushing back when his feet slowly sank into the dirt. *What the actual fennel?* "Ig. Something fudging weird is happening."

"Sulfuric weird? Where are you?"

"Now, now." An unfamiliar voice came from behind Lalo, and a stranger reached out to pluck the phone out of his hand. "Let's not make the game too easy for the half-breed demon."

Lalo had gained two muddy feet. The ground had swallowed his legs up to his calves. "What—"

"What? Not who? It's always 'who are you' with most humans. I'm Buer. Demon. The earth and I have an accord." He sneered at Lalo, crushing the phone in his hand, then tossing it absently over his shoulder. "I demand. Nature responds."

The fear simmering in his belly roared to life. Lalo fought desperately to free himself, for even the hint of freedom to move his legs. It only made his predicament worse.

In his heart, Lalo couldn't help feeling as though his garden had betrayed him. What would be worse? If the ground swallowed him whole, or being left at the mercy of the demon?

"Cry for me. I love human tears, capable of quenching the greatest thirst." Buer casually strolled around Lalo, leaving him far too much time to observe the demon, who stood close to seven feet tall with broad shoulders. His pale skin made his dark eyes and bright green hair stand out all the more. "When you scream, be loud enough for Ignatius to hear you. He so loves to play the hero. Pity. One could almost admire his skills, disgustingly good-natured as he is."

Lalo didn't want to scream. Not even when a thousand invisible thorns punctured his flesh. Not as the crisp air froze the breath in his lungs. And not when his blood seemed to boil in his veins. He controlled nothing but his own voice.

And he wouldn't scream.

Lalo had always experienced pain with a slight detachment. He had a high threshold as a result, and now that came in handy. "Are you done?"

Please be done.

Please go away.

Can I have a meltdown in the middle of being tortured by a demon?

Will I even notice?

"What a dark horse of bravery you are. Such courage." The demon cocked his head to the side, observing Lalo in the same way Wendy often inspected her experiments. "You will break. Ignatius won't appreciate my gift if you don't."

Despite being trapped by the ground itself, Lalo writhed

in agony. He clenched his teeth tightly to avoid uttering a sound. Buer wanted a reaction, so Lalo desperately wanted to give nothing to him.

Go suck on a rutabaga.

"What a stubborn little weed you are." Buer leaned in close enough for Lalo to choke on the putrid scent of his sulfuric breath. "I'll pluck you from the ground like all the others."

Self-preservation eventually kicked in; Lalo withdrew mentally, losing track of time. He'd done so as a child, retreating into his mind when life got too hard to handle. He reminded himself the bad only lasted a moment. Soon enough he'd be through to the other side.

One way or another.

Agony flooded Lalo's system, ebbing and flowing with every stroke of the torturer's brush. Buer continued his flowery, sinister speech to his audience of one. Lalo's vision flickered, and he drifted into a semiconscious state.

"Lalo?"

He forced his eyes open through the immense agony coursing through his body. "I…."

Trailing off uncertainly, Lalo managed to get his eyes to focus enough to find a worried Iggy learning over him. He tried to make sense of everything. His mind struggled against his attempts to remember.

The demon.

Wait, why am I lying on the ground?

Lalo found no sign of the demon's presence aside from the faintest whiff of sulfur and ash burning in his throat and nose. He winced at the pain from swallowing. *Did I eat salt?* "The demon? Did you find him? Where is he?"

And what did he do to me?

"Don't talk." Iggy tenderly wiped Lalo's face, brushing through his hair as well. "I handled Buer. Burnt the fucking dickhead into ash."

"Ig. Not your fault." Lalo didn't always understand facial expressions. He did know Iggy intimately enough to realize he'd immediately blame himself for the attack. "Not your fault. *Love you, Ig.*"

The excruciating pain Lalo had managed to avoid came flooding back with a vengeance when he tried to sit up. He uttered the scream he'd almost broken his jaw by clenching his teeth to avoid earlier. Iggy's eyes going wide was the last thing he saw before losing consciousness.

Faint echoes of sound drifted by him. Lalo heard Iggy pleading with him to wake up, Father Sal whispering prayers, Lydia quietly reading, and Ramon's encouragement. He tried to open his eyes to no avail, even when Maria's crying touched his mind.

The effort seemed more than anyone could bear. He mentally dragged himself away from the brightest light. Instinctually, he knew the peace found on the other side would be permanent.

Lalo pried his eyes open eventually when he heard Iggy begging him to quit screwing around. He took stock of his body; despite the still present ache in his bones, all his limbs worked. His fingers flexed slightly, causing the hand holding his to tighten. "Holy crumbs."

"Lal."

Lalo tilted his head to the right to find Iggy seated beside his hospital bed in an uncomfortable-looking chair. "Ig. I…."

Lalo trailed off. What words adequately expressed waking up alive after being tormented by evil incarnate? None. He turned tear-filled eyes toward Iggy, who squeezed his hand gently, using his other to reach out for a button hanging near the IV drip.

"Nurses will want to know you've woken up." Iggy wiped the tears from Lalo's cheeks. "I ran every light and stop sign to get to you. Almost broke the gas pedal."

"Thank you." Lalo wanted to erase the worry evident on Iggy's face. "I was brave."

"Very." Iggy grinned weakly at him. "Very brave. Lal?"

"Hmm?" He tried not to shift in the bed to avoid hurting himself.

"I…. All the lights and sounds are probably overwhelming, but there's a shitload of people who are loitering in the waiting room to see you." Iggy nodded toward the closed door. "We've been taking turns keeping you company. Talking to you. Pretty sure Father Sal read every prayer in his little book."

"Ig?" Lalo patted the hand covering his, annoyed with the amount of effort the simple touch required. Iggy seemed to want to run from the room. "Thanks for saving me."

"No. Don't." Iggy struggled to speak. He nodded a few

times before standing up. "Who do you want to see first?"

"Ig."

"I'll get someone." Iggy fled before Lalo had a chance to say anything else.

Relaxing into the pillow, Lalo stared up at the off-white ceiling tiles overhead. He'd never seen Iggy so emotionally overwhelmed. How bad had his injuries been?

He wanted to lift the sheet to check, but fear paralyzed him.

How close to death did I dance?

Never.

Never tell Iggy why Buer didn't just end my existence.

It'll kill Iggy to know I was tortured because of him.

As a gift.

"Oh."

Lalo lifted his head tiredly to find Ramon leading his wife and aunt into the room. He had a strong arm around each woman. "I'm okay. Gardening was a little rougher than usual."

"Oh, Lalito." Maria sank into the chair Iggy had fled when her legs gave out on her despite Ramon's arm. "What did they do to you?"

"Pollito." Lydia moved away from her nephew to the other side of the bed. She clutched Lalo's hand gently in both of hers. "I came home as soon as Ramon called me."

"Not a chicken," Lalo muttered.

The next hour went by in a socially exhausting blur. Lalo appreciated his loved ones' concern. He wanted to kiss the nurse who chased everyone out insisting he needed rest.

He did.

Mostly, Lalo wanted time to realize the torture was over.

Lalo had been alone in the room for less than ten minutes after the doctors finished with him when Iggy snuck inside. "Ig."

"Won't make a sound," he promised, taking up his seat again. "Just let me sit with you, all right?"

"Only you. Don't want to be alone." Lalo stretched his hand out toward him. He drifted off to sleep with Iggy holding his hand.

Safe.

CHAPTER TWENTY-FIVE

IGGY

~JESUIT JOURNAL, 1922

From his chosen spot next to the hospital bed, Iggy watched the rise and fall of Lalo's chest. He found himself unable to turn away from the sight. The tangible proof Lalo hadn't died.

I don't want to be alone.

Lalo's words as he drifted off to sleep swirled around in Iggy's mind. At first, the attack had made him seriously reconsider their relationship. He brought danger to Lalo's life, but on reflection, he also didn't want to be alone.

For the briefest moment, Iggy had faced the stark reality of life without Lalo—and instinctively realized even a short time was better than none at all.

The doctors hadn't told Lalo in depth about his injuries. They didn't know. The damage to his body hadn't been visible to the naked eye—or to X-rays.

Demons tended to be clever that way. Iggy doubted the doctors would ever be truly able to categorize his injuries. Outside of the visible bruises and obvious shock, Lalo's body didn't show the torture he'd endured.

His mind went back to the frantic call from Lalo. The dead silence on the phone had made his heart stop. Iggy had spent a panicked five minutes attempting to figure out where Lalo had gone.

After reaching one of the other gardeners who volunteered with Lalo, Iggy managed to find his schedule for the day. Lalo never strayed from his plan, so Iggy'd immediately taken off.

He had arrived in the garden to find Lalo near death, buried in the mud up to his neck. He didn't think the image would ever leave his mind. Whenever he closed his eyes, all he saw was Lalo's body.

A smug demon had stood at the edge of the forest. Iggy hadn't wasted time, launching a rake into his heart and pinning him to a tree before setting him on fire.

With the ash floating away on the wind, Iggy had rushed over to help Lalo. He'd shouted for help, finally gaining the attention of the elderly homeowner. Iggy had no idea how the man hadn't heard any of the struggling outside.

He'd dug him out and wiped him off as much as possible while Lalo's frantic elderly client yelled at the 911 operator.

He'd done CPR when Lalo lost consciousness for a second time. And mostly, he'd spent his time praying to anyone who would listen.

Now, seeing the prone figure on the bed draped with sheets. Iggy wondered why Lalo had been left alive. Buer had no reason to keep him alive.

Why wait for Iggy's arrival?

A message?

"Think Ramon and Maria would sneak me a cupcake?"

Iggy jolted out of his thoughts, lifting his gaze from Lalo's body to find his eyes open. "They'd bring their entire food truck out here to feed you cupcakes every hour on the hour if you asked. I'll bring a whole bakery."

"Just a cupcake." Lalo eased himself up, and Iggy darted forward to adjust the pillows to support him. "Maybe two."

"Mr. Pavia?" One of the many doctors who'd puzzled over Lalo stepped into the room. "How are you doing this afternoon?"

Lalo shrugged, wincing a second later. "Can I go home?"

"Not quite yet."

The doctor moved over to the bed, checking the chart the nurses updated on their visits. He didn't acknowledge Iggy beyond a nod of greeting. Lalo gripped the sheets covering his legs, pulling them up higher.

"When can we take him home?" Iggy decided to intervene to give Lalo a break.

According to the doctor, their main confusion came from the internal damage without any external wounds. They wanted Lalo to stay in the hospital for observation.

Lalo desperately wanted to avoid staying; Iggy didn't even need to hear him vocalize his desire to know that.

It came as no surprise to him that Lalo immediately wanted out of the hospital. One, insurance only covered so much, and a lengthy stay would definitely be more than his meager monthly earnings could handle. Two, the sensory assaults had to be adding to his physical discomfort, as well as slowing down his healing.

Leaving Lalo to speak privately with the doctor, Iggy sat in the hallway outside of the room. He still had dirt under his nails two days after digging Lalo out of the dirt. The entire time since then had been spent in the hospital.

He needed a shower.

Wendy shifted from her seat across the hall to one beside him. "Why don't you go home to change? You're starting to smell like one of Lalo's compost bins."

"Any new info on your gene research or Alexandra's delving into all her precious texts?" Iggy scrubbed a hand across his face. He hadn't been so exhausted in ages. Maybe ever. "Anything at all?"

"Maybe now isn't the time?"

He had to get his mind off Lalo's dead eyes when he'd found him in the dirt. "Just distract me, for fuck's sake."

"Yes, because burying your emotions is such a healthy coping mechanism." Wendy rested a hand on his shoulder.

"Better my emotions than burying Lal." Iggy shoved down the tears. He didn't have the luxury of releasing his emotions. "I'll cope how I always cope."

"Not at all then?" Wendy sent a knowing glance at him.

She raised her hands in surrender when Iggy glowered at her. "Alex, brilliantly stunning woman that she is, found a few mentions of Daddy Lucy in several texts. One in particular suggested a sensitivity to several plants. We hoped our plant man might have suggestions for finding them."

Iggy glanced toward the closed door. "He might not want to even see a garden, let alone think about plants."

Trauma affected everyone differently. Iggy worried Lalo might find working in a garden hard to face. If he did, it would be a cruel follow-up to his brutal assault.

"He won't be alone." Wendy squeezed his shoulder. "Listen. Go shower and change. See if you can get a change of clothes for Lalo—maybe his favorite pajamas. He'll want comfort and familiarity to settle himself."

She spent a good ten minutes convincing him. Iggy finally agreed to leave when Ramon showed up with a box of cupcakes (for everyone, but mostly Lalo.) He went home for clothes and a shower, drove over to Lydia's to pick up things for Lalo, and lastly to the hotel to update Shell, who'd somehow worked their magic to keep the Presidential Suite open for them to stay.

The shower helped him feel more human. Pun intended. Iggy sat in his Trailblazer in the hospital parking garage, having picked it up, trying to process the last few days.

Why Lalo?

Why now?

Demons had watched him for years, probably since childhood. Lalo's importance in Iggy's life hadn't exactly been a secret. Why choose now to attack him?

He grabbed his phone when it rang. "Father Mark."

Father Mark Edwards had been one of the priests who survived the fire at Sedalia. Other guests staying at the retreat had survived, but Lucifer had gone out of his way to devastate the Jesuits. Iggy hadn't heard from any of them while they recovered from smoke inhalation and burns.

"Father?" Iggy prompted after a few seconds of silence.

"We heard about Lalo. Father Sal called. I wanted to check in with you." Father Mark had always been kind, though not overly involved in either of their lives. "I've a theory."

"About?"

"The attack on Lalo. I assume it was a demon—not Lucifer himself." He continued without waiting for Iggy to comment. "We know their numbers are dwindling. They had no great reason to be concerned until news of Lucifer's escape. They locked him up. He'll turn his eyes to them eventually, likely once he's gained sufficient control over the city. They're intelligent enough to understand that fighting both you and Lucifer divides their already stretched strength."

Oh.

Fuck.

"There's one of me." Iggy hadn't even considered that aspect of the attack on Lalo. "With me out of the way, they can focus on Lucifer and whatever faction he's built."

"And assaulting Lalo has two immediate effects. It draws you out into the open, and sends you into an emotional rage," Father Mark agreed. "They won't stop. I imagine

Lalo remains high on their list."

Iggy grunted in answer then disconnected the call. He slammed his phone against the dashboard. "Fuck."

His flare of temper drew the attention of a few other visitors walking by. Iggy waved an apology at them. He needed to get a grip.

Father Mark had a point; the demons wanted him emotionally distraught. Making mistakes. He refused to play so easily into their hands.

Striding purposefully to Lalo's room, Iggy found him in intense debate with two doctors. Ramon and Maria stood nearby, not directly involving themselves but clearly offering support.

After a fair bit of back and forth, the doctors finally accepted they had no reason to hold Lalo. He wanted to sign himself out. Friends and family promised to keep an eye on him.

What could they do?

In truth, Iggy wanted Lalo out of the hospital as well. The longer the doctors had to consider the oddities of his injuries, the more their curiosity might cause issues for everyone involved. They couldn't afford the attention.

Demons and Lucifer, also a demon, are enough for me to deal with right now.

I don't need the government deciding to stick their nose into our tiny sulfuric issues.

They'd gotten lucky thus far, despite centuries of fighting demons. The police had yet to truly realize what was happening in Denver. Iggy had no doubt they'd eventually notice.

Someone would.

A journalist or some random kid with an iPhone.

"Ig?"

Iggy shook his head to clear his thoughts and found a concerned Lalo eyeing him. "Thinking too hard."

"You might break something."

Iggy snickered with Lalo, who held his side in pain. "You ready?"

Halfway out of the hospital, Iggy regretted agreeing to take Lalo out. He was breathing heavily and leaning against Iggy. The doctors had clearly been right to be concerned about his recovery.

They made the journey to the Trailblazer. Just. Iggy had wondered if he'd have to carry Lalo. He doubted the suggestion would've gone down well.

"Lal." Iggy watched with growing worry as Lalo breathed heavily, clutching the staircase railing like a lifeline. "Can I help?"

"Don't say it," Lalo snapped. He had the stubborn steel in his voice that said they'd be making it to the Trailblazer if he had to drag himself along the ground. "I want cupcakes and soda."

Because that'll help you heal. Iggy wisely decided not to comment on his diet. "I've got a box from Ramon and Maria waiting at the hotel."

"Home—"

"Home isn't safe." Iggy had pooled money with Shell and Wendy to get a few pleasant surprises for Lalo at the hotel.

He hoped the good would outweigh his discomfort at not being in his usual space. "You liked the Presidential Suite."

"Not home."

"I know." Iggy dragged a hand through his hair, reminding himself to be patient.

"How's a hotel safer?"

He had a point. Lucifer had set fire to two relatively public places within the last week or so. The demons tended to be more cautious, not drawing attention to themselves, but with their prisoner on the loose, tactics might change.

"I feel safer." Iggy shrugged.

"Irrational."

"When have I ever been rational?" He waited until Lalo was comfortably situated in the back seat, stretched out with a decidedly annoyed glare on his face. "Let's get to the hotel. I can't imagine you're comfortable there even with the leather upholstery."

Despite his knowledge of Denver roads, Iggy swore they hit every single rough patch on the drive from the hospital to the hotel. Lalo said nothing, but he grunted periodically. His pinched expression also spoke volumes.

Damn it.

Maybe he should've stayed in the hospital.

Not helpful, Ig, we're here now.

Shell waited for them with a luggage cart. They convinced Lalo to go for a ride instead of limping his way through the hotel. Iggy grinned gratefully at their friend; he'd dreaded yet another plodding journey filled with pained gasping from Lalo.

When they finally made it into the suite, Lalo disappeared into one of the rooms. Iggy followed, only to find him already in bed, pillows arranged to offer support to his body. He decided to leave him to rest, and placed Lalo's earbuds, tablet, and snacks within easy reach. "Hey, Lal?"

"Hmm?"

"Love you."

"I know." Lalo dragged one of the ten pillows on the bed over his head.

Iggy snickered at the muffled "I love you" he heard on his way out of the room. "I'll be out here if you need anything."

Silence.

Iggy closed the door, sunk down to the floor, and leaned against it. He'd almost lost Lalo. *What the fuck are we doing?*

What the hell am I doing?

Is this what it will feel like as he grows older and I don't?

Complete and utter devastation?

CHAPTER TWENTY-SIX

LALO

In the event of the destruction of the order, protocols have been put into place. Brothers from outside of Denver should be contacted. Only the trustworthy. A secret shared has a chance to be unmasked.

~ *JESUIT JOURNAL, 2003*

Lying in the comfortable bed with luxuriously plush pillows around him, Lalo listened to Iggy breaking down on the other side of the door. His chest hurt and his stomach rolled uneasily. He made himself get off the mattress; easier said than done, given his sore and aching body.

I can't let him suffer alone.

Couples don't do that, right?

Right.

Ramon wouldn't let Maria suffer.

Lalo shuffled across the carpet and opened the door. Iggy fell backwards into the room, and Lalo stared down at him. "You're muttering."

Iggy got to his feet quickly, brushing a hand roughly across his eyes. "You're supposed to be resting. This isn't resting."

"Can't sleep. Why were you sitting on the floor?" Lalo managed to stop himself from complaining about Iggy's talking under his breath so loudly. The older he got, the easier he found it to keep from hurting people's feelings with blunt honesty. "Do you need a hug? You seem like you do. Cupcake? Soda? Blowjob?"

"Blowjob?" Iggy wrapped an arm around Lalo's waist and guided him over to the bed. "I want you to heal."

They compromised. Iggy dragged the blankets and pillows from both of the hotel rooms into the living area. Lalo found the sofa with extra pillows more comfortable than the bed itself; Iggy made himself at home in the recliner next to the couch, allowing them both to watch TV.

Lalo watched.

Iggy napped.

Turning the sound down slightly, Lalo shifted his gaze from HGTV to the snoring man beside him. He'd never seen Iggy so utterly exhausted. Pale. Worn. The assault had taken a toll on all of them.

How long does it take to heal from trauma?

Despite the limited time to process, Lalo thought he

should've at least been able to accept that the attack had happened. When he closed his eyes, he felt the phantom thorns digging into his flesh. The smell of fresh dirt lingered in his nostrils—a once happy scent now caused him intense anxiety.

He had no idea how to erase the connection in his mind between the two.

I'm alive.

I hurt, but I'm alive.

I can cope.

I will cope.

Somehow.

He had to, for Iggy if nothing else.

"Hey, Ig?"

Nothing.

Lalo watched him sleeping for a few minutes. "Don't care what you say. Being apart would definitely be worse than me dying first."

Definitely.

No matter how hard Lalo tried, his eyes refused to close. He'd thought being away from the overwhelmingly bright and sterile hospital environment might help him rest, but the terror of facing the demon lingered even in the lavish comfort of their suite.

Social workers and therapists had flung the phrase post-traumatic stress at him in the past. It was something autistics frequently developed simply from living their lives. Lalo figured the demon attack served to add to his.

What in the basil is that sound?

"Ig." Lalo stretched a hand out to shake Iggy by the shoulder. "*Ig.*"

"What?" Iggy shot up. He peered around blearily. "Something wrong?"

"Snakes." He pointed toward the slithering menaces moving rapidly toward them. "Lots of them."

"Aapep," Iggy hissed the name like a curse. He grabbed for the duffle bag on the coffee table. "Get to the bedroom."

Lalo didn't honestly believe any room in the suite would be safer than being beside Iggy. He also recognized Iggy might be distracted by his presence. "Should I call the cops?"

"And say what?" Iggy had retrieved his fighting gear from the bag. "Just go, Lal."

Rushing while every muscle in his body hurt didn't work well. Lalo struggled to get off the sofa. He hobbled into the bedroom, locking the door behind him and collapsing on the bed.

One of the things that bewildered the doctor had been how with no drastic visible injuries, almost every muscle in his body appeared to be strained or stressed. Lalo hadn't offered any explanations because his memory wasn't reliable. He'd hidden away in his mind during the assault.

But now, every movement hurt. He'd refused strong medication, preferring to stick with the lowest dose possible. *This isn't helping Iggy.*

"How can I help him?" Lalo grabbed his phone, started to text, and set it down. "Who's going to manage a demon if Iggy can't?"

And stop talking to yourself out loud.

Breathe, Lalo, you can't have a panic attack right now.

A faint hissing had Lalo pulling his legs up onto the bed and wrapping a blanket around his body for protection. *Because nothing stops a snake like a thick quilt.* The terrifying noise thankfully came no closer.

The lack of other sounds worried Lalo more than the snake. If Iggy had engaged Aapep in battle, he'd expected to hear some sort of crashing or shouting. The dead silence, aside from hissing, scared him.

Lalo stared at the clock on the nightstand, watching the seconds tick by one at a time. A knock on the door startled him badly enough to fall off the bed in a heap. "Son of a cabbage."

"Lal? You okay?"

Lalo tried to stand, but his legs refused to stop shaking. He crawled across the carpet to unlock the door, revealing Iggy on the other side. "Hello."

"Need a hand?" Iggy crouched down beside him. "Shell's on their way up to give me a hand with the snake bodies."

"Snake bodies?"

"Aapep's ash. No idea how the smoke alarm didn't deafen us, but I'm not complaining." He grasped Lalo under his arms and lifted him up onto the bed. "There are about twenty dead snakes in the living room."

"Shell hates snakes." Lalo remembered the time they'd gone hiking in the mountains. Shell had hidden in the vehicle after spotting a little snake slithering along the path ahead of them. "Are you trying to traumatize them? You're covered in guts."

"Snake guts."

"Still gross." Lalo shuddered. He wondered how Iggy planned to explain the presence of deadly snakes to Shell— or anyone else, for that matter. "We're not safe here."

"Obviously."

He glanced up at Iggy, avoiding his eyes and settling on his eyebrows instead, which appeared to have bits of snake in them. *Gross.* "In theory, we were just as safe at home as we are here."

"Yes. Maybe." Iggy stuck his tongue out at Lalo who grinned. "I admit the suite at the Four Seasons might have been an unnecessary expense."

"Might?"

"When do we ever splurge?" Iggy shrugged, getting a bit of snake on the carpet. Lalo made a mental note to leave a large tip for the cleaners.

"We?" Lalo never splurged on anything. His camera had been the one big purchase of his entire life. "You have animal chunks in your hair."

"Everyone's a critic."

CHAPTER TWENTY-SEVEN

IGGY

MODERN DEMONIC ENTITIES ARE AKIN TO CULT LEADERS.
LIMITED IN QUANTITY AND REQUIRING VAST NUMBERS OF
FOLLOWERS TO TRULY ATTAIN THE PINNACLE OF THEIR
POTENTIAL POWER. AS FEAR OF THE OCCULT HAS DECREASED,
THE RISE IN THEIR ABILITY TO DRAW IN THE
VULNERABLE HAS ALSO INCREASED.
A TERRIFYING COMBINATION OF CIRCUMSTANCES.

~ JESUIT JOURNALS, 1996

"What the actual fuck? Shell peered around the room in disgusted awe. They stepped gingerly toward Iggy, avoiding the snake guts strewn about. "Are we suddenly in *The Craft* or some horror film?"

You're not far off.

Iggy doubted Shell would believe the actual truth. He

tried for a more plausible reason for the disaster zone that his fight with Aapep had created. "Someone dumped a bag of snakes into our room."

Not completely wrong.

Half a lie was always more believable than a whole one.

Aapep had created the snakes, sending them off to do his bidding. They served mostly as a distraction. When Iggy destroyed the demon, his minions went off like slithering time bombs.

He'd gone straight for Aapep, knowing his creations would die with him. *Why couldn't the hissy bastards disappear instead of blowing chunks? Literally.* He'd taken the demon by surprise with a glass vase, which lay shattered on the floor underneath the ash.

"Someone 'dumped' snakes on you," Shell drew each word out. "Randomly, for no reason. Are any of these even local species? What did you do to them? Molotov cocktails?"

"Can you get me one of those carts with all the cleaning shit? I'll do my best to make this less of a crime scene before anyone else sees it." Iggy didn't respond to any of the questions Shell threw at him. He had no believable answers to offer. "I'm sorry. I swear I didn't implode a snake colony on purpose."

"Implode or explode?" Shell snickered, then grimaced when a snake piece dropped from the ceiling onto their shoulder. "Right. Cleaning cart. How's Lalo?"

"Hiding in the room. I'll check on him after we clean up." Iggy didn't think Lalo would handle the disgustingly slimy gunk strewn around.

While Shell went to borrow a cart from one of the cleaners, Iggy tried to come to grips with the mess. His body hadn't relaxed from fight mode yet. How could it, when another demon might appear out of the shadows at any time?

With every demon turned to ash, Iggy always wondered when it would be the last. Of the named and known ones, he had only a handful left to deal with. How many more might come crawling out of the darkness?

Though truthfully, Iggy found Lucifer's new plot more terrifying than the old remnants. Tracking half- or three-quarter demons was far more difficult. For one, he didn't sense them as clearly, which made tracking them down infinitely harder.

Iggy glanced over when the door opened to reveal Shell with the cart, along with Wendy and Alex who'd obviously wrapped up their research at the university for the day. "Watch your step."

"We come bearing—" Alex cut herself off, covering her mouth and shielding her eyes with her hand. "Oh my God."

"Going for the post-apocalyptic butcher vibe?" Wendy clutched a paper bag to her chest. "We brought food, but I'm suddenly not hungry."

Two hours of cleaning had the suite normal enough for housekeeping to manage the rest on their usual rounds. Iggy hoped no one ever had a reason to use a black light or luminol in the room. The hotel would have a hard time explaining all the blood, even if tests proved it to be from animals.

Would it, though?

Is demonically conjured snake blood the same as from a natural born one?

Wonder if Wendy would run a test for me?

"Another demon?" Alex asked after Shell had returned to work at the front desk, leaving them alone.

"Aapep." Iggy nodded.

"Aapep." Alex grabbed her laptop out of her backpack, sitting cross-legged on the couch with it balanced on her knees. "Egyptian deity."

"Demon."

"Demon who masqueraded as a deity in Egyptian times." Alex smiled over the top of her laptop screen at Iggy. "Appeared in a lot of art as a serpent; suppose that explains the snakes. A few different spellings of his name. A god of chaos who opposed light. Fitting for a creature of darkness."

"Damn." Iggy was blown away by the extent of her knowledge as Alex continued on for almost ten minutes. He looped an arm around Lalo's shoulders when he joined them.

"How come you don't know all of that, demon boy?" Wendy teased. She sat beside Alex and opened the bag, placing the containers on the coffee table. "Did you take your pain meds, Lal?"

"Makes me tired." Lalo shook his head with a familiar air of stubbornness. "Lydia's bringing her homemade bath salts. They'll do more for the muscle ache and won't turn me into a Lal-zombie."

"Lal…." Wendy trailed off and raised her hands in surrender when both Iggy and Lalo glared at her. "All right then. Dinner?"

"Osaka Ramen?" Lalo leaned forward to peer into one of the bags.

"Yes, we got bacon fried rice." Wendy reached in to hand a container to him. "Two, actually, since I know you won't share."

"Mine." He clutched the container tightly. "Beef Bento?"

Wendy hunted through the bag again to pull out the requested bento. "You're welcome."

Silence reigned while they ate. Iggy kept an eye on Lalo, who'd been more withdrawn than normal since leaving the hospital. Understandable. He worried, though, about the lasting effects of being almost buried alive in his beloved garden.

A knock on the door had Wendy hopping over the back of the sofa and heading to answer before Iggy could even set his ramen down. She peered through the peephole. He got up to join her.

"Priest-o-gram?" She snickered after opening the door to reveal a bandaged Father Sal. "It's for you."

Iggy dragged her away from the open door, shoving her toward the living room. "Father Sal? Should you be out of the hospital?"

"I'm in no danger. One of the sisters told me you'd been staying at the hotel. Young Shell sent me up." Father Sal followed him inside the suite. He offered a wave to Stony and Alex before greeting Lalo with a gentle hug.

"Are you well?"

"Fine." Lalo eased away and returned to scarfing down his rice.

"And by fine, Lal means every part of his body hurts." Iggy knew he had a tendency to minimize his pain. *Not that I'm any better.* "Ramen?"

Father Sal waved off his offer. He lifted the small satchel from his shoulder and held it out to Iggy. "Journals Josiah didn't manage to steal from us."

Iggy took the bag, setting it safely away from the open containers of food. "How are you doing?"

"Tired." He lowered himself into the cushy chair beside the sofa. "Our retreat will take years to rebuild. I'm saddened by the loss. Most of my priesthood happened within the beauty of the foothills. We'll be sad to leave."

"Leave?" Lalo put his bento box aside. "Where are you going?"

"We've been told not to rebuild. Others will take over the retreat in another location. As you're the last and only child given into our care, we're being sent to other missions." Father Sal reached out to pat Lalo's knee gently. His attention, however, remained on Iggy. "You've learned all your lessons from us. We're not fighters. The back of our order was broken in the fire. Brother Mark and I aren't enough to bridge the gap. They may change their minds with time."

They weren't. Iggy had always maintained a pragmatic approach. If anything, he thought they'd ended up holding him back.

And the added intrigue hadn't helped with Father Josiah, ex-Jesuits, and Titus.

Leaving the others to chat with Father Sal, Iggy made his way into the bedroom. He needed a shower. And time to think. They'd missed something.

Iggy's instincts told him that somewhere in all of the chaos of the past few weeks, they'd missed out on something. But what? He stripped out of his clothes, leaving them in a pile on the floor, and sat on the edge of the bed.

What the fuck am I not seeing?

And how the hell is it going to bite me in the ass?

CHAPTER TWENTY-EIGHT

LALO

~ JESUIT JOURNALS, 1915

Food made Lalo sleepy. He left Wendy and Alex with Father Sal. They could handle social niceties; his tolerance had been reached.

Pain always made his ability to play allistic almost impossible.

He wanted to disappear in the garden for days without anyone to bother him, except just thinking about plants, dirt, anything outdoors sent shivers of fear up his spine. He rubbed his eyes tiredly, deciding to deal with his new phobia later. *How can I fight demons?*

How do I help Ig?

At the heart of it all, Lalo most wanted to be a help and not a hindrance to Iggy. He might not fully understand love—and being in love. Lalo did, however, completely grasp the raw desire in his soul to do everything in his power to ensure they lived long lives together.

And fudge the demons.

And Lucifer.

Fudge them to Hell.

Stretching out on the bed, Lalo plotted while listening to Iggy shower. There'd been several mentions in the journals of finding a natural, organic solution to the demonic problem. Plant-based. Despite his impulse to hide away, he forced his mind to consider the options.

They had to stop both Lucifer and the remnants of the demons who'd attempted to rebel against his rule by locking him away. How many years had the Jesuits been fighting in Denver? Lalo had the strangest feeling if their little group didn't win now, they might never.

And if Iggy died in the fight?

Who'd pick up the mantle of mile-high hero?

No one.

With the destruction of the retreat, the priests had clearly decided to cut and run.

With Daddy Lucy's intense charisma, Lalo doubted the Denver police or even the federal authorities stood a chance. They'd fall. Quickly. *And what happens after we slide down the sulfuric slippery slope?*

Bad things.

All the very bad things.

He had to get back into the garden at the retreat. The greenhouse had been mostly spared by the fire. If their rarer plants had survived, he might discover something. Alex might also have ideas with her historical texts, and Wendy, with her lab work, could help in the experimentation process.

Demon death by poultice?

"Lal?"

He tilted his head to the side, getting a wonderful view of a completely naked Iggy. His body responded. Well, part of it; the rest protested with an aching sort of pain. "Plants."

Iggy glanced down at his dick. "Eggplant?"

"Baby carrot, maybe," Lalo teased, rolling away from the damp towel thrown in his direction. He immediately regretted the move. "Ow. I hurt."

"Maybe a cucumber?"

"Not the one between your legs. Actual plants, herbs, and flowers, Ig." He shoved the damp towel off the blanket. "We need to head to the retreat."

"Now?"

"Maybe get dressed first?" Lalo reached for his backpack from the floor next to the bed and made himself stand up. He had to ignore the ache in his muscles whenever he moved, pausing to enjoy the sight of Iggy moving around the room naked. "It's important."

Returning to the living room, Lalo found Father Sal and Alex in a heated debate about myths and facts as related to Lucifer. Wendy had her eyes glued to her laptop. He cheered silently when he found his bacon fried rice untouched and slumped into his previously abandoned seat. "If I were demonic, what sorts of herbs, flowers, any greenery really, would I avoid?"

Alex paused in the middle of her debate to stare at him. "In the 1800s, they used to burn mullein to ward off evil."

"Sixteenth-century texts within the church mention the use of rue as a repellent for many kinds of evil." Father Sal added his two cents.

The two went back and forth, trading information from their studies. Lalo and Wendy both took notes. He had no idea if any of it would be useful.

As Lalo saw it, they had two goals. Take as many of the plants at the retreat as were still viable, and do research in the journals and with the greenery itself to find something. Anything useful. Time wasn't on their side.

"Council of war?" Iggy joined them, still towel drying his hair. "Are we preparing for battle or a secret mission to the retreat?"

"You watch too many movies, young Ignatius." Father Sal sipped from his glass of water. "The police have finished their investigation. The garden and the buildings, what's left of them, are open to you."

"Take everything or just what we need?" Wendy asked.

Lalo glanced down at the initial list they'd made of potentially useful herbs and flowers. They didn't know what all they'd find in the retreat's garden. All the samples he'd gotten the first time had been destroyed at the fire at the university before Wendy had managed to test them. "Everything."

"Everything?" Iggy questioned.

"Nothing." Lalo thought about the greenhouse, and unwanted memories of his attack flooded his mind. "I don't want to go in the garden."

Iggy rested a hand on Lalo's shoulder. "I'll be there."

"You'll be fine." Father Sal shifted forward in his seat and patted Lalo on the knee. "I'll pray for you."

Over the years, Lalo had heard Iggy grumble at the priests' inaction. They taught. They prayed. And left playing warrior to children. He'd never fully understood Iggy's bitterness over it until now.

Then again, what can old men in cassocks do?

What can a gardener do?

More than just pray.

Part of Lalo wanted to call Father Sal out for leaving them. He didn't. What would be the point?

Father Sal was a kind, caring man who'd looked out for him over the years. At his age, what actual difference could he make? Maybe he thought prayers would do something.

I'll keep you in my thoughts and prayers.

How does it help? Makes him feel better? That's something, right?

No.

"Are we going?" Iggy had started tying the laces of his sneakers.

"Sleep first." Wendy pointed to the dark sky out of the window. "Get some rest. We can head out early in the morning, grab breakfast, and make our way to the retreat with the light of day to help our search. What's the point of going now?"

"Getting it over with?" Iggy shrugged. He caved to the glares sent his way. "Fine. Morning it is."

After Father Sal left, they sat around the living room, chatting about nothing and everything. Shell joined them around midnight with pizzas and soda. They all eventually passed out at around three in the morning, leaving a grumpy quartet to wake up at seven when the alarm went off.

The drive to Sedalia went quietly for Lalo. He'd put his earbuds in to drown out the conversation between the others. Each bump of the road jolted his aching muscles.

He tuned out the pain by reading through one of the Jesuit journals from the 1800s that Father Sal had brought with him. The 1840s in particular had been a time when massive numbers of demons had been destroyed. The priests had obviously discovered some weakness to take advantage of.

The journal belonged to a Father Edward Walsh of Ireland, who'd run an apothecary before joining the Jesuit order. He'd created, amongst other things, the concoction Iggy used in his tranquilizer darts. What else had he come up with?

In some ways, Lalo felt kinship to Father Edward. According to some of the more personal notes in his journal, the Irish priest had been considered a laughingstock for what others considered outrageous ideas. They hadn't taken him seriously—and his story and possible solution to the demonic problem had been lost in the archives.

Lalo flipped to the next page of the journal, frowning at a drawing of angelica in full bloom. *Why this one?* It wasn't exactly a rare or obscure herb.

The intricate sketch included several variations of the herb. Alex had mentioned angelica in her lecture on historical myths and religious folklore. A monk had supposedly dreamed up a cure for the plague after a visit from an angel.

Are Jesuits superstitious?

Additional pages contained notes on parsley, fennel, and a few other common kitchen herbs and vegetables. No recipe, but sketches of a copper pot, along with notes on stirring and temperature. *Am I going to play with potions? Does that make me Snape?*

Always.

"Lal? Why are you snickering at the journal?" Wendy twisted around from the front seat to stare at him. "Lalo?"

Waving off her concern, Lalo continued reading through the journal. He jotted notes in the notebook Wendy had given him. He hoped they'd find time to test some of the ideas.

"Alchemy, alchemy, alchemy," Lalo sang under his breath. "Alchemy for me, alchemy for you. Alchemy."

"If you're done serenading us, do you want another biscuit?" Wendy held out the bag to him.

They'd stopped for biscuit sandwiches at the Denver Biscuit Company before heading out toward the foothills. Lalo's favorite had to be the Dahlia: sausage, egg, apple butter, and dripping with maple syrup. He found his second one at the bottom of the sack and returned it to Wendy.

He'd stretched out on the third row of seats in the Trailblazer. Alex had journals and books spread across the second, leaving Wendy and Iggy in the front. The two had argued most of the drive on whether sausage or bacon made the best breakfast sandwich.

Lalo tried to ignore their increasingly heated debate over meat and continued hunting for more ideas in the journal. "Alchemy, alchemy, alchemy."

CHAPTER TWENTY-NINE

IGGY

THE DANGERS OF UNBALANCING THE WORLD REMAIN UNKNOWN. THE DANGERS OF ALLOWING LUCIFER AND HIS DEMONS TO EXIST ARE CLEARLY KNOWN.

~ *JESUIT JOURNAL, 1892*

"Hey, Iggy? Wendy? Check this out." Alex waved them over to a half-burned painting hidden behind a ruined tapestry. The mural showed a winged Lucifer in all his glory standing guard over a globe. The earth had been divided in half by light and shadow. "Have you ever seen this?"

"Never." Iggy frowned at the partially melted artwork. He bent down to pick up the tattered remains of the tapestry that had always hung from the wall behind the church's altar. "Why hide it?"

Alex traced the depiction of Lucifer. "The symbolism

is intriguing. They've portrayed him as a hero of sorts or a vengeful guardian. Not an imprisoned enemy or a fallen angel."

"Yin and yang. Just a Jesuit version." Iggy eyed the globe with interest. "Maybe he's corrupting the world?"

"Or guarding the balance between the sun and shadow?" Alex fished her phone out of her pocket to begin videoing what remained of the mural. "The darkness is centered— not overtaking the light."

What if the demons had sealed Lucifer up to wrest his control away?

To attempt to disrupt the balance in their favor?

Iggy shook his head. A single painting didn't change what he knew. Not yet. They needed more than a half-burned mural hidden away on a wall in the church. "Maybe we're overthinking it."

"Why paint the mural at all, though?" Wendy kicked at the charred fabric on the floor. "If you're only going to cover the art up?"

"So which came first? The painting or the tapestry?" Iggy wondered if any of the surviving priests had an answer. And would they tell him the truth he asked? Probably not. "My guess would be the painting."

Alex shook her head. "I'm not sure. Not enough of the tapestry remains to accurately judge the age. They might easily have painted over the mural to keep it hidden. Why use fabric?"

Leaving the two women to debate the painting and explore the church, Iggy made his way over destroyed benches out the door. He wanted to check on Lalo in the garden. They'd left him to relax a bit.

Iggy found him outside of the garden, sitting on a tree stump. "Lal? You okay?"

Lalo started in surprise. "I'm afraid of dirt."

He knew fear could cripple anyone, and his heart broke for Lalo. *We shouldn't have left him on his own.* "Why don't we conquer the dirt together?"

Lalo shrugged.

Or not.

Iggy sat beside the tree stump, leaning against it and grimacing at the damp seeping through his jeans. "Why don't I video the inside of the greenhouse, then you can tell me which plants to bring out to you? I'll be your gofer."

Lalo shrugged.

"Or we could fuck over Father Ricci's desk instead? Always wanted to desecrate his office." Iggy nudged Lalo's knee gently with his hand.

He shrugged again, then Iggy's words seemed to actually filter through. "Seriously? Father Ricci's desk? Didn't the fire destroy everything?"

"What's a little ash amongst lovers?"

"That's not a quote." Lalo snickered with him. "Not sure we should desecrate a place where people died."

"Fair point."

"And I think your horns are showing." Lalo stretched a hand out to poke him in the head. "I'm not having sex where…. We're just not."

"Not even a hand job?"

"Ignatius." Lalo smacked him in the arm. "No. Your worst idea to date."

"Worse than pope on a rope for Christmas gifts to the priests?"

"No, that was your best idea to date."

Iggy smiled as Lalo broke into hysterical laughter. "Ready to tackle dirt?"

"Why would I— You didn't mean literally tackle dirt," Lalo corrected himself midsentence. "I suppose. You'll basil it up if I let you handle the herbs."

"Basil it up?" Iggy always found the lengths Lalo went to avoid actually cursing to be hilarious. "Basil it up."

One of these days, I'm going to make a thesaurus for all the made-up cursing Lalo does.

I shall call it herb-a-swore.

Ducking under caution tape, they made their way across the ruined space. First responders had obviously used the well-tended garden for a shorter path to hot spots. Lalo grumbled to himself while carefully stepping between the rows; he dragged Iggy along behind him to keep from causing further damage.

The greenhouse had managed to escape the fire. Iggy wondered if Lucifer had been aware of the plants within. He'd likely have gone out of his way to burn the building and the contents to the ground if he had.

Moving into the greenhouse, they discovered looks could be deceiving. The back half had been completely destroyed. A part of the wall of the adjacent building had collapsed into it.

"I'm sad." Lalo carefully stepped over fallen pots and tables to the wall of debris blocking off half of the greenhouse. "All our effort, gone."

How do I respond?

He's not wrong, and without the priests, the garden will never return. They'll probably demo the entire fucking retreat. Cowardly dickheads.

"Do you hear a fountain?" Lalo tilted his head to the side. "Is it raining? I didn't see any clouds or anything on the weather channel about storms today. Where's the dripping coming from?"

While Iggy didn't hear rain, he'd learned from experience not to discount Lalo's super senses. He glanced through the windows but saw no rain. The sun was still shining brightly, glinting off the undamaged glass.

Seconds passed while Iggy strained his ears to listen for rain. *Nothing.* He almost jumped out of his skin when water flooded through the greenhouse from the debris. A waterfall of muddy liquid quickly rose up to his ankles.

Fuck.

"Lal?" Iggy sloshed over to grab him by the arm, dragging the protesting Lalo toward the door. "We've got to get the fuck out of here. Now. Will you quit grabbing flower pots?"

"Herbs."

"Okay, Mary Jane." Iggy ignored the glare and forced Lalo to the exit. He kicked through the glass door when the handle wouldn't budge, shoving Lalo through first. "Find Wendy and Alex."

"Ig?"

"Please. Go." Iggy didn't know if Lalo would survive another face to face encounter with a demon. And he knew of only one being who controlled water with such deadly efficiency. "Come out, come out, wherever you are, Little Mermaid."

"Always with the delightful repartee." She laughed at him—an unpleasantly sensuous sound. Her voice always reminded him of silk, if the fabric had been dragged through a deadly poison first.

He watched her glide down the hill to stand a few feet from him. "How's Sebastian? Do you want to go where the people are?"

"I am *not* a Disney princess."

"Yet you've clearly watched the movie." Iggy smirked when she practically growled at him. "More like the evil stepmother. How is your spawn doing?"

"Far superior to your weak flesh."

"Doubtful. Titus lost in every one of our sparring matches. His offspring isn't likely to be any better." Iggy had always been the strongest of his siblings. "Did Titus know who you were? He had to sense you. I'm struggling to believe he voluntarily put the d in the demon."

She growled, again. Her eyes darkening even further. "I will—"

"Do nothing." Iggy hooked his foot under an abandoned rake on the ground and kicked it up into the air. He caught the garden tool easily in his hand to spin around in front of him. "Daddy Lucy might miss you. Who's going to do all the dirty work for him when you're gone? Does he know you're here? Aren't you a glorified secretary for him?"

"Lucifer gave me a task. Find another way to build his army. No guidelines. Whatever I've done has been to forward his cause. And you, little boy, are just an obstacle in my path." She practically vibrated with angry energy. "A pestilence to be exterminated."

"Okay, Dalek."

In his experience, angry humans made mistakes. Demons were spawned ticked off. He still enjoyed the adrenaline rush of manipulating them into losing their tempers.

He was playing with fire.

Not fire, water.

Aapep had his snakes. Other demons had fire or nature at their disposal. Siren enjoyed water sports.

Despite expecting something of the sort, Iggy went under the tidal wave in an instant. Watery fingers wrapped around his ankle, holding him under the churning liquid. He fought with every ounce of his strength to surface for one brief breath of air.

I'm never living this down if I die from drowning in the middle of the garden.

From one instant to the next, the water evaporated around him. Iggy collapsed on the muddy ground, coughing up sulfur water. His eyes stung, but he forced them open and rolled onto his back, staring up at the three concerned faces peering down at him. "Miss much?"

"While you swam with the fishies, Lalo tapped into his inner pyro." Wendy knelt beside him. "You all right?

My CPR is rusty."

"Keep your lips on your history nerd, Stony, and away from me." Iggy shoved her face away from his. He sat up slowly to find Lalo carrying what appeared to be a makeshift flamethrower. "How the fuck?"

"Father Sal and I had a secret project for two years." Lalo shifted uneasily in front of him, lowering the weapon to his side. "I won't be helpless again."

"He's a secret pyro," Wendy whispered. She grabbed Iggy's hand, tugging until he got to his feet. "Another one bites the dust. Literally. No ash to be found."

"Lucifer's going to go on a rampage at losing Siren." Iggy shook his head, sending water flying. His clothes stank of sulfur, and a steady pool gathered at his feet. "Did we lose all the herbs in the greenhouse?"

They were on the edge of what felt like a final battle. Iggy knew their little skirmishes with demons had only been an appetizer. Lucifer wouldn't make the end easy, whatever happened.

"I saved a few of the plants." Lalo lifted his backpack by one strap. "Enough to test my ideas for a way to combat Daddy Lucy's power."

"The Four Seasons won't appreciate our turning the Presidential Suite into a lab." Wendy looped her arm through Alex's as the group walked away from the waterlogged garden. "University's too obvious. None of our places will do for the same reason. So, where else can we go?"

"Doesn't Shell's cousin run an essential oil and perfume business? She's got a little chemical kitchen of sorts. It would work." Lalo handed his slightly warm weapon to Iggy, who placed it carefully in the back of his Trailblazer, hidden underneath the shelf. "They might help."

"Shell will have questions." Iggy didn't know if they'd believe his implausible story. "What do you need at the bare minimum to experiment?"

Lalo and Wendy went back and forth naming off equipment. A copper pot seemed critical. Iggy had no idea where they'd find any of it.

"It's all theoretical." Lalo eased into the first row of back seats. "I don't know if any of my ideas will actually do anything other than smell nice."

"I'll make a list," Wendy slipped into the row of seats behind his. She leaned forward to rest her elbows on the back and speak to him. "Between the two of us, I imagine we can come up with everything necessary. I still have Titus's hair to check out as well at some point."

Shell, it turned out, believed in a great many things, including supernatural phenomena. They took the concept of demons walking the earth in stride. And their cousin did run a well-stocked lab for making perfumes and natural body sprays.

After promising to allow Shell to join their merry band, Iggy drove through the aggravating downtown lunch traffic. He dodged construction and road closures. They eventually made it to the hotel so he could get out of his mud-crusted jeans and Shell could leave with them.

I might enjoy a stiffy in my jeans, but I don't enjoy them being stiff.

CHAPTER THIRTY

LALO

The many faces of Lucifer should never cause a moment of doubt. We must not be misled by the prince of lies. For every generation, the devil has seen fit to reinvent himself.

~ *JESUIT JOURNAL, 1977*

Lalo had never excelled at sports, but if he had, watching Iggy shower would've definitely been his gold medal event. He sat on a bench against the wall to enjoy the view through the glass doors.

"Want to join me?" Iggy leaned against the floor-length glass divider, his entire body on full display. "Plenty of space. Walls seem sturdy."

"Sturdy until the glass breaks and cuts your eggplant off." Lalo remembered Shell saying the glass shower had been repaired after a panel had collapsed, narrowly missing a guest. "Don't slice off anything you might miss."

"Not funny."

"A bit funny." Lalo, despite his grumbling, allowed Iggy to drag him into the shower. "We're not leaning against the glass. One hospital stay is enough for me."

Iggy's hands were gentle when they guided Lalo toward the warm spray. "I'll take care of you."

Still sore from the demonic assault, Lalo didn't really think his body capable of engaging in anything more than a shower. Iggy dropped to his knees in front of him, clearly ready to test the waters. He grabbed Iggy's shoulders to keep balance.

"Ig." His fingers tightened on Iggy, who was putting his mouth and tongue to good use.

"Just enjoy." Iggy grinned up at him.

"I'm trying."

Losing himself in the sensation, Lalo had to focus on Iggy. He struggled to tune out the sound of the water. Drowning out the racing thoughts in his mind was even harder for him, but he managed.

After sharing pleasure, showering, and drying off, they sat side by side on the edge of the bed. Lalo kept a small space between their thighs. He tried to center himself and actually hear what Iggy was saying.

He failed.

"Lal?" Iggy prompted. "Did I lose you?"

He nodded.

"Where?"

"No idea." Lalo shrugged. He hadn't been able to keep up with the conversation. "What are we doing?"

"I'll tell you on the way."

After they'd gotten dressed, they headed out with Shell to meet up with their cousin, Shirley. Iggy teased Shell about their family's choice of names. Given their experience in foster care, Lalo nudged Iggy to quiet him down.

He never meant to tease too much.

Lalo tended to be more sensitive and thus more aware.

Splitting up had *not* been Lalo's idea; it always ended badly in the movies. Shirley's lab happened to be fairly small, and they didn't want to overcrowd her—or Lalo.

Shell stayed with Lalo and their cousin. Wendy and Alex went with Iggy to pick up supplies from the university. *Why would we need an experienced research-type person?*

We wouldn't.

Clearly.

It'll be fine.

Why did Iggy have to jinx us with famous last words?

It'll be fine.

Shell and Shirley left Lalo to sort out his thoughts. For a while, he simply stared at the plants laid out on the stainless steel countertop. *What am I doing?*

Why didn't I ask Wendy to stay and help me?

Because I don't know how to ask my friends for help.

"Lal?"

He glanced behind him to find Shell and Shirley hovering at the end of the table. "Yeah?"

"What are you trying to do?" Shirley stepped up beside

her cousin. "Maybe I can show you an easier method? I've done a lot of experimenting to get my oils, sprays, and perfumes perfect."

It couldn't hurt.

Pushing his notebook across the counter, Lalo showed her the recipes put together with Wendy's help, inspired by the notes from the journal. Shirley muttered to herself before moving around her little lab. They separated the plant samples into different piles, hoping to get the most out of what they had.

With a little guidance, Lalo managed to create four liquid versions of what Shell called evil repellant. He'd had the idea to use water balloons. Iggy could use his dart gun, but Lalo wanted to have some sort of defense of his own.

David had a slingshot, according to Father Sal. I'll use the herby-juice water balloons.

"Do I want to know what these are for?" Shirley asked while holding the balloon Shell was filling. They'd found a pack of them at a nearby party store. "It's not the weirdest thing I've created in here, but it's damn close."

"Lalo." Shell's uneasy call drew Lalo's attention away from the last of the demon repellant. "You have a visitor who definitely hasn't come in peace."

The imposing figure of a tall, olive-skinned, dark-haired man loomed in the doorway. Shell shoved their cousin behind him. They both glared at the stranger, not that Lalo thought he seemed at all concerned about them.

"Ah, you know me." He practically preened, reminding Lalo of strutting peacock he'd seen at the zoo once.

"Throwing a party for someone? Are the balloons for me?"

Lalo hefted one in his hand up, throwing it squarely at the demon, who simply dodged to the side. The juice splashed harmlessly against the wall, and the few drops that hit his trousers didn't seem to have any effect. *Distract him, so we have a second chance.* "Do you have a name?"

"Dagon."

Dagon.

Dagon.

Why is that familiar?

Searching his mind, Lalo remembered Alex briefly mentioning an ancient deity from Mesopotamia with the same name. She'd said something about agriculture and fertility. He doubted this Dagon had come to help any of them have kids.

The name had also been on Iggy's list: Dagon was the last known demon in Denver. Lalo didn't want to think about whether the sulfuric hordes had spread across the country. There weren't enough water balloons in the world to deal with all of them if so.

The last demon aside from the big, bad Lucifer.

Just one small issue to handle.

Focus, Lalo.

One genetic anomaly at a time.

Lalo still wondered about the demonic label the Jesuits used. There were no angels or other mythological creatures. Why only demons? He'd yet to see any actual proof one way or another.

They didn't have horns or turn red.

I watch too many movies. Are demons mutants of some sort? Or aliens? Shell would be thrilled if they are.

The demons obviously believed in their own existence. They fit historical depictions. He wondered if any of them would survive long enough to determine the whole truth.

Not the Jesuit version of the story.

Or Lucifer's version of it.

Lalo's mind raced while keeping a cautious eye on the demon. Dagon paced the small space in the lab. He seemed intent on telling them how they'd die—and how the demons would take over the city.

His fingers found another of the balloons. Dagon, like Buer, enjoyed the sound of his own voice, which had provided Lalo with the chance. A small one. He hoped it was all they'd need.

"Hey, horn-head." Shell kicked a small trash can directly at Dagon, providing Lalo with the perfect opening to launch another attack. "Son of a—"

"Holy Crumbs." Lalo cut them off. He stared at the glistening, smoldering pile of ash where Dagon had stood. "Oh, my basil."

"Fuck." Shell grabbed Lalo's arm, shaking him slightly. "You evaporated the evil dude. Don't glare at me. Something stronger than 'oh my basil' is required."

"What the hell just happened?" Shirley had come out of the corner to stare down at the mess on the floor. "I have questions. Lots of them."

As Shell tried to explain to their cousin, Lalo sent a slightly frantic but succinct text to Iggy. **Good News:**

dead demon. He walked over to pluck the busted balloon out of the ash. *Well, at least I know this works.*

Death by water balloon.

How in the name of fennel did it work?

Distracting himself from the hushed conversation between the cousins, Lalo figured out which of his herbal tinctures had succeeded in ending Dagon. He closed his eyes, trying to replay the moment. Everything had happened in such a dizzying blur.

Angelica, fennel, and parsley with a dash of the original liquid from Iggy's tranquilizer dart, the supposed holy water.

Would it really be as simple as dousing Lucifer with his concoction?

What was Iggy always saying about Occam's Razor? *All things being equal, the simplest idea is the best one?*

Deciding to make up a larger batch of demon juice, Lalo tried not to consider if killing a demon made him a murderer. *No body, no murder?* The police probably wouldn't agree with his assessment.

He'd managed to make a decent batch for balloons and tranquilizer darts before Iggy arrived.

"Done." Lalo grabbed his earbuds. He'd used up the energy rush, and now felt a sudden shutdown dragging him down. "I can't finish."

"Lalo?" Shell ushered him toward the tiny alcove Shirley used as an office. "Why don't you take a moment to breathe? I'll clean up the ash, and we can wrap up the rest of your demon juice."

Is killing a demon justifiable homicide?

It's self-defense, right?

CHAPTER THIRTY-ONE

IGGY

Our brothers in other cities have yet to report any demonic activity. Either their attention has remained in Denver, or the demons' subterfuge has been more successful.

~ JESUIT JOURNAL, 1995

Iggy arrived at Shirley's expecting the worst. Shell immediately directed him to the cramped office in the back where Lalo sat with his head in his hands. "Lal?"

Nothing.

"Lal?" Iggy crouched down beside him. He waved a hand slowly in front of Lalo's face. "Were you hurt? Do you need to go to the hospital? Lal?"

"Breathe, Igster."

He raised an eyebrow at Lalo in disbelief. "Me? I'm not

catatonic in a chair in the corner."

"Catatonic. Good word. Catatonic. Do cats drink tonic?"

Iggy couldn't hold back the snort of amusement. "Pretty sure that is *not* the derivation of the word catatonic."

"Cat-a-tonic." Lalo drew it out. He sometimes seemed to practically taste words he liked the sound of. "Can cats even drink tonic?"

"Lal? Not the point." Iggy sat on the ground in front of him, resting his feet between Lalo's. "So, not hurt then?"

"He evaporated the demon," Shell added helpfully.

"Evaporated?" Iggy didn't think that was possible.

"Eviscerated. Extinguished." Shell grinned when Iggy glanced toward them. "He did."

"Ash was left," Lalo muttered defensively. "Ash and the remnants of my water balloon."

"You killed an ancient demon with a water balloon?" Iggy felt like Christmas had come early. "You're a fucking genius."

"I threw a water balloon. It's not rocket science." Lalo clearly didn't have the same level of appreciation for his success. "I made more."

"Rockets?" Iggy stood up, holding his hand out to pull Lalo up.

"No." Lalo pointed to a nearby counter that contained a large jug of clear liquid and a bag of colorful balloons. "You can fill your tranquilizer darts with it. Maybe we'll get a lucky shot on Lucifer."

"Question." Wendy joined them in the small lab. "Have we confirmed demonic genetics are the same as Lucifer's?"

"Why—" Iggy cut himself off. He didn't actually know for certain. "No, we haven't."

Leaving Alex and Wendy muttering to each other about science versus historical data, Iggy considered their options. They'd had it easy thus far. The attack on Lalo aside, they'd successfully destroyed the demons who'd come after them.

Lucifer would be different.

Even with Siren gone, Lucifer had Titus Junior and the ex-Jesuits. And who else? How many other people, human or otherwise, had been dragged into his sperm donor's scheme to populate the earth?

There had to be scientists.

And security.

The idea of security worried Iggy the most. They tended to be armed with more than water balloons. And if they were human, the tranquilizer darts would have no effect on them at all.

And all the priests who'd supposedly dedicated their lives to guiding him had already hopped on planes out of Denver to separate retreats, being absorbed into other Jesuit groups across the country.

He needed to think, which wasn't happening in the cramped room.

They had a few more nights booked at the Four Seasons. Was it the height of laziness to waste the day away in a luxury suite? The quiet would allow him time to plan their next course of action.

I could go for another round in the shower (or anywhere else) with Lalo.

No, focus, Ignatius.

Daddy Lucy has to know about Siren.

I'll be surprised if he's not also aware of the other demon's demise.

There's no time to play with Lalo—much.

A glance at Lalo told him sex was definitely off the table. He might not be catatonic, but he wasn't fully aware either. *Okay, he needs alone time to decompress.*

Decision made.

Easily.

Lalo's health and sanity came before anything else, even a chance at Lucifer. Iggy, unlike the Jesuits, refused to sacrifice his loved ones for any cause. It was a line he refused to cross.

The close calls had also brought their relationship into sharp focus. He'd expected danger to make him want to distance himself. Instead, Iggy found himself wanting to draw Lalo even closer.

To enjoy their time together.

Maybe Lalo will be taken away from me eventually by age, but fuck if I'm not going to take advantage of every single second I have.

The world can burn around me before I throw Lalo to the wolves.

And it might.

We need to get moving.

With a promise to get Lalo set up with food and his favorite show, Shell left with their still bewildered cousin and Lalo in tow. Alex and Wendy joined Iggy outside the store. They carried half of the proven demon-killing juice.

Lalo and Shell had the other half.

Better to be safe than sorry.

"Can you really extract anything useful from wisps of singed demon?" Iggy opened the rear door of his Trailblazer. He grabbed his hunting kit and dumped out the liquid from the darts to refill with Lalo's new version. "Where are we going?"

"Lunch, first. Then north. One of my professors retired and now runs a research project out of a lab in Arvada. I already called. I can test the ash." Wendy slipped into the back seat with Alexandra. "If there's any chance of extracting genetic material to compare with Lucifer's, I want to try."

They decided to stop by Manneken Frites for hotdogs and fries. Traffic in Olde Town Arvada was a nightmare, but Wendy ran inside while Iggy made several loops around the area. He made a mental note not to tell Lalo about the trip. Lalo had been talking about wanting to try the various dipping sauces at the Belgian restaurant.

"We won't tell Lalo." Wendy hopped back inside with several bags. "Smells better than I even thought it would."

"Definitely not telling Lal."

Wendy directed him to the lab less than a mile away from Olde Town. "Are you waiting?"

"Yep." Iggy grabbed the bag containing his lunch. "Have fun."

Dipping his fries in the peanut sauce, Iggy relaxed in the Trailblazer in the parking lot. Alex and Wendy disappeared into the lab to work. He stayed outside eating, grabbing his tablet to continue his research into the building, since a friend had finally gotten access to records.

Xavier Ricci, their excommunicated Jesuit, was listed as the owner. *Interesting.* The name of the company attached to the building was Daemonium Incorporated. *Really? I mean, really?* He rolled his eyes at the pretentiousness of using the Latin for demon.

Daemonium.

How the hell did we miss that?

Iggy dug into the sack from Manneken, only to find all the fries gone. "Damn."

He wanted more. Wendy and Alex might spend a few hours in the lab. They wouldn't miss him if he snuck over to the restaurant.

Another large order of frites can't hurt, can't they?

And more sauce. I could drink this shit.

Wonder if they sell Kate's Peanut Sauce by the gallon?

Maybe when the demons are gone, Lal and I can have a date here? Might be fun. Or we should do it now; life's too short to keep putting things on hold for when we're supposedly safe.

The short drive back to Olde Town Arvada hadn't dissuaded him from his craving. He deftly eased through traffic, frowning at honking behind him. A vehicle seemed to be trying to catch up with him.

I have an overactive imagination.

He made a circuit around, attempting to find parking. The lunch crowd hadn't thinned out yet. A familiar Dodge

Charger caught his attention on a side street off Old Wadsworth. *Wait a second. Titus Jr. What's he doing in Arvada? Was he following me?*

A quick illegal U-turn had him going in the same direction when Titus pulled onto the main road. They continued down Wadsworth. Titus hung a sharp left onto 55th and went into a strip mall parking lot, swinging around to face Iggy.

Iggy followed, not bothering to maintain any sort of distance. Titus knew he was there. He stopped in the middle of the parking lot and they stared each other down. "Well, Junior? What's it going to be, kid?"

Why am I talking to someone who can't hear me?

With a rev of what sounded like a V8 engine, Titus drove directly toward Iggy. *Well, fuck.* Iggy slammed into reverse, narrowly avoiding a row of parked cars. The Charger skidded by him, shooting back out onto 55th.

Who's chasing who?

Iggy followed as closely as possible, hoping Titus didn't speed up enough to draw police attention. He'd rather participate in the slowest car chase in history than wind up with a massive drama going on in Arvada. "I just wanted fucking fries. Damn it."

They slipped onto a narrow neighborhood street, Titus picking up speed despite the sharp left followed by a sharp right. They wound up on Reed heading toward 52nd. Iggy held his breath through the quiet road, hoping against hope no kids came running out.

Barely slowing down for a stop sign, Titus roared onto 52nd. Iggy had to be careful making his left off Reed. The Trailblazer outweighed the Charger by a good thousand pounds. He didn't have the ability to stop on a dime.

Iggy followed Titus's son from a distance down the road, watching the Charger swerve between vehicles. "What the fuck are you trying to do?"

Why am I still yelling at someone who can't hear me?

On the surface, Iggy tried to remain calm and focused. In the back of his mind, he couldn't help wondering how this chase might end. *If it's him or me, can I kill Titus's son?*

Is he really Titus's son?

Does Siren being the mother make him any less my nephew?

They went under 76 across Sheridan before finally taking a right on Tennyson. Sirens in the distance caught Iggy's attention; Titus Junior's as well, as he slowed down significantly. The Charger went under the highway for a second time before turning left onto a side street.

Iggy once again found himself holding his breath while they began to pick up speed to almost sixty, careening through a small neighborhood. *I can't let him get away, but I'm creating a problem.* "Shit."

Weaving their way around, Iggy frowned as Titus pulled onto West 47th. That dead-ended in a cul-de-sac past the parking lot at Rocky Mountain Lake Park. *Where the fuck is he going?* He slammed on his brakes when Titus drove up onto the walking path around the lake.

"Well, shit." Iggy eased forward, then hit the brakes for a second time. He reached up to hit the emergency call button for On-Star. "I do not have a reckless regard for human life."

And I never will.

I'm not my fucking father.

It took him a few seconds to convince the On-Star representative that someone was indeed driving around the jogging path at the lake. Iggy inched back into one of the parking spaces. He hoped no witnesses had reported him following Titus.

If they had, he'd have to convince the police he'd been following the dangerous driver. *Not stalking him. Or chasing him. Or contributing to the problem. Not me, I'd never do something like that.*

Maybe I should practice a little more before the police do show up.

The police had apparently already been contacted several times by concerned joggers on the walking path. Iggy had a front row seat for the excitement. He didn't understand why Titus didn't cut across the grass to get onto 48th and sneak onto the onramp for the interstate.

He seemed intent on making the full circuit of the lake. *Does he know I'm not following him anymore?* The Charger suddenly veered sharply to the left, narrowly missing a couple walking with their dog. The vehicle skidded on the dirt, spun out of control, and went right into the lake.

Well, shit.

You absolute dumbass.

Iggy watched the police vehicles with sirens blaring come from both sides of the path, sending walkers scattering. They converged on the slowly disappearing vehicle, fishing Titus out of the lake. He immediately began to struggle with the officers. He'd obviously inherited his mother's temper. "Stupid son of a demon."

Titus, with his amped-up strength, easily threw off the first officer. He slipped on the grass and dirt, soaked from the lake. The police now had him at gunpoint, clearly not wanting to risk injury.

"Oh, come on." Iggy considered his options. Did he involve himself in the mess? Or let the authorities deal with Titus. "What an absolute clusterfuck."

Shaking his head, Iggy slowly drove away from the lake. He dodged the growing police presence. His interference wouldn't serve any purpose at all, and getting arrested wasn't high on his priority list for the day.

I just wanted fries.

CHAPTER THIRTY-TWO

LALO

THE END GAME FOR OUR ORDER IS TO SEE THE COMPLETE DEMISE OF DEMONS IN OUR LIFETIME. ONCE EVIL IS VANQUISHED, WE MUST ASSESS THE NECESSITY OF OUR WORK—AND THE CHILDREN. THEY MUST BE MONITORED TO ENSURE THEY DO NOT CAVE TO THE LESSER NATURE OF THEIR INHERITED GENETICS.

~ *JESUIT JOURNAL, 2003*

"What the parsnip?" Lalo sat up on the couch, grabbing the remote to turn the sound up. He stared at aerial footage of an incident at one of the parks near Arvada. The camera zoomed in on a Dodge Charger being lifted out of the water. "Is that—it can't be."

"I'm always dismayed at the lack of intellect often shown by so many of my progeny."

Lalo narrowly avoided falling off the couch. He twisted around so quickly, all of his sore muscles complained loudly. "What the fennel?"

Lucifer stared at him unblinking for several seconds before breaking into a smile. "He did choose well, didn't he?"

"You killed the priests." Lalo shifted down the couch, holding a cushion like a barrier against the distinguished-looking man who'd appeared beside him. "Dead. Killed them dead."

"Is there another way to kill them?" Lucifer shrugged indifferently. "They won't be missed. You mourn men who didn't give you a second thought. And balance had to be restored. If you'd seen the future, their sacrifices wouldn't even seem a drop in the bucket of pain and loss coming."

I am having a conversation with the devil. I am having a conversation with the devil. I am having a conversation with the devil.

"Done panicking?" Lucifer seemed highly amused.

"No." Lalo tried to move away from the ticking time bomb who'd taken a position on the other end of the couch. "Shouldn't you be making me burn now?"

Lucifer laughed.

And laughed.

Lalo couldn't help glaring, Prince of Hell or not. "This entire month has felt like a century. Just get on with it if you're going to."

Lucifer continued to laugh. He wiped tears from his eyes. "You're safe for the moment."

"Is there a God?" Lalo decided to ask one of the questions that had always plagued him, since Lucifer didn't appear to want to murder him immediately. "Out there somewhere?"

"Somewhere out there?" Lucifer laughed yet again. He shrugged when Lalo rolled his eyes. "I'm not sure. I've forgotten."

"How do you forget if God exists?"

"Lost my memory in the 80s."

"Too many drugs?" Lalo sat on his hands to keep from covering his mouth like a child. He hadn't meant to retort sarcastically.

"Concussion from being hit by a car while helping a grandmother across a road." Lucifer smirked wickedly when Lalo huffed. "Don't believe me?"

"You burned down a church and a university building."

"Touché." Lucifer stretched his legs out, apparently deciding to get more comfortable. "I woke up in a hospital in Nevada with a hell of a headache. Patches of my memory are gone. I've no idea if there's a higher power that made all of this possible. Maybe they've moved on to a new evolution of another planet?"

"So, how do you know you're the devil?"

"Magic."

Lalo shifted uneasily. He hated small talk, and this was a million times more stressful than a casual conversation at the grocery store. "You forgot about God."

"Doesn't everyone eventually?" Lucifer leaned toward him, making Lalo feel like a cornered rabbit in the crosshairs of a wolf. "What are your intentions?"

"What?" Lalo blinked in confusion.

"Toward my son. Your intentions. Going to break his heart?" Lucifer seemed completely serious, which only confused Lalo further. "He's delicate."

"Iggy? Delicate?" Lalo managed to keep his repetition of the word in his mind instead of voicing it out loud. "I'm not going to break his heart."

"Good. Any other burning questions?"

Lalo ignored the choice of wording. The devil was toying with him, or teasing him at the very least. "How did the demons lock you up?"

"They didn't."

"What?"

He reached out to grab one of the sodas sitting on the table. "Can I?"

Lalo nodded in a bit of a daze. He was fairly certain he'd stepped into the twilight zone. "They said…."

"Did they? Or did the priests tell you? I was never sealed away, not by those weak vestiges. They used my less than convenient disappearance in the hospital to their advantage. Clever demons." Lucifer held a hand up when Lalo went to ask another question. "Now, now. Magicians never give away all their secrets. Not at first."

"But…." Lalo trailed off when Lucifer vanished.

What the fennel?

What the actual fennel?

He pinched himself to make sure the encounter hadn't been a dream. *Ow.* Lucifer had actually sat and talked with him. *What the fennel?* Maybe if he repeated himself a few more times, it wouldn't be so surreal.

Iggy's never going to believe this.

Collapsing on the couch with a groan, Lalo tried to find his cozy, warm calm again. He couldn't. Nowhere seemed safe to him, and being alone in the suite had lost some of its attraction.

The silence, despite the volume of the television, slowly eroded Lalo's nerves. He tried every chair in the living room. The bed didn't work either.

Lucifer had destroyed the sanctity of what Iggy claimed to be a safe space, even if the powerful being had been oddly pleasant. Lalo didn't even want to sip the soda left on the table. Anxiety boiled under his skin; he had to do something.

Okay.

This isn't helping.

In order to lower his stress and avoid triggering a meltdown, Lalo knew a change of scenery was required. He packed his camera, the snacks, and his tablet into the bag. Lydia would be thrilled to have him home.

"Lal?" Shell caught up to him halfway to the door. "You all right? Run out of soda?"

"Home." Lalo ducked by them. Shell knew him well enough to not take offense at his struggle with words. "Home."

Once outside, Lalo realized his car was parked at Iggy's. *Fudgsicle.* He scrolled through the contacts on his phone, trying to decide what to do. A bus might get him close to Lydia's, but public transport definitely wasn't autistic-friendly.

And he'd had enough stress for one day.

Or for the whole year.

"Want a ride?" Shell joined him by the valet stand. "I've got an hour break. Should be plenty of time to get across to Lydia's."

"You—"

"I'm sure that it's not a bother. Let's go," they promised. "We don't even have to talk. You can do your quiet thing while I drive."

He did do his quiet thing, all the way to Lydia's. She took one look at him and bustled him into the garden. *Technically hers, but I keep it alive.* Shell returned to work with three Tupperware containers filled with tamales because Lydia had been cooking.

Lydia liked feeding people. It ran in her family, given Ramon and Marie's food truck. She left him in the garden to relax.

Lalo had to breathe through an initial cold rush of panic. He clenched his fingers painfully tightly around the trowel in his hand. *I can do this. This is my fudging space, and I won't allow a sulfuric brussels sprout to ruin it for me.*

Two hours in the garden worked wonders for his state of mind, even if the first thirty minutes had been filled with panic. Lalo had made decent progress on the herb section. Lydia eventually knocked on the kitchen window to wave him inside.

In the house, Lalo carefully cleaned off in the downstairs bathroom. He washed the dirt from his hands, using a brush to carefully get it out from between his fingers. Lydia enjoyed the end result of his garden but not having it trailed all over the carpet.

"Sit. Eat." Lydia had plates already spread across the table. "You pushed yourself too hard, *pollito*."

"Not a chicken. And I didn't have a choice." Lalo grabbed the glass she set in front of him and drank down half of the soda. "I can't always avoid what stresses me out."

"We should try harder to help you." Lydia stepped over to the oven, pulling out a tray of shell-shaped sweet bread. "I made conchas for you."

Lalo found himself cheering up almost immediately and snatching for the bread. Lydia made her conchas with the perfect amount of cinnamon. "Hot, hot."

"*Pollito*." Lydia shook her head while he juggled two of the extremely hot pieces of bread. "Patience."

"Not a chicken. Not patient."

CHAPTER THIRTY-THREE

IGGY

THE FIRST RECORDS OF OUR ORDER WITHIN THE JESUITS WERE LOST IN THE MID-1800S. THE INFORMATION LOST MAY HOLD THE CLUES TO SOLVING THE DEMON PROBLEMS. WE MUST FIND A WAY TO REDISCOVER WHAT OUR PREDECESSORS KNEW.

~ JESUIT JOURNAL, 1982

By some miracle, Iggy managed to avoid the police presence around the lake to return to the lab. He decided not to risk a second attempt at more fries. Wendy and Alex were probably starting to wonder where he'd wandered off to.

Stony's never going to believe this shit. On the plus side, Titus 2.0 has been taken off the table for the moment. One less issue for me to deal with.

When Iggy pulled into the parking lot, Wendy and Alex

sat outside on the curb waiting. From the grin on Wendy's face, he knew they'd found out about the car chase. Or, at the very least, they knew Titus had taken a plunge into the lake.

"Shell texted me. They dropped Lalo off at Lydia's. Heard you had a front seat for Titus turning his Dodge Charger into a submarine." Wendy wasted no time in teasing him the second she'd gotten situated into the back seat with Alex. "What happened? It can't be a coincidence that you were at the park."

"Minor car chase across Arvada," Iggy admitted reluctantly. "What about you two? Any luck with your tests?"

"I see you, Ignatius, trying to change the subject. What exactly do you mean you had a minor car chase?" Wendy leaned forward, resting her elbows against the back of the front seats. "Spill. How the hell did you wind up chasing the clone?"

"Not technically a clone, and I wanted fries." Iggy paused at a red light. He glanced over his shoulder to grin at his glowering friend. "What? I'm serious about my potatoes."

"Okay, Dan Quayle," Wendy snickered.

"Dan Quayle?" Alex sounded a little lost.

"Bonus points for the obscure political potato reference." Iggy fist bumped Wendy, then turned back to driving as the light changed. A quick check of his watch told him they'd arrive at Lydia's in time for dinner. "About the accident."

After detailing his brief chase across Arvada, Iggy returned the conversation to the genetic testing. He had serious doubts the answers would lead to an advantage over the demons. They might, however, offer a clue into himself and his connection to them.

He snickered when Wendy began singing "Lucy in the Sky with Diamonds," altering the last word to demons. "Very punny. Can we get back to the DNA stuff?"

"Lucy is your father."

"How did you convince the university to give you a grant for research?" Iggy rubbed a hand tiredly across his eyes, laughing a bit helplessly at her mimicking Darth Vader. "A little help, Alex?"

"Lucifer is your father," Alex offered.

"Very helpful." Iggy paused to flip off a driver who'd cut him off. "Tell me something I don't know."

"Lucy is *not* the father of the demons. I'd need more time and my own lab equipment to tell you more. In simple terms, their nucleotide bases are arranged differently. Some of their molecules within their DNA don't match up with any human strand I've seen." Wendy went on for another twenty minutes. Iggy tried to listen but struggled to keep up.

"That's simple terms?" Iggy slipped onto the highway to make their journey to Lydia's faster. Shell hadn't explained why Lalo had left the hotel, and he was starting to worry. "What the fuck is a nucleotoid base?"

"Nucleotide," Alex interjected. "Your DNA molecule is made up of four of them."

Wendy waved to stop Alex from explaining further. "Let's say your DNA is a novel. The demons' structure is written with a few chapters missing and in a completely different order. Lucifer's is closer to yours but still significantly altered. Strangely enough, you're also more similar to Lucifer than Titus's son. In fact, even with Siren's addition to the mix, I would say your brother differed from you as well."

"Aliens?" Iggy didn't necessarily believe in extraterrestrials, but then again, he had super strength that most people would struggle to accept outside of comic books and movies.

"Or demons?" Wendy shrugged. "I can tell you the similarities and differences on a genetic level. I can't tell you if the supernatural exists."

"So, same but different." Iggy narrowed his eyes on another vehicle trying to cut in front of him. "Dickhead."

"Use your words, Ig."

"Dick. Head."

"Wait. Hang on. Did you say Titus and I likely had different genetics?" Iggy tried to wrap his mind around the concept. "I'm closer to Lucifer?"

"Only a theory." Wendy nodded.

What if Lucifer had spent all this time spawning children in the hopes of finding one exactly like him?

They drove in relative silence for a while. Alex and Wendy whispered in the back about their findings. Iggy was, despite everything going on around them, genuinely thrilled one of his best friends had found someone who understood her, even when he didn't get her ramblings on all things science.

"Ready to face the Aunt Lydia music, Stony?" Iggy asked.

He turned left at a light; they had less than a mile to go.

Wendy's eyes widened instantly. "She'll smother us with food and hugs."

"There are worse ways to go." Iggy knew Lydia would love Alex, probably pepper her nonstop with questions about her knowledge of ancient religions. "Hugged and fed? Not a bad end."

"Maybe we can hug Lucy to death?" Wendy broke into raucous laughter with Alex. She wiped tears from her eyes. "Can you imagine?"

"I'm trying not to." Iggy was tempted to try it, just to see the look on Lucifer's face. "Death by public display of affection. Feel free to try next time we run into him."

"You first." Wendy managed to get the words out around her snickering. She sobered up as he pulled into the driveway behind Lalo's little car. "Do you think there are more demons out there?"

"Aside from the ones I know by name and have already dealt with?" Iggy parked his Trailblazer, turning it off and twisting around to stare at her. "The Jesuits would say no. But my experience tells me that I've only touched the tip of the iceberg of the demonic world."

And we're completely fucked if they all come out to play.

Not enough water balloons in the world to deal with them.

After smothering them in cinnamon-scented hugs, Lydia bustled them into the kitchen. She had an array of baked goods and her famous tamales on the table. They feasted into the evening; eventually Lydia left them to chat outside in the garden, enjoying the gentle spring breeze with the temperature in the high fifties, and Lalo shared his run-in with Lucifer.

"He asked about your intentions?" Iggy had repeated his question six times so far. Lalo had patiently nodded; he still struggled to grasp the concept. "Did he hit his head again? Is it even possible for him to have suffered unconsciousness? Or was he fucking with us?"

"It's possible." Alex glanced up from the journal she'd been perusing to compare with other ancient texts on her laptop. "Whatever superpowers and strange genetics make up their existence, Lucifer has a human form. It isn't a complete stretch to say his body might be at least partially affected by a physical ailment."

"The flu?" Iggy grinned.

Lalo shushed him with a wave of his hand. "Maybe not small foibles. But a direct impact to a sensitive area? If he wasn't lying, he definitely healed far more quickly than I would if a car hit me."

"I'm more intrigued by his talking about balance." Alex flipped her notebook to a page where she'd sketched the hidden painting from the retreat. "This can't be a coincidence."

No, it can't.

But I have no fucking idea what it means.

Balance. Lucifer. The priests. Demons.

What the hell am I supposed to do with this?

Iggy sipped the warm coffee Lydia had made for them. He stared up at the stars peeking through the scattered clouds.

"Tomorrow morning, I'm getting into that building near the university. We need answers. And fucking around isn't getting them for us."

CHAPTER THIRTY-FOUR

LALO

"I'm having a sense of déjà vu." Iggy slid out of the Trailblazer to join Lalo on the sidewalk. They stared at the eerily familiar plumes of smoke in the direction of both the university and the building owned by Daemonium Incorporated. "What the fuck?"

"Drone?" Lalo went back to the vehicle to grab his backpack. He'd made sure to bring his little flyer in the hopes of giving an aerial view into the mysterious building. "Think Lucifer did this?"

"I'm not sensing him around. Since the firefighters are making headway with the fire, he probably took off once he'd built the flames up enough." Iggy shifted closer, looping an arm around Lalo's back. They both leaned forward to watch the screen of the tablet as Lalo carefully maneuvered the drone overhead. "If it was dear old Dad, why do this? All of his research gone in a puff of smoke. I don't get it."

With the relatively limited battery on his drone, Lalo did his best to capture as much footage of the remnants left by the fire as possible. He kept away from the streams of water from the hoses. They had a slightly smoky view of smoldering beams and what appeared to be a lot of ruined equipment.

Lalo tuned out Wendy's explanation of what she believed each item to be. He had to focus carefully to keep the drone from either crashing or interfering with the firefighters. They didn't need unnecessary attention from authorities either. "I can't get any closer."

"Beautiful, isn't it?"

"For fennel's sake." Lalo lunged to catch the tablet that he'd dropped in surprise. He glared from father to son while trying to save his drone from crashing, complaining to Iggy, "Your extra senses didn't see him coming?"

"When he arrived, yes," Iggy muttered. "I can't feel him traveling on the wind."

"On the wind? Does he fart his way through the shadows?" Lalo glanced back over to Lucifer when he cleared his throat loudly as Iggy choked on a laugh. "Is it flatulence related? I mean, demons do smell of sulfur.

Would Bean-O stop them from traveling?"

"I am *not* windy." Lucifer clenched his jaw so tightly that Lalo winced at the sound of his teeth grinding together.

"Well, there's a sentence I never thought the devil would utter." Iggy wiped tears of laughter from his eyes.

"Jesuits, even excommunicated ones, can't help themselves. They want order from chaos, but nature *is* chaotic." Lucifer clearly wanted to draw the conversation away from the ridiculous and back to the fire. "They try my patience. An amusing distraction at first became more of a stumbling block than comedic relief. Siren's offspring had none of the intelligence of his father. Running around the city trying to chase you down. He followed you and managed to stumble right into the police. Tragically amusing."

"Tried my patience," Lalo repeated. He enjoyed the sound so much that he tried to mimic Lucifer's exact intonation. "Tried it. Tried. Tried."

From the shaking of his shoulders, Lalo knew Iggy was laughing behind the bag he held up in front of his face. He didn't quite understand why. No one had said anything funny; Iggy had never made fun of him or his verbal quirks before.

So it wasn't that.

Lucifer seemed perplexed, a reaction Lalo understood more. The bewildered expression on the devil's face made him want to snicker. *Maybe Iggy finds his reaction funny and not me.*

He'd ask later when the prince of Hell wasn't glowering at them. "Why burn down your own building?"

"You're clever boys, but not enough. So close to the answers." Lucifer disappeared in a wisp of smoke.

"Dickhead." Iggy flipped off the empty space where his father had stood. "I wonder what he meant."

"That we're not smart enough to keep up with him?" Lalo frowned, processing Iggy's words. "Oh, wait, not what you meant."

Iggy wrapped his arm around Lalo's shoulders again. "Daddy Lucy is either fucking with our minds, or he's hinting at not being the mastermind behind Titus Junior. Alternately, he started something and Josiah, et. al. ran with it in an unexpected direction."

Lalo leaned into Iggy. "Another question to add to our never-ending list of mysteries."

"Should we rescue your drone before the first responders decide to grab it?" Iggy grabbed him by the wrist and led the way down the sidewalk toward an alley that ran parallel to the road. "Where'd you park your flying machine?"

"By the—" Lalo cut himself off, twisting his hand around to clutch Iggy's arm and yank him behind a dumpster. "Priests. *Fudgsicle.* They've got my drone."

"The priests?"

"Xavier, Josiah, and several large men in suits." Lalo hadn't gotten more than a glimpse of the group congregating at the end of the long alley. They were obviously watching the firefighters trying to get the blazer under control. "They have my drone."

"Can you download and delete the footage via the app?" Iggy inched forward to peer around the edge of the dumpster.

"Dumpster stains on jeans are definitely worse than grass ones."

"Random." Lalo didn't glance up from trying to make his tablet work faster. "Got the footage saved, trying to remotely reset to the factory setting. It'll hopefully keep them from identifying the owner."

"I'm going to get closer." Iggy stood up slowly, grimacing at the stains on his jeans.

"And what? Have a friendly conversation?" Lalo never understood Iggy's ease in going headlong into what he considered dangerous situations. "I'll stay here."

Iggy bent over to kiss him on the top of the head. "Maybe I'll just listen into their *friendly* conversation."

Well, this is going to end badly.

Very badly.

Definitely badly.

CHAPTER THIRTY-FIVE

IGGY

Despite his best efforts, Iggy hadn't managed to hear anything useful between the former Jesuits. Xavier and Josiah had spoken with one of the firefighters before being driven off by who Lalo referred to as the stuffed shirts in black. The excommunicated duo had obviously brought security along for the ride.

Fuck.

I can't destroy human security with demon juice.

Might blind them, though.

Iggy had backed cautiously away, avoiding the attention of the first responders. "What now? Early lunch?"

Lalo waved his phone. "Wendy wants us to go to

Alex's apartment. They're making lunch for us."

Iggy eyed Lalo with concern. Change often led to meltdowns of varying degrees. "We can say no."

"I'll be fine."

"Fine? Or actually fine?" Iggy asked once they'd gotten into the Trailblazer.

"Is there a difference?" Lalo had his tablet out, going over the video from the fire. "Fine is fine is fine."

"Is fine?" Iggy eased the Trailblazer out of the parking lot and onto the street. "Fine. If we keep saying fine, it's going to stop being a word."

"Not sure language works that way." Lalo went on a lengthy ramble about linguistics. "Quit laughing at me."

"Define laugh." Iggy grinned when Lalo huffed and returned to his tablet. "I'm laughing with you."

"I'm not laughing."

"Don't be pedantic." Iggy held up his hand. "Yes, I know you hate the word. Can we focus on something important?"

"What?"

"Are you *actually* fine?" Iggy took Lalo reaching for his earbuds as a sign joke time was over.

"Definitely, completely fine."

Content with the sound of Lalo's muffled snickering, Iggy left him to the quiet of his music. They drove in silence the rest of the way. He resisted the urge to stop for donuts, mostly because they'd have to share.

Sharing is caring except with donuts.

Lunch, they discovered, had been a labor of love by Alex. She'd made a spread of Greek dishes for them to try.

Lalo fell on the tomato fritters, taking the entire plate for himself. *Tomatokeftdes.* Alex had repeated the word for the seasoned fritters, but Iggy couldn't wrap his tongue around it. Lalo had been convinced to allow them to taste one as well. He'd grumbled about it until Alex promised to give him the recipe.

Or Lydia, since we'll probably set the kitchen on fire.

Iggy, on the other hand, thought he could eat the *melomakarona* for breakfast, lunch, and dinner for the rest of his life. The gooey treat reminded him of baklava in cookie form. "I don't even care if all my teeth rot. This is fucking delicious."

"Alex has a theory." Wendy practically glowed as she stared at her girlfriend. Iggy had to resist the urge to tease her. "A good one."

"Oh?" Iggy sat forward, reaching for another cookie. "What have you found?"

"Patterns." Alex slipped off the loveseat where she'd squashed beside Wendy. "Patterns and parallels."

"I'm going to need more words." He tapped his fingers against his leg and considered the plate on the table. How many cookies were too many? Alex distracted him by spreading out several sheets of paper, including a massive Venn diagram with multiple interlocking circles. She'd clearly used them to track the connections. "What's this note about a Vatican artifact?"

Wendy exchanged a glance with Alex. "According to one of the oldest journals, the priests claimed a holy relic led them to the locations of the children of Satan."

"I sense a 'but' heading my direction," Iggy prompted when she hesitated. He glanced down when Lalo stretched out on the sofa to rest his head on Iggy's knee. "What?"

"The *palevis de nominibus*, or font of names, was a leather-bound handwritten book." Alex flipped to a journal from the 1900s; one of the pages contained a sketch of the relic. "The handwriting remained the same from the first name until the last."

"The last being mine." He glanced between the two women who believed they'd found something earth-shattering yet obvious. "What am I missing?"

"Names appeared. No one ever saw the writer. Not a single entry was ever witnessed." Wendy pulled the plate of cookies out of his reach. "Save some for me, Igster. What if Lucifer wrote the names, mothers, and locations down?"

"That makes no sense." Iggy tilted his head back to stare up at the ceiling while he thought. "Why?"

"If Lucifer wanted his children raised together and trained to fight, what better choice? He watched from afar. He pitted demons against Jesuits, playing everyone while maintaining some semblance of control." Alex shuffled through her notes to pull out a page. "I've found multiple obscure references all the way back to before ancient Egypt. All about a mysterious being balancing good and evil. What if this is simply an extension of that?"

"So? It can't be that simple. Or complex. Lucifer's the embodiment of a universal yin and yang? And my siblings and I were a distraction? Collateral damage?" Iggy tried to wrap his mind around the concept. "Why is this important?"

"Lucifer played the demons against the Jesuits."

"So you hypothesized," Iggy retorted sharply, then stopped and took a breath. "Sorry."

Alex waved off his apology. "He stopped with you."

"And moved on to Titus 2.0."

Wendy shifted forward and cut him off. "What if the test tube babies weren't his idea? He set the ball rolling, allowing Siren leeway. We think Lucifer had them looking for something—or someone in particular."

"He wanted an army, didn't he? Or did he?" Iggy glanced incredulously at them when Wendy pointed at him. "Me? Seriously? Why me?"

"No clue. It's a theory." Alex shrugged. "An incomplete one. If he wanted an army, why stop with you? Sure, he had an accident, he claims, but why not start up again?"

Iggy shook his head. He was going to need an entire platter of cookies to help process their idea. "Isn't it possible Daddy Lucy burned the building down to keep us from realizing his plans?"

But had he?

Lucifer's words about having his patience tried came back to Iggy. The devil certainly had the devious nature to lead Xavier and Josiah into believing he approved of their project. Siren might've even started it as a way to prove her loyalty; she could have easily drawn the priests away.

Layers upon layers of deception.

Had Siren drawn the priests away? Offered them what they believed to be a more proactive solution to the demon problem. How long would it have taken to twist their ideals?

And I'm still on the problem of why me.

Why me?

If he stopped with me because I'm the closest to him, whatever that means, why?

What do I offer to his plan?

"I am so confused." Iggy slid down on the couch with a groan. He grabbed Lalo, who almost rolled off. "Sorry. Am I the chosen one?"

"Okay, Harry Potter. Settle down." Wendy grinned with him. "We, and by we I mean Alex, found some tale from Rome in something-something BC. All about a god created for the purpose of maintaining balance. Maybe Lucifer evolved from that?"

Or maybe he started it.

Or it began with him?

And if so, why the hell did he choose Denver of all places? Or did he simply follow his children?

Which came first, the devil or his offspring?

A knock on the door distracted them from their debate. Alex checked the app on her phone to see who'd disturbed them. She immediately twisted the screen around to show them the two large security guard types filling the hallway; Iggy spotted the former priests behind their bulk.

Fuck.

"Out the back window with us?" Alex quickly gathered up all of the documents. She stowed them away in a folder. "Or do we want to confront them?"

"You call the cops. I'll confront them." Iggy sent the others into the bedroom, telling them to lock the door.

"Well, this is either going to be genius or a disaster."

Grabbing a handful of food, Iggy went over to open the door and leaned casually against the frame. He shoved one of the cookies into his mouth. The four men in the hallway didn't seem to know how to respond to his relaxed consumption of his crumbly Greek treat.

"We'll take ten boxes of Thin Mints." Iggy sprayed the bodyguards with crumbs. He held on to his laughter when they recoiled from him. "Not selling cookies then?"

"Take him," Josiah snapped angrily.

Iggy gave a wicked grin when the bodyguards shifted forward. "Oh, good, I get to play."

CHAPTER THIRTY-SIX

LALO

The names have stretched across centuries. No priest has ever seen one written; yet they always appear. We've traveled far and wide. Our order chose the retreat in the mountains to provide safety and security on the chance the children prove to be lost causes. We have yet to truly lose one to evil despite strong temptation, but the threat remains.

~ *JESUIT JOURNAL, 1921*

Gunshots jolted Lalo from his thoughts even through the earbuds. He ignored Alex and Wendy, who tried to stop him, and bolted from the room. His fingers trembled on the handle before finally yanking the door open.

Lalo didn't know what he'd expected to see. Father Josiah unconscious on the ground wasn't it. He stepped around the former Jesuit and inched down the hall toward the parking lot. "Ig?"

As Wendy tried to shush him, Lalo stubbornly continued forward. He stayed crouched to the ground to allow the brick wall to block him from view. Alex and her muttering girlfriend joined him.

"We're going to die."

"Everyone dies." Lalo lifted up on his knees to peek over the wall. He spotted Iggy across the lot behind a truck. One of the bodyguards lay passed out on a bush. "We're missing a priest and another one of the armed suits."

Another shot sounded, causing the trio to crouch down further. Lalo couldn't help peeking a moment later. He thought the bullet had come from behind a large SUV with blacked-out windows.

Xavier or the nameless suit with gun?

Nameless suit.

"Where are the cops?" Lalo nudged Wendy, who shrugged.

Given the multiple shots, Lalo knew the police would arrive in a rush. They couldn't have been the only ones to call in the emergency. He hoped they arrived quickly to prevent Iggy from having to hurt the guards.

They'd have a lot of explaining to do if there was evidence of Iggy's superhuman strength. Lalo still remembered all the practice Iggy had done as a teenager to gain control over himself. He'd had the hilarious habit of crushing cups, cans, and just about anything else without meaning to.

"Not today, dickheads."

Lalo shot back up to watch when Iggy launched himself around the vehicle. He practically flew across the parking lot, using the roof of a Fiat to leap over the SUV and tackle the armed guard. "Holy fudgsicle."

Knowing Iggy had skills and seeing them in action was two very different things. Lalo watched mesmerized while Iggy barely exerted himself disarming the thug. Wendy dragged him down when another shot rang out.

"Let me up."

"You won't help him." Wendy kept her grip on his wrist. "Iggy knows how to handle himself."

Sirens had all three of them peering up over the bricks. The police arrived moments after Iggy subdued the last of the security guards but not Xavier. Lalo let the others give their statements. He stayed behind the brick wall, hidden from view, toying with his camera and waiting for the drama to be over.

He heard the hushed whispers of Iggy and Wendy explaining to the officers why he hadn't come out to speak with them.

He ignored them.

As long as the police left him alone, Lalo trusted Iggy—and Wendy, for that matter—to deal with the authorities. It wouldn't be the first time they'd handled conversations for him. Lalo had learned to accept their help.

Most of the time.

Turning the camera over in his hands, Lalo hated how time to garden or take photos had been restricted ever since Titus died. His death had triggered the slowly evolving chaotic nightmare. A roller coaster Lalo desperately wanted to get off.

Life has to return to normal, right?

Right?

"Lal?" Iggy vaulted over the wall and landed beside him. "You okay?"

"Me?"

"What? I dodged the bullets. Went all *Matrix* on the jerk." Iggy seemed inordinately pleased with himself. "Xavier Ricci escaped."

"Alone?"

Iggy shifted closer, so they were sitting with their legs pressed against each other. "I'm not sure."

"Ig?" Lalo remembered something he'd read in one of the journals earlier. "What if the named demons we know of aren't the only ones out there?"

Iggy seemed to agree with him. "We're going to need a fucking vat of demon juice. And a plan."

"A plan?" Wendy sat on the wall, legs dangling beside Lalo. Alex stepped up behind her. "Your idea of a plan or mine?"

"Mine. You can all bask in my brilliance." Iggy flicked Wendy on the leg when she practically fell off the wall laughing. "I scored higher than you on my SATs."

"You cheated," she insisted.

"Bitter, much?"

Lalo waved his hands around, wanting to stop the tired old playful argument from reaching full force. "Do you have a plan, Ig?"

"I have half a plan." Iggy got to his feet and reached down to help Lalo up. He still felt sore even without any evidence of his demonic assault. "And half is better than none."

Wendy exchanged a grin with Lalo, who turned away when the eye contact became uncomfortable. "Why don't we go back upstairs and think it through carefully?"

"No faith at all," Iggy complained.

CHAPTER THIRTY-SEVEN

IGGY

CARE OF THE CHILDREN BEGAN AS A MEANS TO AN END. WE GUARDED OURSELVES AGAINST ATTACHMENT TO ENSURE OUR ABILITY TO THINK CLEARLY IF THE WORST-CASE SCENARIO BECAME FACT.

~ JESUIT JOURNAL, 1969

"Ig?" Lalo squeezed underneath the eighteen-wheeler with him. They'd hidden behind one of the tires. "What do we do?"

"Live the rest of our lives on the ground in a pool of oil?" Iggy hadn't stopped to consider the impact of not only neutralizing the rogue Jesuits but the demons. "It's cozy down here."

"Ig." Lalo rolled slightly on his side to level the full weight of his annoyance at Iggy. "*Iggy.*"

"I'm thinking."

"Think faster." Lalo twisted around again, peering through the darkness.

Plans had gone badly. *Catastrophically wrong.* There were more demons. And he had a sneaking suspicion they'd be showing up in droves.

Iggy wondered if the Vatican had ever considered making Murphy a saint. They'd certainly proved his law to be true. In all honesty, driving around to find Xavier Ricci was more of a road trip than an actual plan.

Saint Murphy.

The patron saint of plans doomed for failure.

Isn't there already a patron saint of lost causes?

I don't believe in saints.

Focus, for fuck's sake.

We're not under the truck playing hide-n-seek for the fun of it.

Shell had gate-crashed their brainstorming meeting at Alex's. They'd brought pizzas and insisted on joining them. Shell had been the one to suggest seeing if the business that had owned the destroyed building held any other properties in the area.

They'd found one in Commerce City, another Denver suburb, near a truck stop.

The plan.

The plan had been to use Lalo's drone to survey the spot from a distance. After confirming Xavier was alone, Iggy intended to secure the building and interrogate the former priest. He wanted answers.

The plan.

Arriving in the middle of a battle between Xavier—along with additional security—and demons Iggy had never seen before had definitely *not* been part of his plan. He wanted to be out there fighting but thought the better part of valor would be to observe.

From under a truck.

In a puddle of oil.

Shell, Alex, and Wendy had gotten separated from them in the vast trucking parking lot. Iggy hoped they stayed close to the Trailblazer and kept water balloons on hand. Demons wouldn't pick and choose their targets.

"Stay here." Iggy slid out from under the truck slowly. He heard Lalo following. "*Lal.*"

"I have balloons." Lalo swung his backpack around his body and unzipped it. He grabbed one out. "Might need them."

Rows and rows of eighteen-wheelers provided ample opportunity to hide. Iggy took advantage of the darkness and raced between the vehicles, easily outpacing Lalo. He grabbed a large side mirror, catapulting himself over the hood and leaping up onto the truck parked beside it.

"Ig?"

He peered over the edge down at Lalo. "*Lal.* I'm trying for smooth hero."

"Okay, fine, but you have a plastic bag dangling from your foot." Lalo continued forward between the vehicles. "Go on with your smoothness."

Iggy pinched the bridge of his nose. He scraped the bag

on his foot off on the side of the truck. "For fuck's sake."

Playing leapfrog across the parked trucks, Iggy managed to reach the outskirts of the parking lot, where the battle had shifted toward an open grassy area. He was shocked to see the demons hadn't simply eviscerated the bodyguards. Had the former priest developed a method to kill demons?

Sirens in the distance told him someone around the truck stop had noticed the fight.

Why aren't the demons using their powers?

"Enjoying the show?" Lucifer appeared next to him, sitting casually on the edge of the truck. "Fascinating. New to the world. Jesuits never considered how destroying demons might attract more to Denver."

"Is your secret weapon cryptic statements? What do you mean, new to the world?" Iggy growled. "Shouldn't you be creating mayhem or killing?"

"Balance, Ignatius." Lucifer waved grandly at the fighting groups. "I could return the demons to shadow, but restricting their powers is far more entertaining. Aren't you trained to fight the monsters?"

"Which ones?" Iggy leaped off the truck. He closed a door that was opening, urging the driver to stay in the relative safety of the cab. "Someone has to stop this."

"Why?"

The callously casual one-word question didn't shock Iggy. He'd never expected any sort of kindness from the devil. Iggy also knew Lalo and the others would insert themselves into the fight whether he played hero or not.

And they were inserting themselves by flinging water

balloons haphazardly at the brawling demons and guards.

"I feel like we're one coconut away from a Monty Python movie." Iggy squatted down beside Wendy, who'd taken command of Lalo's drone. "Are you seeing anything useful?"

"Demons aren't being demon-y."

A shout from Lalo drew Iggy's attention away from Wendy. Shell had been inching closer to aim at a specific demon who'd spotted him. Lalo threw multiple balloons; the demon shifted away to dodge the projectile.

Iggy started toward Shell, only to realize Lucifer had taken one of the balloons directly to the face. "Oh, fuck."

Dead devil.

That's good, right?

Why does it feel both bad and good?

"They left me in charge. Whoever you want 'them' to be." Lucifer coughed violently. He dropped his head back on the ground. "I created balance. Pulled the hapless people from the brink of self-destruction over and over. Now it's your turn. My perfect replacement. I waited centuries, playing Jesuits against demons, all in the hopes one of my offspring would have potential. And you were the closest but not enough."

"What the fuck are you?" Iggy knelt beside him. "What are you talking about?"

"I found another solution—your Lalo. Found a way to gift him with my curse of balancing the world." Lucifer convulsed on the ground. He grabbed Iggy's wrist with surprising strength to yank him closer. "They'll come for him, expecting you to be too weak to protect him. Defeated by a water balloon."

Iggy watched his father's body splinter into shadowy ash, swirl around Lalo, and seem to sink into his skin before vanishing into nothing. "Cryptic dickhead. Lal? Are you all right?"

"What did he do?" Lalo whispered. He hadn't moved since throwing the balloon. Iggy rushed over to him, grabbing him tightly by the arms. "Oh, my crumbs. I killed the devil."

Iggy shook him gently. "Are you okay?"

"I think so. I *killed* the devil."

"Is that a hundred years of bad luck?" Wendy teased. She joined them with the others. "Demons took off. Cops arrested the bodyguards. Xavier had a heart attack."

"Lucifer wasn't a mirror." Iggy crushed Lalo into a hug. He didn't know how to feel about his father dying. There hadn't been a relationship between them. Mourning the amoral being didn't seem appropriate. "His last words were fucking useless."

"This might not be." Shell picked up an envelope from the ground. "Has your name on it."

The letter Lucifer left offered a tantalizing clue—a key and an address. They played the innocent, terrified bystanders until the police had questioned and released all of them. The key burned a hole in Iggy's pocket the entire time.

Would it explain his ominous words?

By the time they rolled back into Denver proper, the sun

had just begun to glint off the buildings. Iggy stopped at a drive-thru for coffee and bagels. He ate his dry, choking it down with coffee as a chaser.

The luxuriously decorated apartment rivaled the penthouse suite they'd been inhabiting at the hotel. Iggy wasn't at all surprised Lucifer lived in the most expensive building in the city. They spread out to search through the massive open space.

"Ig?" Lalo held up what appeared to be a manual or reference guide. "Think this is for us."

Iggy choked on a laugh at the words on the cover. "*How to balance darkness and light to keep them from destroying the world for dummies*? Catchy title."

"You're co-owners of this place." Wendy wandered over with a folder of documents. "He put your names on it and several bank accounts."

Iggy collapsed onto the plush leather sofa in the living room area. "So, we've got no priests, a load of fucking demons, and a manual for being Lucifer?"

"And apparently enough money to buy an island." Wendy twisted around a bank statement. "Ig. Have I ever mentioned how much I adore you?"

"Found a letter." Lalo had disappeared into the kitchen to hunt for soda and returned with the envelope. "Pinned to the fridge. Got your name on it."

"Ignatius." Iggy read the letter to himself then decided to summarize. "He doesn't remember how or what created him—and the demons. He lost pieces of his memory after the accident. Lucifer claims he fucked his way through half the women in the world in an attempt to find a child who could balance good and evil once and for all, since he'd failed. Stopped with me because he thought I was the best chance."

"Classy." Wendy leaned down to read the letter over his shoulder. "So, what do we do?"

"Take a nap." Iggy sank further into the sofa. "Then figure out what Lucy did to Lalo and help him save the world?"

EPILOGUE

LALO

In the year that had passed since Lucifer's passing, life hadn't drastically changed in the city. It had for Lalo. Denver itself hadn't changed much at all.

The hustle and bustle in the Mile High city had never seemed fazed by the demonic activity. Suspicious deaths always wound up being termed accidental or ended as a cold case. Lalo felt sad for the families who'd never get answers.

Never know how their children died.

The city remained the same.

They hadn't.

With the additional wealth from Lucifer, Iggy had decided to turn their thrown-together group into something more official. The swanky apartment became part office, part research lab, and part living space.

Iggy had sold his apartment and moved in immediately. He'd invited Lalo to live with him three months later. They'd been on a photography date up in Estes Park when he asked.

He'd said yes despite Wendy texting him to play hard to get. Allistics were strange. They'd dated for over a year. Wasn't it too late to play coy?

Lydia had been sad to see him go. Lalo hadn't understood the fuss. He was moving in with Iggy, not climbing Everest.

Aside from his volunteering and photography, Lalo had taken land bought by Iggy and created the perfect garden space. He grew all of the plants required for Wendy's experiments, plus a few others just for the pleasure of it. Iggy often had to come and drag him away.

They'd also gone through the journals and all the information scattered around Lucifer's penthouse. Reading over and over, looking for the needle in the haystack. Lalo had eventually been the one to find hints about a location in the mountains outside of Denver.

After making a list of potential spots, they'd begun their investigation. Iggy had assumed his chili-senses would prove to be a secret weapon in locating the demon source. They hadn't.

Hiking through one state park after another had made for many days on the trails and several nights camping. Alex called them the most Colorado double dates of all time. Shell occasionally enjoyed them.

"Lal?" Iggy eased down beside him on the sofa. He handed over the bowl of popcorn and a can of soda. "Ready?"

Lalo held up his tablet. He'd gotten a camera attached to a remote control vehicle. "Wendy's going to kill us."

"If she insists on proposing in her lab in my apartment,

we're watching. Drive." Iggy leaned forward to watch. "They're adorable."

"But deadly." Lalo had no doubt if they ruined Wendy's romantic moment, she'd find a way to eviscerate them. "Any news about Josiah?"

"Died after being released from jail." Iggy grabbed a handful of popcorn. "He went from prison to the hospital after suffering a massive stroke and never recovered."

Since assuming the mantle from Lucifer, Lalo had begun to develop powers of a sort. He'd gotten premonitions that turned out to be painfully accurate. They'd also noticed his strength increasing.

Lalo remembered the first time with embarrassing clarity. They'd been hunting through yet another state park. It had been the third-to-last on their list.

They'd accidentally stumbled onto a cougar's hunting grounds. *And scared the shiitake out of ourselves.* Lalo had leaped back away from the predator, only to find himself almost thirty feet across the forest behind a tree.

He'd shadowed. Or whatever it was the demons did when they vanished into wisps of nothing. They'd completely forgotten the cougar in their surprise.

Iggy and Lalo had been completely stunned. Wendy had had the presence of mind to begin shouting at the cougar while Shell threw rocks and sticks. The predator slunk off into the forest, probably more bewildered than afraid of the wildly flailing two-legged fools.

Despite numerous attempts, Lalo hadn't been able to deliberately repeat the shadowing. It continued to happen randomly, at inconvenient times. Iggy had almost cracked his head falling off the bed laughing when Lalo's lower half disappeared mid-sex.

Lalo hadn't seen the humor. It was disconcerting. None of them had been able to figure out a way for him to successfully control the ability.

What happens if I partially vanish in the middle of a story?

What the fennel do we do then?

"It happened again." Lalo decided to bite the bullet and tell Iggy.

Iggy turned his head immediately toward him. "Disappearing?"

"Just my hand." Lalo wiggled his fingers. "Damn guide didn't mention me suddenly turning into a shadow."

"Has Wendy finished her analysis?"

"My DNA is changing. Shifting closer to Lucifer's and yours." Lalo's arm around his shoulder squeezed tightly. "What if I'm no longer human?"

"We'll cross the demon bridge when we come to it. Oh, look, she got on one knee." Iggy pointed to the screen where Wendy had begun her proposal. "Do you want to marry?"

"Wendy?"

Iggy pinched the bridge of his nose. "Me."

"Not really." Lalo had never seen the point of marriage.

"Lalo."

He held up his hand to stop whatever speech Iggy had prepared. "I'll be happy with the time I have. A stressful wedding with lots of people I don't like, a ring I'll never wear because I hate jewelry, and a piece of paper I'll never see because it'll be in a drawer? No, thanks. Do we need marriage to have love and sex?"

"No, we've managed to christen every surface in this apartment without a wedding." Iggy gestured toward the large picture windows. "I'm particularly fond of those."

"Not while Wendy and Alex are here." Lalo glanced back to the tablet, only to find Wendy had obviously found the camera and switched it off. "Did you see the group message from Shell? They've noticed a new YouTube star in Aspen gaining a following, not unlike Siren. Want to head up to the mountains tomorrow? Get a sense for what the demon is trying to accomplish?"

Iggy drew Lalo closer, carefully setting the bowl of popcorn on the coffee table. "We've wanted to see if demon juice would freeze in the mountains."

"No, we tried it in the freezer." Lalo batted away the hand trying to poke him in the side. "But, yes, Shell found a camping site for all of us. We'll leave in the morning."

While Denver hadn't changed, Iggy had. Lalo had seen a massive difference in his boyfriend. Iggy had made a concerted effort to create calm and balance in their lives.

They'd spent some of their inherited funds to soundproof every room in the penthouse. It allowed Lalo to relax completely without fear of sensory overload. Iggy had done everything humanly possible to develop the perfect autistic space.

The intimacy Lalo had feared never being able to appreciate flowed naturally between them.

With the lab and office set up, they'd made demon hunting their business. Wendy focused on improving the demon juice and trying to decipher the genetic differences. Alex continued to hunt through historical texts and the many journals at their disposal. Shell joined in when they could to help out, particularly with keeping track of demons on social media.

The following morning they headed west out of Denver toward Rifle Falls State Park. The beautiful space had a lot of caves and forest. It was the second-to-last on their list.

"Why are we voluntarily awake at four in the morning?" Shell grumbled from the very last row of seats in Iggy's extended Trailblazer. "Just why?"

"Park opens at eight to non-campers. It's a three-hour drive, maybe less with the Igster's speed demon ways. We've got coffee, donuts, and every chance of finding our spot to set up the tents before anyone gets in our way," Wendy explained for the third time. "If you ask are we there yet one more time… I'll think of something creatively threatening later."

They managed the journey in a terrifyingly short time. Lalo refused to look at the speedometer. He didn't want to risk a panic attack induced stroke.

With his headphones on, Lalo tuned all of them out. The speed, Shell and Wendy teasing each other, and Iggy and Alex debating Lucifer myths. He rocked in his seat to the music while reading through the vague hints left about where the supposed demon gate in the mountains was.

Demon gate.

Portal.

Random hole in a tree. Focus, Lal, this isn't Winnie the Pooh.

Son of a Basil.

What if all of this is Lucifer's idea of a joke?

After hiking out to the campsite and setting up their tents, they left Alex and Wendy behind to head north toward the first set of caves. The crisp air kept their scrambling around in the forest from being oppressive. Lalo tried not to get distracted by all the flora.

"Ig?" Shell drew their attention to where they'd jogged ahead. "Check this out."

Lalo and Iggy caught up to Shell. They'd stopped outside of what appeared to be a collapsed cave. "What am I missing?"

They carefully edged over a portion of the rubble to point to a faded painting of what looked like a feather. "Remember the hidden painting? The style is remarkably similar to the image Wendy showed me."

A quick text to Wendy followed. She immediately messaged them the saved image from her phone. The three explorers crowded around Shell's phone, glancing from it to the cave multiple times. Lalo had to agree with them— someone had done a remarkable job copying the style of the feathers.

"Coincidence?" Shell eventually broke the silence.

"I believe in them, but I don't think this shit is a coincidence." Iggy reached into his backpack to hand Lalo the drone. "Let's get aerial footage of the area. Shell and I can try to clear some of the rocks. Maybe Wendy and Alex know someone who's a geologist or something. Is there such a thing as a caveologist? We can't clear a path inside only to have it collapse on us."

It took a week to find someone Wendy trusted enough to ask about the excavation, a friend and colleague from the university who wouldn't get overly interested in why she was asking. Shell rented the camping site for three weeks. Tricky, and expensive. Then they returned to the falls to begin digging their way to the bottom of the mystery of the cave. It was less digging and more shifting rocks from one pile to another.

Three weeks of tedious work made worse by their need to not draw the attention of park rangers. Their excavation eventually revealed what Shell nicknamed the energetic portal of weirdness, a strange sliver running the length of a partially hollowed-out wall of rock.

Not quite a door. None of them could widen it, not even Lalo or Iggy. They camped outside of it for weeks hoping to see something. The group took turns, always armed with their weaponized herbal concoction.

On their fifth camping trip to watch for demons, Lalo had begun to give up on the possibility. He'd brought Lucifer's notes in the hopes of maybe finding another spot. They couldn't indefinitely visit the same spot in a national park; rangers would start to get suspicious.

"What the fuck?"

Lalo glanced up at the demon suddenly standing in front of him. The sliver in the rock glowed, likely from having been used. "Fudgsicle."

Reacting on instinct before Iggy or Wendy had a chance to respond, Lalo fired his Nerf gun at the demon, who hadn't quite recovered from her surprise at their presence. A splash of juice. No demon. They'd done it.

They'd found the entrance. The reason Denver had been the home to the Jesuits—and the start of the demons. They now had to devote all of their energy to finding a way to seal the demons inside.

First, they'd tried covering the area with the herbal concoction. It didn't last. Lalo hadn't expected their first attempt to produce results.

They'd set up cameras to observe the area since they couldn't realistically spend month after month sitting outside of a cave in a national park. Lalo and Wendy spent long days in the lab.

They experimented with his demon juice. Their compared efforts developed a way to permanently coat the cave. Similar to cooking a sauce, they'd simmered the liquid down into more of a syrup consistency, then combined it with a concrete-like substance. Once coated on the rock, it hardened.

And they waited.

Four months later, they'd yet to see another demonic appearance in the city. But they'd continue to watch. And wait. Forever if necessary to keep Denver safe— and maintain balance. To their knowledge, only three demons had been left in the area. They'd systematically hunted each one down. The goal was to keep humans and demons separate. With a little luck, they'd prevented the Armageddon-like event Lucifer had claimed was inevitable if a solution wasn't found.

And they'd done it together.

In the end, Lalo wondered if Lucifer had really been interested in a solution. They'd managed—in a relatively short amount of time compared to his centuries on the planet—to develop a way to seal off demons from humans. He couldn't complain; he now had an extended lifetime of peace to enjoy, thanks to the laziness of the prince of darkness.

"I love you."

Lalo sat up to eat another handful of popcorn. "I love you enough to ignore you drinking my last soda."

And enough to spend my life with you even if we live forever.

Enough to live in the same house—even when you drive me crazy.

"You're complaining about me in your head again, aren't you?" Iggy grinned at him.

"We're having sex." Lalo thought they'd made quite a few changes in the past year. "We've made sure the demons stay locked away. Lucifer isn't spawning more siblings for you. No more clones of Titus."

"And we're fucking."

THE END

THANK YOU

Thanks for reading *Here Comes The Son*. I hope you enjoyed the story. I appreciate your help in spreading the word, including telling a friend. Before you go, it would mean so much to me if you would take a few minutes to write a review and share how you feel about my story so others may find my work. Reviews really do help readers find books. Please leave a review on your favorite book site.

Don't miss out on New Releases, Exclusive Giveaways and much more!

JOIN MY NEWSLETTER:

HTTP://EEPURL.COM/Q0N0X

LIKE ME ON FACEBOOK:

FACEBOOK.COM/DAHLIADONOVAN

JOIN MY READER GROUP:

FACEBOOK.COM/GROUPS/1326515147425106/

FOLLOW ME ON TWITTER:

TWITTER.COM/DAHLIADONOVAN

ACKNOWLEDGMENTS

A massive thank you to my brilliant betas who deserve overtime for helping me on this one. A massive thank you to Becky and Olivia, who kept me going while I struggled with this story and a family medical emergency. To all the fantastic people at Hot Tree. And also to my beloved hubby who keeps me from losing my mind while I'm stressing over word counts.

And, lastly, thank you, readers, for following me on my writing journey. I hope you enjoyed *Here Comes The Son.*

ABOUT THE PUBLISHER

Hot Tree Publishing opened its doors in 2015 with an aspiration to bring quality fiction to the world of readers. With the initial focus on romance and a wide spread of romance subgenres, Hot Tree Publishing have since opened their first imprint, Tangled Tree Publishing, specializing in crime, mystery, suspense, and thriller.

Firmly seated in the industry as a leading editing provider to independent authors and small publishing houses, Hot Tree Publishing is the sister company to Hot Tree Editing, founded in 2012. Having established in-house editing and promotions, plus having a well-respected market presence, Hot Tree Publishing endeavours to be a leader in bringing quality stories to the world of readers.

Interested in discovering more amazing reads brought to you by Hot Tree Publishing? Head over to the website for information:

WWW.HOTTREEPUBLISHING.COM